C000131467

This book is a work of fiction. Names, ~~~~~~~

product of the author's imagination or are used fictitiously. Any resemblance to act~~

persons, living or dead, or events past or future is entirely coincidental.

First paperback edition May 2024

Cover design by Edward Frizzelle

Cover photo credit – iStock.com/Gyro

ISBN 978-1-7385308-0-9 (paperback)

ISBN 978-1-7385308-1-6 (ebook)

PEGGY

Carole L Pollard

Rebecca

Best Wishes

Carole Px

For my family, and for Georgia and Charlie
without whom this story would still be a series of notes

ONE

Peggy had never loved her husband of forty-two years. She would say she had no idea what love might feel like, and thought she probably never would.

But she did know resentment, anger, bitterness, and she was acutely aware of her own pitifully fragile sense of self-worth. That, she felt, was a start.

Had she heard him fall on that sunny August morning?

Yes, definitely.

Had she been aware that the damage inflicted to his head might prove fatal, as it struck the edge of the ancient bath he refused to replace with one of a more modern forgiving construction?

As she had decided to be honest with herself this morning, she agreed that yes, she had realised and hoped that as she heard his body slump to the floor, her marriage might finally be over without the need for a legal process she had no funds or energy for.

Was she responsible for his death?

No, she didn't think she was. She had told him many times to walk carefully in the bathroom when the lino was wet. Well, again, if she was being honest she had warned him once, many years ago. Since then, maybe she had been hoping he hadn't listened to her.

Anyway, fall he did, fatal it was, and die he did. Not immediately, but just after the emergency services deposited him in an Accident and Emergency side ward. She accompanied the fast-fading Leonard in the ambulance, relishing the silence, and minutes after arriving by his bedside found herself listening quietly while a doctor expressed his sorrow in hushed tones. Her natural blank expression seemed to re-assure the staff that she was dealing stoically with the dreadful news, and she gratefully accepted their offer of tea and biscuits.

His last cohesive words to her had been to instruct her it was time to change the ancient sheets on their bed. As she walked out of the hospital she thought about that, and about how none of us know when our last moments will be. What our last words will be; our last actions, or the last words we might read. For Leonard, his last words were,

'I don't know what you do all day, you get lazier with every year.'

His last action, before the fall anyway, was to pull the plug out of the bath. She might have thought more kindly about him if his last action had been to wipe the ring of greasy hair cream and dead skin

2

deposits from around the bath, but no – as ever that was to be her job.

Leonard was not a book-lover, so the last words he read were probably from the sticker on the back of the soap. That amused her.

She was still wiping away laughter tears when her taxi pulled up and the driver called out her name. The hospital visit had been consigned to memory and it was a cheerful Peggy who jumped into the back seat of the smart blue car, surprising the bored driver by announcing,

'Shopping Centre please. I'm going to buy myself some new bedding.'

Peggy stripped the bed of old worn sheets on the morning after Leonard's death, and re-made it with her new Egyptian cotton bedding, lovingly washed in fragrant washing powder, and dried in the warm breeze of a late summer afternoon.

She was plumping her new pillows, arranging them as she had seen them in the shop display, when there was a knock at the door. It was Joe, their neighbour – her neighbour now, hers alone.

He thrust a bunch of flowers at her as she opened the door,

'We saw the ambulance, me and Tracey. How is he? Mr Thomas? They kept him in?'

Joe seemed embarrassed, his face was flushed red and beads of sweat were forming on his forehead.

'He's dead Joe. He won't be coming back. Won't be complaining about your hedge trimming anymore.'

Peggy was triumphant. This was the first time she had voiced her new arrangements out loud.

Joe was taken aback, unaccustomed to this approach to the death of a loved one.

She beckoned him into the front room, and offered him Leonard's old chair.

'Would you like a whisky with me Joe?'

Brushing off his protests mainly about the time of day and Tracey waiting to go shopping, Peggy poured two large whiskies into tumblers, added a splash of water from a jug and offered a glass to Joe, exchanging the whisky for the flowers.

'Thank you for these, just what I needed to brighten up the place a bit.'

She thrust them into the jug of water and sat in a leather chair by the fire, facing her astonished neighbour.

'I was going to ask you a favour actually Joe. I wondered if you'd burn his chair for me. I spoke to the undertakers when I got home from the hospital and they said even if I broke it up, they wouldn't burn it with him.'

Joe shuffled in the chair, 'I guess I could, if that's what you really want.'

He took a swig of his drink, wincing at the heat from the fiery liquid, stuttering a preference for beer and feeling the heat rise in his cheeks.

After his condolences had been passed on and they had shared a few moments of friendly conversation, Joe scuttled back to an impatient Tracey waiting on the path with her reusable shopping bags. Peggy closed the door behind her and looked around. Her home now, all hers. She would have a good clean up and rinse every bit of Leonard's DNA out of the house. Then she would sit down with one of her new leather-bound notebooks and plan the rest of her life.

Peggy had always kept notebooks – years ago scribbling down her teenage thoughts, then burning the pages if she had written anything incriminating or words anyone might taunt her with.

She was the middle child of three and for the first years of her life she had a brother, Ray, who was her hero. But Ray had been killed in a motorbike accident two days after her 14th birthday. He had taken a bend too fast the police said, lost control of the bike and was killed instantly.

Peggy had been inconsolable at the loss of her brother. Her notebooks were full of memories of him, and full of her anger at the god she had spoken to every Sunday of her life, who had deserted her family. She still had her younger brother Paul but he was only eight and his life seemed to carry on. Yes, he spoke of Ray occasionally but maybe at that age he hadn't understood the finality of death.

Peggy's mother refused to leave the house and would not speak to anyone for a year after Ray's death. Sitting in her eldest son's bedroom for hours, she argued violently with anyone who tried to challenge her behaviour. Finally the doctor had been called in. Peggy had no idea what was prescribed and although the bright, intelligent woman Peggy had known never returned, she saw small positive changes in her mother after each of his visits.

Her father had dealt with his grief in his own way, a way that included new friends Johnnie Walker and Timothy Taylor, both enjoyed to excess in the Black Lion on the High Street.

Peggy's happy family life never returned and when a fairly good-looking lad on the bus to work started paying her attention, and talking to her, she was flattered. Flattered became engaged, and engaged became married. Then the good-looking lad turned out to be nasty Leonard. Leonard successfully alienated her from her family and to Peggy's shame she let him do it. On and on he went until she had no-one left but him, and he was no friend to her.

It took Peggy five full days after Leonard's death before she began looking through his paperwork for a will – she knew there was one. They had visited the solicitors together, and she had signed the will that mirrored his – on his death everything to her and on her death everything to him. She didn't have anything apart from a pile of bank notes in her locked box, the small amounts she had hidden from him if there was anything left from the meagre housekeeping money he handed her every month.

The wills – hers too – were at the bottom of an old shoe box and she was pleased to see that yes, everything of his became hers on his death.

At the bank she managed to hide her surprise when she was told there was a joint account because he had always insisted it was in his name only. Why had she never questioned that? She had so many questions to ask the version of herself that had existed until Leonard's death.

She made an appointment to visit the solicitors on the day after the funeral - a quiet affair, few flowers and fewer mourners, just her and their neighbours including Joe with his wife Tracey and two boys Liam and Mark. How respectful they were, and how undeserving Leonard was of their time and consideration.

If the Peggy Leonard had been married to for all that time was one person, and the Peggy after his death was another, then the Peggy who walked out of the solicitors' office was a completely different person altogether. This was a Peggy with money, not just the bank account, there were savings, shares, investments. It struck her how busy he had been saving all this money secretly, presumably because he believed he would outlive her and get to do what? No friends, no interests and if she was gone no-one to run around after him. She had survived him and got to spend his money and that made her feel very happy – an emotion she had not felt for many years.

Thanks to Leonard and the years of misery she had spent with him, she suddenly had enough money to travel, to go to places where she would be able to speak in the many languages she had learned from library books – study carried out while Leonard was at work, believing his wife to be polishing wood floors, or whitening the heavy lace curtains he had insisted on. He had never noticed that the floors were not polished and the curtains remained a dingy shade of grey so she was always pleased that she had not spent any of her precious time on them.

Maybe for her next birthday Peggy would plan a trip to Bulgaria, out of season, because she had heard they don't encourage any English to be spoken when the tourists aren't there. No English menus, no help at the bus stops or the shops. She was looking forward to practising her languages.

Peggy liked to read, all the time, and no longer needed to hide her books or foreign language dictionaries under the floorboards or behind the bath panel. Since his death she would definitely be found reading at 5.30pm every weekday, when in life Leonard would walk through the door, all self-important and in desperate need of 'a cup of Yorkshire tea, and a small piece of Dundee Cake.' Every day the same ritual of plumping the thin tapestry cushion on the back of his chair, settling his pompous self down for what he thought was a well-deserved rest.

'That's just what a man needs when he gets in from the coal face.'

On a chilly September morning some time after the funeral and bank visit, Peggy picked her way through the overgrown gravestones at the edge of the churchyard, clutching Leonard's remains in her right hand. The harsh edges of the container scratched against her fingertips, and she was speaking to him in a hushed whisper, explaining their mission.

The local community had been busy identifying local dignitaries among the occupants of the churchyard, and many of the graves proudly displayed metal signs beside the stones, detailing the life and achievements of each departed soul.

She was interested to read about the people who had lived in her town, many years before she was born. Some she recognised. There was the local butcher who had cut all the fingers on his left hand off while chopping up a pig for display. This wasn't mentioned on the notes, but Peggy remembered staring at that fingerless hand as a child when her mother had taken her in to buy chops and bacon, or mince – sometimes even a whole chicken. The butcher had other claims to fame, apart from his lack of digits – he had been mayor of the town for ten years apparently, and had used personal funds to build a community centre. He would spin in there she thought, staring down at the soil, if he knew he had simply provided a secluded space for alcoholics and drug takers to gather on a Friday evening.

She wandered among the graves, taking care not to stand on any raised earth – she enjoyed a graveyard and knew the rules.

People had been very busy investigating the lives of these forgotten heroes, and she found it fascinating – would this have been paid work, or something completed in the researchers' own time? Maybe this was something she could be involved in. She stopped and took a notepad out of her handbag, removed the silver pen from its elasticated fitting, and wrote 'Research local dead', on the first empty page.

The churchyard was deserted apart from the hunched figure of a woman tending a grave set against the far wall. Peggy felt safe in the presence of this stranger. She knew loneliness from her time as Leonard's wife, but she was still not accustomed to being completely alone.

She watched as the woman stood, running her fingers through straight grey hair, cut in a tight bob. She pushed the fringe away from her face as she looked up towards the cloudless blue sky, but she did not have the air of sadness normally surrounding mourners at gravesides. She seemed weary, tired, but not heavy with grief. She was short, and the buttons on her peacock blue woollen coat were straining. The woman sensed she was being watched and turned her face towards Peggy, her dull expression turning to delight.

Peggy instinctively looked away, embarrassed by the thought of social interaction with a stranger. She started to walk away, but there was something about the woman's face she recognised. Could it be?

Apparently it was.

'Peggy? Peggy Underwood? Is that really you?'

There was a moment when Peggy could have carried on walking, with Leonard secure in his box, but the pre-Leonard parts of her were slowly returning and she longed for company, especially female company.

'Yes Ros it's me, me and him, my dead husband.'

Peggy nodded towards the heavy cardboard box now tucked under her arm as she walked towards her old schoolfriend.

'I'm looking for somewhere suitably dismal to dump his ashes. I can't have them in the house, I feel like he's watching me if I leave the lights on or turn the heating up too high.'

Ros laughed,

'Same here.'

She nodded towards the wooden cross.

'Mother. I had to get rid of her before I moved into my new place, I didn't want her setting a foot in there. You'd probably be able to get him a plot down this side of the wall – no sun shines here, it's damp and not much grows apart from ivy. It's not very popular with the bereaved.'

The two women made small talk, asking about the lives each had led since their last meeting.

'I have a flask here, there are two cups on it – one of them has never been used. And I have homemade brownies. Shall we sit?'

Ros gestured towards a commemorative bench under the rustling leaves of an enormous sycamore tree, and two hours later they were still there, talking and laughing. Post-school years melted away and the two women shared their experiences of growing older, both in sad circumstances, both living with people who made them feel worthless, hopeless.

At times sad, but mostly breathless from laughing, the two enjoyed a roller-coaster of emotions they had not experienced for many years.

Ros had taken a job at Latimer's alongside Peggy, but after just a few months of pay packet independence she had left to care for a mother who had convinced herself, Ros, and the medical profession that she had not many months left. Thirty-five miserable years later, she had finally turned up her toes and left Ros to get on with what was left of a wasted life. Her mother had been manipulative, a misery, and a bully. Ros had remained with her initially out of a sense of duty. An only child with no other immediate family, she had found herself unable to leave the house for fear of each period of absence being the cause of her mother's demise, or the dread of guilt that she might not be there when her mother needed her most. After years of enduring this maternal torture, she found she no longer had the energy or the inclination to seek the company of others and had resigned herself to a life of solitary crafting and gardening.

When the mother's last hours finally did arrive, they were spent in cheery fashion, similar to the farewell of two people, each knowing they were about to embark on a more enjoyable existence. They exchanged pleasantries and Ros politely lied that her mother had been as good a parent as it was possible for her to be. The mother, without apologising outright, talked of her regret that she had occasionally spoken in a harsh manner to her only daughter.

They parted as one might leave a temporary job where no proper relationships have been formed, but with an acknowledgement that time had passed together.

After a twenty-minute period of final noisy breathing under the watchful eye of the ever-patient Dr Miles Emsworth, the older woman had slipped away, and both the doctor and the daughter breathed sighs of relief.

'What happened to your dad Ros? He was still alive when we worked at Latimer's wasn't he?'

Peggy was keen to know everything about her old friend's life since their time at school and work. Was it wrong to be delighted, hearing she hadn't been the only one to have endured years of misery?

'He cleared off, that's why I had to leave the job. Went off up north somewhere. Mother said she'd heard he'd died not long after but she might have just been saying that. What about you? You packed up work I heard, and married lovely Leonard from Accounts.'

Peggy laughed, spraying brownie and coffee into the air.

'Lovely? Leonard? They're two words I've never heard in the same sentence before. I suppose he was handsome wasn't he? In his own way, and he dressed OK – for the office anyway, but lovely? Definitely not Ros, definitely not. There was not one shred of lovely about him. I learned a new word the other day, came up in a play on the radio. Odious. As soon as I heard it I thought, that's the word for Leonard. He was an odious man.'

Peggy filled Ros in on some of the background of her married life, not all of it was suitable for a public airing, but saying some of the stuff out loud made her feel better. And she knew Ros had held back some of the stories about her mother – admitting to being bullied and manipulated all your life can be humiliating. She knew when she heard stories about people in documentaries on the television she had little patience for their whining, that if things were that bad why didn't they get out?

But really she knew why. Because she hadn't, and nor it seemed had Ros.

Some details, she decided, were best private.

Ros was living in a ground floor flat in nearby Sovereign Court, with its neat well-maintained gardens nudging alongside the old walls of the graveyard. Constructed on the site of the old Ribbon Factory, Sovereign Court was a new exclusive complex, set at the higher end of Ribbon Lane around a large white central property, and had the appearance of a country estate for the landed gentry. There had been uproar and protests in the town when the developers' plans to rip down the old factory building and replace it with this modern monstrosity were announced. Peggy remembered signing a few of the petitions thrust at her as she tried to remain anonymous on her occasional walks into the High Street. If she'd been honest with the earnest campaigners, she didn't really care what they did with the building. She could see the silhouette of the place from her bedroom window at night when the moon was behind it. She had no idea if anyone lived there or if it was empty. It had no impact on her – let the developers do what they want. The campaigners could spot a lonely soul from a mile off, she thought. They knew that a brief chat on a Monday morning might be the only social interaction a person would have – they took advantage for their own purposes. Both parties were aware of the interaction and both gained something.

When Peggy was a child, living with her parents and two brothers in their bow fronted terraced house just off the main road, the Ribbon Factory was the town's main employer – there was work on the production lines, and some of the women, including Peggy's own mother had worked both in the canteen and in the offices, either cooking or shuffling papers.

Ribbons from the factory were sent all over the world in the good old days, adorning hats, dresses and hairstyles of many glamorous men and women. The owners had no idea about a future world where quality handmade ribbons would not be a priority purchase, but despite a few unsuccessful diversions into other clothing accessories, that world hit them in the late-seventies. The demise of the empire was quick and the building had been empty for many years, finally becoming a haunt for local drinkers and general troublemakers.

Now this hub of industry found itself occupied by a few young professional couples scattered among ageing and monied locals. This included Ros, who had benefited handsomely from her mother's frugal existence.

The women parted company with none of the modern demonstrative hugging and kissing Peggy had seen among the teenagers in the town. They smiled at each other and alluded to meetings in the near future – much as they had fifty years before after walking home from school. Then, Peggy would wander off to her happy family home and Ros to the solitude of life as the only child of desperately unhappy parents.

Time had slipped away and Peggy found herself laughing as she wandered back to her cottage with Leonard still tucked under her arm, and Ros's telephone number written in her notebook.

She was humming to herself as she approached the cottage and was surprised to see Joe at the door.

'Ah, Mrs T – I was wondering if you were OK.'

'I'm fine Joe, thank you, fine. I may have found somewhere to bury the old sod, so all good here.'

Still not quite accustomed to his neighbour's casual attitude to the death of her husband, Joe shuffled his feet and plunged his hands deep into his pockets.

'I'm, er, I'm thinking about having a bonfire on Friday evening. You know, you said about the chair, about burning it. Are you still thinking about doing that?'

'Of course!' Peggy laughed.

'Of course I am. I've pushed it to the side of the room, but it smells a bit and I keep thinking he's still sitting in it, watching me. I definitely want rid. Shall we have a bonfire party?'

Peggy enjoyed Joe's discomfort. He was a kind man and she couldn't imagine him wanting anyone dead, but he agreed to send his eldest boy Mark round the following day to collect the chair, and pile it on top of his garden waste, ready for the big burn. Once Joe had returned to his own cottage next door, Peggy made herself some pasta, poured a large glass of Malbec and sat in her chair absent-mindedly spooning in garlicky pasta bows, and thinking about her meeting with Ros. In just a few hours, she felt some of her old self had come back. She emptied her bowl, took a large swig of wine and settled down for a nap.

Sleep wouldn't come.

Now his physical form was out of her life, she couldn't stop herself thinking about Leonard, about how little she knew of him.

She knew that he had started in an accounts office at the age of 16 and by the time he died at 58, he was head something or other, or so he had told Peggy.

She realised she knew nothing about his past; where he had come from, or where he was born. She had no idea whether he had other family still alive. He also, she realised, never spoke about the future. That seemed odd to her, now she was giving some space in her mind for him – something she had not done before. Surely most people their age would have some idea what they wanted to do with their time when they retired, but he had never spoken about plans or hopes for retirement and beyond.

On his last morning she had heard him fall, but she had remained in her chair, pulled up to the fireplace, with her latest library book – *Bulgaria – Culture and Language*.

The ambulance and paramedics, once she called for them, had arrived within 30 minutes. Leonard had been taken to hospital and deposited in a side room off A&E. The doctors tried their best but could not revive lifeless Leonard. The nurse was sympathetic, kind and efficient. Was there anyone she wanted to call? She shouldn't be alone apparently. Why not she thought, she had been alone for most of her life.

The doctor sat her down in the Relatives Room. He exuded sympathy and condolences on her, clearly concerned Peggy was in shock judging by her response to Leonard's death.

'I'll call a taxi, don't worry.'

And that's what she did, as soon as the police had asked her a few questions, without explicitly asking her to remain in the country, she was free to go. She called a local firm whose card was cellotaped above the pay phone in the waiting area and stopped off at John Lewis on her way home to buy some new bedding and cushions with her remaining housekeeping money.

There had been a couple of visits from a friendly and very young police officer, scribbling her comments in his notebook.

Why had it taken so long to call the ambulance? Had she moved him before the ambulance arrived?

Each time she told him the same story, a version of the truth, she had heard him fall, but didn't want to disturb him in the bath – Leonard was not a man who appreciated being disturbed while in the bathroom.

On his demise, Peggy instantly felt herself change into a happy widow. She knew the house was paid for, and he had contributed to a handsome pension all his working life – presumably believing he would have many years to enjoy the fruits of his labours. She thought she might be fairly comfortably off, something he would be furious about. To some extent, more important than the money was the fact she would never again hear him call her PegBag, mocking the slightly old-fashioned name her mother had given her. Her mother had her reasons – she admired Peggy Lee's singing voice and wanted her daughter to sing too. She had disappointed her mother in that area, certainly never living up to the warblings of Ms Lee.

But she would never again sit shivering in a freezing cold house because of the fury any hint of wasting money on heating might ignite. Maybe she would get a job, yes, a job – that would be a good idea. There were many things she could do – she had been secretly learning languages while Leonard was at work – maybe she would travel and work as a translator somewhere.

Leonard had never had a good word to say to Joe, and Peggy knew her neighbour would enjoy watching the chair burn, maybe visualising Leonard sitting in it as the flames licked around that skeletal face, sneering down from the top of the fire, and still complaining about something.

She was right.

Peggy and Joe met on the allotment at 7pm exactly. Peggy had brought cigarettes, whisky and two crystal glasses.

'Ready?'

Peggy nodded as armed with a box of long matches, Joe gently approached the firelighters and crumpled newspaper balls he had laid on the flattened red pile of the seat pad, worn shiny by the daily visits of Leonard's bony backside.

The thin, sinisterly embroidered cushion caught first, the Celtic snake design disappearing into a scorched circle.

Flames gripped the back of the chair, and ancient dry fabric disintegrated before their eyes, laying bare the wooden frame, and spitting orange fireworks of horse-hair and stuffing into the sky.

Spindles of smoke curled high above the fire, momentarily taking on the shape of lifeless Leonard, and filling the air with old memories.

'Did Leonard wear Pinewood Aftershave?'

'Yes, he smothered himself in it, maybe to disguise the smell of internal decay. That and cheap hair cream – his signature fragrances.' Peggy laughed as she poured single malt into the two glasses and passed one to Joe who wasn't laughing.

'Oh, I don't really...'

'Are you going to let a lady drink alone Joseph? No, I didn't think so. Tell your wife I forced you.'

Peggy smiled at Joe as he took the glass, watching as he took his first sip. He winced but she was pleased to see he didn't give up and they stood close together watching, from the first glimmers of blue and orange flame, through to the deep red of hot springs and smouldering remains.

'I didn't really know your old man. I only ever saw him when he was walking around the garden, checking I'd trimmed the hedges OK. He usually had something to say about it, not usually very nice comments.'

'He wasn't a very nice man Joe. Did you notice that no-one from his firm came to the funeral? He'd worked there for nearly 43 years, and not made a single friend. Not even made anyone like him enough that they would come and pay last respects. What does that tell you about him? They sent flowers – a mean looking bunch of chrysanths and thistles. It's sad isn't it? Top up?'

Ignoring Joe's signals that he had had enough, Peggy poured a tot more into Joe's glass, and a large shot into her own.

'Do you smoke Joe?'

'Not really, but, well it is an occasion isn't it, thanks. Here I've got matches.'

They stood together in silence, smoking one and then another cigarette.

'I'm packing up smoking now – no need to escape into the garden when there's no-one to escape from is there?' Peggy drained her glass for a second time and seeing that Joe wasn't actually drinking anything, she tucked the bottle back into her bag.

The two of them waited to make sure the wood had turned to ash for Joe to sprinkle on the earth beneath their feet. In the receding light of that autumn evening, the last fingers of smoke reached out for them, circling around and behind, trying to pull them into the dying embers. Peggy took a last drag of her cigarette and flicked the butt towards the fire, shuddering to think of Leonard, but she was becoming more able to make herself think about her own home and her own new furniture – no tapestry, no ancient red fabric, dust, or fragrance of soulless man.

'Anyway, he seems to have been on a surprisingly good salary. He never trusted me with information like that – me just being a woman and all that. We had a workhouse lifestyle. Never gave me much for housekeeping, but he kept it all to himself and now it's mine. All that bitterness, it's gradually going. Now I'm left with a daily love of waking up every morning excited, not nervous, for what the day may bring. '

'I never knew you were that miserable.'

'I don't think I knew to be honest. When you live with someone who constantly tells you you're useless, that you have no value, you just go along with it.

He said I should be grateful because he rescued me from my life before, and I believed him, for a while anyway, until I realised too late that there was nothing wrong with my life before. Nothing bad at all.

Now though, I just thank him for his quick, fairly young death that leaves me time to have another chance at life, to maybe you know, move on.'

Joe's thoughts were clearly elsewhere and even Peggy had the sense to realise that she was perhaps confiding too much to this man who was only a neighbour. Maybe it was the whisky, or maybe it was how solid and real he seemed. So honest, and down to earth.

She knew she wasn't necessarily looking for a husband. Joe was a married man and would definitely not be interested in an older woman like her but how lovely if there was someone she could care about; someone who, if they were sad, she would feel sad for them, not just irritated by them.

'I think about that day he died you know. I woke up not knowing how my life was about to change. We had breakfast and he was going on about how grateful I should be to him, that I had an easy life and that the sheets needed to be changed. That was my job for the day.'

'Did you change the sheets then?'

'I chucked them. Brown and grey check, worn thin where his thick toenails rubbed along the edges, and those pillowcases with ingrained yellow oily stains on them, smelling like vinegar.

Anyway a couple of hours later, I'm sitting with free tea and biscuits in a hospital relatives room, he's pronounced dead and I'm a liberated woman. I took a taxi to John Lewis on the way home and bought some new sheets – all flowery and lovely they are. Bloody marvellous. I was supposed to be the grieving widow, but I felt great, like when the sun comes through the clouds after a massive storm that you thought would last for days, then it just stops and you look around and you're seeing the world for the first time, all over again. And you know it's a good place.

I suppose you think I'm awful.'

Peggy threw another cigarette butt into the smouldering remains of the fire and watched as Joe poked at the ashes with his spade.

Turning slowly away from the fire, Joe handed the still half full glass back to Peggy,

'I'll be honest with you I didn't think much of him. No disrespect but he was quite petty. Always moaning at me about what he thought was my substandard hedge trimming. But I never saw him doing any of it.'

Joe was well into his stride. Just two sips of alcohol and he had lost all his inhibitions.

'Come to think of it, I don't ever remember seeing him smile, or laugh.'

He took back his glass and sipped again at the whisky, thoughtful.

'What I think, Peggy, is that it sounds like you've had a tough time living with that man, and I wish you well now he's gone. What I think too, is that you need to make some plans. Go places. And get yourself a taste for something other than whisky – the devil's water my mum used to call it.'

'What would be an acceptable replacement Joe? I've become reliant on the stuff lately.'

'Exactly. That's not good. I'll think of something.'

Embarrassed suddenly, that he may have gone too far,

'What are you up to now anyway? Still learning your languages? I suppose you could travel a bit now couldn't you?'

'I have a trip in mind actually. To Bulgaria, next March. Practise my Bulgarian.'

She frowned,

'Actually I had an odd experience the other day at the bus stop. There's a woman I often see there. She never speaks, never smiles. Small and grim-looking, she's always wrapped up in layers of coats and has a big flowery scarf wrapped all around her head. She's the spitting image of the woman on the cover of my language book.

Anyway, I approached her and asked her in my best dialect, if she thought it would rain later. She had no idea what I was saying and was quite rude when I said she wasn't from around here, quite common English accent actually. So rude.'

Joe stifled a laugh,

'See you shouldn't judge people by how they look should you? Especially if all you know is an image on the front cover of a very old book.'

'Clearly not. I told my friend Ros about the exchange and she said she thought the woman was from elsewhere too. Ros has spoken to her at one of her classes. Turns out her family are local through and through and having done some family tree research, she believes she's related to Henry VIIIth. How true that is I can't be sure, but I suppose there must be the descendants of a lot of illegitimate children of royalty running around.'

Joe had abandoned the spade and was absentmindedly jabbing at stubborn pieces of chair leg with a long iron pole.

'Anyway, I shouldn't keep you.'

Had Peggy ranted on for too long? She was aware her social skills were sadly lacking.

'Thank you Joe. You have been a good neighbour to me, although I am thinking about a move and we might not be neighbours for much longer. I hope we can keep in touch in between my travels. I'd only be a short walk away, across the fields or five minutes in your car. There's plenty of parking. I'm thinking about a place in Sovereign Court – you know, the old Ribbon Factory.

She smiled, encouraging, hoping the ample parking might entice him to visit.

There was no sign that a farewell hug would be appropriate, and a handshake seemed too formal, so Joe merely handed his glass back, now empty, and touched his cap in a mock servant fashion.

Peggy nodded appreciatively, tucked the glasses into her handbag and moved away, through the far gate of the allotment and into the fields beyond, back to the row of cottages where she had lived with Leonard for so long, and where she soon hoped she could leave all memories of him.

As she opened her front door, she looked up at the outline of Sovereign Court, with its lights blazing from all the windows. The white of the building glowed a pale pink in the reflection of the setting September sun. Maybe she should consider Ros's suggestion of moving herself into that community, and away from this house full of memories of her life with Leonard. For a few moments, as the sun finally set, the windows in Sovereign Court reflected its final rays and were shining gold.

Joe turned to face the fire, threw a few handfuls of sand onto the embers and then walked through his allotment, collecting the last of the runner beans, before turning and heading home. Home, where his wife would be waiting, sitting in the half light of Midsomer Murders; slippers and ulcerated legs resting on the old leather pouffe.

TWO

There were other reasons for Peggy's desire to move away from the house she had shared with Leonard. She felt his presence in every room, particularly the bathroom where he had breathed his last gulp of air.

She could no longer enjoy a soak in the bath, and had taken to washing in the kitchen. She spent as little time as she could in the bathroom and frankly that was taking its toll on her inner workings.

The bedroom they had shared for so many years still smelt of him; of his hair cream and his after shave, no matter how many times she had washed the sheets, adding fresh fragrances to the wash each time. She had taken the curtains to the dry cleaners and used litres of Zoflora on the hard surfaces, trying to wash him away, but still essence of Leonard lingered.

There were times she heard him fall in the bathroom, when she was sitting quietly reading and when she knew he wasn't there. Sometimes when she came back into the house after a walk into town, she could swear that one of the chairs had moved, or maybe the dent in a cushion would be in a different place.

One Saturday afternoon, after a long ramble in the nearby woods, she had returned home to find the house was filled with the aromas of beef, tomatoes, good stock and an assembly of root vegetables coming from her new slow cooker. She hung her coat in the porch, kicked off her boots and lit the fire.

There was a book Peggy was eager to finish, about a woman who had driven to the north of Scotland to escape a violent husband, but he was following her every move on the tracker he had installed under her car. Peggy felt sure the story would end well and was pinning her own hopes on the plight of this fictional character. If Bryony could escape wicked Wayne, then surely she could move on from lousy Leonard.

Her eyelids were heavy and she was struggling to stay awake when there was the sound of someone knocking loudly on the bathroom floor above her. She sat up, the room was icy cold and the knocking grew louder and louder. Holding her hands over her ears she tried to stand but couldn't, something heavy was holding her down, not letting her move. Her hands were cold and clammy against the side of her face. There was shouting, someone and it sounded like Leonard, was calling her name.

'Open the door Peggy, open the door.'

There was movement at the window, was it Joe? She tried again to stand and this time she could. Her book fell from her chest to the floor, and she moved towards the front door, peeping through the tiny window at the top but no-one was there. She opened it slowly. No Joe, no Leonard, no more noise from the bathroom. She'd been dreaming, that was all. Drowsy from the walk the warmth of the fire and the smell of the welcoming stew, she must have fallen asleep. That was it. She had fallen asleep.

She knew it was probably all in her mind, but it bothered her, and she needed to be away from these rooms, away from these memories and away from Leonard.

For years Leonard had told her she was a bit unhinged. Maybe he was right. Maybe he was the sane one. She would give herself one more chance to see if she could manage without him. She'd rent the house out and move somewhere else, somewhere he had never been and his ghost could never find.

First thing on Monday morning she contacted the local Estate Agent who turned out to be fairly efficient. His rental department found a young couple who fell in love with the cottage at first sight, and he sold Peggy a penthouse flat in Sovereign Court. He assured her that the previous occupants had moved overseas and had definitely not died in the bathroom, although he never questioned why she wanted to know, and he didn't like to ask. There was a handsome commission on the flat. He had no idea if anyone had ever died in any part of the property but the sale would pay off his credit card and there was no way he was going to risk losing that much money by not telling the buyer exactly what she wanted to hear.

Ros recommended a removal firm who packed everything Peggy needed from the cottage and placed it in the new flat, just where Peggy wanted it. New furniture mixed with one or two pieces from her previous life. Her books were proudly displayed on a series of modern bookcases, not shoved under the bath panel.

Peggy's new life consisted of walking, reading, wandering along the High Street window-shopping, cooking and meeting up with her old friend Ros. The two spent many hours laughing about their schooldays, or sharing miserable memories of their lives before the death of their respective tormentors.

'Tomorrow Bulgaria, next week the world!' Ros sat beside Peggy for their morning coffee in a shared garden area beside the extensive driveway to Sovereign Court.

Ros was slightly shorter than Peggy, and would describe herself as comely, but compared to Peggy's stick thin arms and legs, Ros could only really be described as chubby to an unbiased onlooker. They both knew that.

The two women had the same taste in facial furniture – oversized, black-framed glasses in a severe style, sitting just below a sharp, home-cut fringe. Ros had decided years ago to leave her hair colour to Mother Nature who had bestowed on her an ageing shade of dark mouse, never flattering against sallow skin. Peggy achieved the same ageing look by dyeing her long curly locks in a jet black shade bearing no resemblance to her original colouring, and rinsed every ounce of life from her face. She had recently discovered her skin tone could be enhanced with the clever application of blusher, which Leonard would not have approved of at all.

'Have you seen the latest Collette Cooper?'

Ros was waving a hardback book in Peggy's face.

'Dear God, no Ros. I've told you before, I don't read stuff like that. I don't know how you can either. Why don't you challenge yourself?'

Ros chose to ignore the slight.

'It's our latest Book Club read, recommended by that lovely TV couple, you know they're never wrong.'

Peggy shook her head and looked skyward, muttering 'save me' to whoever was up there.

'Why don't you come along to the next meet? You don't have to read this one, I'll tell them I didn't give you enough notice. There's men too! And new members get to suggest a book for the next meeting although I wouldn't recommend you doing that. It's tomorrow night at the Memorial Hall on Grosvenor Road, 7.30. I know you're not doing anything; I saw your calendar.'

'I might not be doing anything worthy of writing onto 'Dogs of the Philippines', Ros, but I might have plans of my own – maybe a restorative spa session in my own bathroom.

'I've told you before Ros, people don't like me. Years of marital solitude have left me with no social skills. I tend to be overly anxious to offer unwanted constructive feedback. You'll be turned out because of your association with me. I can't do that to you.'

Ros laughed,

'I don't mind. If that happens it'll be God's way of telling me to find something else to do on the third Thursday of every month. Go on, you might like it, you might like the other people, they might like you – the possibilities are endless.'

Peggy screwed the cup back onto her new stainless-steel flask and looked up to the cloudless blue sky. She allowed a few moments to pass before turning towards the expectant face of her friend.

'Maybe once, but I'm not making any pretence of reading that book.'

'Good. There's wine, and olives of course. It's a lively evening usually, and as I keep telling you there's men too. You never know, Mr Right might be sitting reading the last page of Collette's 'Anguish' right now!'

'We'll see, but I'm not dressing up.'

The church clock chimed 11, and the two women bent to pop flasks and satsuma peel into their shopper bags. As they headed home, they both knew that Peggy would definitely be dressing up for the Book Club.

So it was that at 7.15pm on the following evening, Peggy found herself knocking on the door of Ros's flat. Well not so much knocking, as repeatedly lifting, and replacing the large knocker with its seasonal wreath attached – a large circle of almost dead greenery and wilting sunflowers, looped at the top with a daffodil yellow ribbon.

And of course, she was wearing her good black dress, with a new blusher and outrageously red shade of lipstick.

'Why aren't you ready? You said 7.15.'

'I am ready – it's a Book Club, not a night on the tiles! You might want to cover yourself up a bit at the front there, like this.'

'Get off woman! I can do it. The wrap-over has just slipped that's all. I'll be fine. I think it can be a big mistake to be under-dressed, but it's never wrong to be slightly over-dressed in a new situation. Come on – leave a light on there, it'll be really dark by the time we get back.'

As Ros turned to secure her front door, Peggy dabbed a tissue onto her 'So Marilyn' lips, tucking it back into her bag before Ros could see.

'It's a lovely walk through the churchyard into town isn't it? So peaceful. I see another sorry soul has been laid to rest over there. I watched them all gathering around the grave yesterday afternoon. Three limousines and so many mourners but I didn't recognise anyone. Binoculars before you ask – they're so powerful! Not much gets past me from my kitchen window.'

Look Peggy, the lights are on – that's good. Someone must be in there already, getting the glasses and nibbles out. Oooh, Mikey, Hi there!'

Peggy was astonished to see Ros suddenly running across the Memorial Hall car park, towards a shabby looking man in a long black coat. He appeared to be wearing some kind of woollen bobble hat and he was carrying a pile of books.

'Darling! You made it. Did she agree to come along? Oh of course yes.'

He lowered his voice and the two laughed together leaving Peggy feeling uncomfortable at their apparent intimacy.

'Might I be introduced?' The man was approaching Peggy with his arm outstretched.

'I'm Mike. You must be Peggy. Välkommen och god kväll'

'Yes I'm Peggy, good evening. I'm sorry, my Bulgarian is obviously not as good as yours.'

'Not Bulgarian, that was my best Swedish – I thought Ros said you had been learning it.'

Peggy shot a quick 'I'll speak to you later,' to Ros and began searching in her handbag for something, anything.

'Oh, I did start, but it's difficult to learn more than one tricky tongue at a time, I find. Of course I will return to the Swedish when I can, but I'm off to Bulgaria next March so I must concentrate on that first.'

'Of course you must, now come on in, let's introduce you to the rest of the gang.'

Gang?

They followed him as he sprinted up the few steps into the Memorial Hall, where chairs had been arranged in a circle. Ros headed straight for the only remaining two seats together, pulling Peggy who was trying desperately not to make eye contact with the rest of the gang, all staring in her direction, she was sure.

The door behind them banged shut, and Mikey headed for the seat at the far end of the hall, facing everyone, grimy library book in hand.

'Now, darlings, did we all love this latest tome from the great Collette Cooper? Did I mention she is a distant cousin of mine?'

The groans around the room were a signal that maybe he had mentioned this before.

Peggy could tell from the cover of the book that it was unlikely to have been included in a literary canon of this or any century. The cover showed a close-up shot of a brash woman with bleached blond hair, huge cleavage, and unlikely pink lips.

'Any questions before I head on with the Reading Group Hints and Insights from the TV Book Club celebrities?'

'I was wondering where the wine was.'

A tall, well-dressed woman wearing a long green bone-hugging cashmere dress and matching silk scarf was holding a wine glass aloft and waving it around to display its complete emptiness.

'You lure us here with talk of wine and then plough straight into discussing this chick lit trash.'

Wow – Peggy and Ros exchanged a look.

'She's fairly new', Ros mouthed, impressed, 'only been a few times, but never been this noisy. She's normally quite subdued–maybe she's had a few wines before she set out.'

There were murmurs of agreement around the circle. Clearly this had been a concern for everyone.

'Well, after last month's disagreements over Mr Rochester's sex appeal that went on long after Lionel had turned up to lock the doors, I thought maybe we would save the wine until after the meeting. I know some of you like to leave early, to get back for the News at 10, but if we draw our discussions to a close by say 9, that will leave us time to have a quick glass of wine and you could be on your way by 9.30. How does that sound?'

'So you can polish off the rest to yourself? No chance mate. Come on, crack the bottle now – it's why we're here!'

A large, rough looking man in navy track suit and black shoes stood up as he spoke, linking arms with the cashmere woman and they both headed for the stage where there were bottles of red and white wine lined up.

Peggy and Ros stayed in their seats.

'Has this happened before?'

'No, it's only Mike's fourth time leading the group – and last time there was a bit of a set-to at the end. He's right I guess, a few people had drunk more than perhaps they should and it did get a bit out of hand, but he keeps trying to make it a bit like a classroom. They won't have it.'

By the time the women looked up from their private conversation, there was a small gathering of bodies around the stage and Mike, wielding the only bottle opener, was trying to restore some calm.

Someone shouted,

'The red's in a screw cap.' They watched as the crowd heaved closer to the stage.

'Come on, or we'll miss out.'

Ros took Peggy's arm and they headed for the throng.

The woman in cashmere was walking towards them clutching a glass almost overflowing with red wine. With her other hand she was struggling to control a pile of crisps and she had a small swiss roll balanced under chin.

'Get in quick ladies, it's going fast and there's no olives - again. Still, any excuse to get up close and personal with Mikey eh?'

'I don't know what you mean,'

Peggy's protestations were interrupted by Ros tugging her arm towards the wine.

'Not much left ladies – red or white?'

They both chose red, took a few artisan crisps from the remaining bag, and started to walk away, but without warning Mike had slipped his arm around Peggy's shoulder and was drawing her towards him,

'Lovely to see a new person here, did I catch the name, ah yes Peggy. Yes always good to see an intelligent person for a change.'

He shot a look at the cashmere woman, and then fixed his eyes back onto Peggy, leaning in a little too close for her liking.

'Well thank you I'm sure, Mike. I don't know if I'll be a regular here – just giving it a try out, you know. I have quite enough to do really.'

She was interrupted by the cashmere woman tapping her pen on her glass,

'Come on lovebirds, let's get on with it.' Then the woman let out the most awful cackling laughter, encouraging others to join her.

Finally, taking their seats in the circle, they followed everyone else and Ros opened the book, leaning towards Peggy so she could share it with her.

'Ooh, perhaps I've got you two wrong!' More cackling from the cashmere woman.

'Come on now. I've got the official question sheet here, shall I start? Now, was the plot believable? What do we think?'

The questions went on and on, about characters, would they have done what they did, which characters were likeable and was the ending what they had expected? Someone wanted to know if everyone had guessed early on that the voice of the mother was only in the girl's head. Peggy felt sure that storyline had been overused recently since its marvellous launch with Miss Oliphant. It seemed that only a few people had read the whole book, some had listened to the audio version and spent their time commenting on the reader's dull voice. Some had obviously only read reviews because the facts they were quoting were being disputed by others.

One woman, with a reputation for always reading the last page first, expressed annoyance that the ending hadn't been clear, but no-one took much notice of that.

'Shambolic Ros, that's what it was. And that cashmere woman, yes Jean, she was awful. When she first stood up and spoke I thought she was marvellous. I actually thought well finally I've encountered someone who might be an intellectual match for me. No offence intended.'

'None taken I'm sure. I felt the same.'

'Really? Well anyway, how common she turned out to be. Hadn't paid full price for that cashmere – I heard her telling that rough track suit man that she'd picked it up in a charity shop for £3. And did you hear her showing off that she pinches vegetables from her neighbour's garden. I feel like telling someone about it. Don't forget to send me the link for the next book will you?'

'You're going to come along again?'

'Of course I am, do you think I'm going to let that Jean think she's scared me off. She's clearly got a thing for Mike, but he's out of her league, even I can see that.'

'OK Peggy, I think you might be wrong about that, but we'll see. Anyway, we've got a different sort of class first, I'll order the book club books. We need to buy some materials for this next one. No wine, but I think there's tea and cake at half time.'

Ros laughed as she headed off for her ground floor flat, leaving Peggy to go through the large oak doors into the reception area of the main building, mounting the wide stairs to the top floor, while nodding at Derek the Receptionist/Maintenance Man/Porter/General Head of Gossip, who stood behind the desk shuffling papers,

She often wished Ros would leave her to her solitude, but perhaps she was right, she did need to get out more. Maybe she would just do a few more of Ros's barmy classes and then when she got back from her trip hopefully Ros would have found someone else to go to all these events with.

Maybe.

THREE

Light snow was falling outside Dolly's coffee shop where Peggy and Ros were finishing the last crumbs of cake. They had cleared steam from the windows to give them a good view of the High Street, and both watched motionless as an elegantly dressed man in his mid-sixties, crossed the road walking towards them. They carried on watching as he slipped down the kerb, and crashed knees first to the floor.

A few workmen who had been drinking tea from disposable cups by their van, rushed to his aid and carried him gently into the coffee shop. By the time he was settled into a bench seat beside Peggy, a cup of steaming tea had been delivered to his table by the previously unhelpful waitress.

'Not sure why she's glaring at us are you Ros?'

'No. She took against us as soon as we walked in here – if she didn't want snow all over the floor in here, maybe she should have got herself out of bed a bit earlier, applied all that make up before she left the house, and allotted some time to provide a more suitable door mat. This lemon and poppy seed loaf cake was a bit stale too. If I hadn't had the coffee to wash it down I probably wouldn't have been able to finish it.'

'Ladies, would you mind moving over a bit please? The Paramedics are on their way. We need to make some space.'

As the two women walked briskly away from the coffee shop, Peggy leant in towards Ros, whispering,

'Did you see that? The accident man put his hand on my arm when I was trying to put my coat on in there.'

Pleased with her companion's startled reaction, she continued,

'He smiled at me, like he knew me. But I don't know him – never seen him before in my life.'

'It'll be the concussion Peggy – don't worry about it. He'll have been dazed by the fall – did you see the state of his trousers? All torn and bloodied, what a mess. The professionals are there now, look – they're carrying him out to the ambulance. Come on – we've stuff to buy. This way – old Reilly has artist materials; we'll get what we need in there.'

Behind the windows of 'Reilly's – We Sell Everything You'll Ever Need', stood Nicky Reilly, wife of the third-generation owner of the shop. She had rubbed a viewing area into the grimy window and was watching the events taking place outside the coffee shop.

'He's had a bit of a fall then?'

'Yes, on the kerb I think. He seems OK, just a bit shaken up but best to check him out I suppose.'

Ros cut the questioning short and ushered Peggy further into the shop.

'Come on, we need sketch pad and pencils, they're this way.'

Ros continued guiding Peggy through the stacked shelves of kitchen equipment, gardening tools and sledges, finally emerging in an open space at the back of the shop with canvases, sketch pads and racks of artists materials arranged around clean, new shelving.

'For our class tonight. Life Drawing. Peter said we needed to bring an A3 sketch pad and a selection of pencils, from H2 through the whole spectrum of hardness, to the softer Bs. B5 is as soft as we want to go I think. Come on, there's a starter set here – see?'

'Who's Peter? And Life Drawing? I thought we were Life Writing – I've been planning a whole memoir about Leonard, you know, cashing in on the current trend for spilling the beans on your experience of mental abuse and stuff like that. What's Life Drawing for heaven's sake? How can we draw 'life' in the confines of the Memorial Hall?'

Ros fetched two large sketch pads from the top shelf, grabbed starter packs of drawing pencils, and steered her complaining companion back towards the till at the front of the shop.

'Do we want this chocolate bar for a pound? It's a special offer because we've spent more than £12. I'll get two – I feel like we might need them.'

'They're nearly up to their sell by date ladies – don't hoard them! I need to get rid of a load of out-of-date stuff so I can fit all the Christmas tat the old man's bought. He was in here earlier.' She waited for a response.

Ros, more sensitive to the social niceties of general chat, fulfilled her obligation and enquired,

'Who? Mr Reilly?'

Nicky Reilly snorted,

'No, him.' She prodded a manicured finger towards the door, 'him who fell. In here asking about your Leonard.' The finger pointed towards Peggy and she could see that the orange nail polish had chipped, revealing dirt under the nail. Nicky continued,

'Said he'd seen the obit in the local rag.'

Peggy, still mesmerised by the jabbing orange fingernail, wasn't sure what to say. In all the years she had lived in the town, she rarely engaged with the shop keepers, and couldn't remember exchanging words with Nicky Reilly since they had sat on the same bus to school, when she was Peggy Underwood and Nicky was Nicola Grainger.

'Asking about Leonard? Asking what? Who is he?'

'I don't know Ros. Just said he'd seen that he'd died. I told him I'd seen you two going into the coffee shop and he wandered over. Didn't get chance to chat I guess?'

'We left when he was brought into the shop Nicky. I'm sure Peggy will catch up with him properly later. Can we just pay for these?'

They paid for their sketch pads and pencils and Ros ushered Peggy out of the shop.

The snow had begun to settle on the pavements and passing cars were throwing muddy slush towards the two women as they headed home.

It was Ros who broke the silence.

'Any idea who he might be?'

'Maybe someone from Leonard's work I guess, although he wouldn't have needed to read about it in the paper would he? Someone he knew before we met perhaps, or someone who worked with him at Latimer's and has left so didn't know all the latest gossip. I don't know. Well I don't suppose we'll hear from him again will we?'

'No, best forget about him for now.'

'Yes, probably that's best. But it'll niggle Ros – you know it will.'

Ros knew.

As they parted at the front door of Sovereign Court, Peggy asked again about their class that evening, but Ros refused to be drawn into a discussion about how it is possible to draw life, which as Peggy tried to explain is a moving thing, in a sketch pad, with no experience of it and just a piece of lead between her thoughts and the paper.

'It'll all be explained later Peggy. Just wrap up warm – it's often chilly in that Memorial Hall, as we found out when we did the 'Liven up your Lunch' session with that chef chap from the Abbey. Although it might be in their best interests to provide a decent heater tonight, or there won't be much to draw. I'll see you down here at 6.30 prompt.'

The women parted at the front door – Ros laughing to herself as she set off for her ground floor flat, and Peggy frowning as she opened the front door of the building, planning to enjoy the luxury of the lift to her penthouse apartment.

'Mrs T', Derek was calling to her as she tried to escape past him. 'You had a gentleman caller. Tall chap in a long coat, said he was from the Book Club. He left you these.'

When she turned, she realised he was holding the box of flowers she had seen on the reception desk.

She thought he had just bought them himself to brighten the place up a bit. She was mortified that they had something to do with her.

'There's a card.'

He was carrying the flowers, holding the card out towards her.

She stared furiously at the display. Derek was waiting for an answer, and was struggling with the weight of them.

'I'll take the card Derek. You keep the flowers. They look better down here. I don't like artificially dyed flowers anyway – it's virtually a crime in my opinion, and lilies give me a headache. You have them.'

Confused, Derek handed over the card and carried the flowers, in their presentation box full of water, back down to his position by the front door, arranging them again so the best side faced him.

'She's a funny one, that Mrs T', he muttered to himself, but he was pleased with the fragrant flowers. It was two days before he realised the headaches he was suffering from might be due to the aromatic floral display, and as he dumped them into an outdoor bin, wondered if maybe Peggy wasn't so daft after all, just brave enough to be honest.

Peggy waited until she was safely inside her own flat before she opened the envelope.

'I so enjoyed your company Peggy. I do hope to see you again very soon. Much love and in hope, Mike.

No kisses thankfully. Disgusted, she pushed the card into the paper recycling bin and the whole business was forgotten by the time she layered up ready for Ros's next adventure.

At 6.30 pm, the women met in the reception area of Sovereign Court and Ros was pleased to see that Peggy had brought sketch pad and pencils with her, in her special see-through V&A carrier bag. She had obtained the bag from a fellow passenger on the train when they were on their way home from an exhibition in London. Peggy refused to pay the £1.50 for the bag at the museum shop, but had talked a young woman into handing one over, using age and infirmity as her weapons of deception and theft. She had never known Peggy to suffer from the ill effects of age or infirmity in her everyday life, but had witnessed how quickly she could adopt an elderly and frail attitude in pursuit of random small items she set her sights on.

The High Street was quiet; the pavements wet with melted snow, and the women's breath hung like icy clouds behind them as they walked.

'We'll get more snow tonight I think.' Peggy suggested. Ros's nervous manner was unsettling Peggy and she wanted to calm her down. Maybe some talk of the weather would help. She did not normally allow Ros to arrange their entertainments without confirmation of agreement, and this Life Drawing was a new concept. She had spent the afternoon wondering she would be expected to draw the life she wanted, or the life she had experienced so far. How would she be able to interpret her thoughts onto paper, without her trusted words?

At the entrance to the Memorial Hall, they were met by a tall thin balding man, wearing grey sweatshirt and matching jogging trousers. He was smoking a cigarette, and held it out to one side as he greeted the two women, as if they were all old friends.

'Guys! Welcome. I'm Peter, your host for the evening.'

Peggy shuddered. Guys! Is that any way to address two women in their late fifties, here for an evening of art? And in her view he did not appear to be dressed suitably to host anything.

They shuffled past him and entered the main hall. There were four electric heaters placed around the room and a circle of chairs surrounding a chaise longue in the centre of the room. The seat had been strewn with a variety of blankets and scarves – Peggy was sure she could see some rather lovely sari fabric sparkling gold between two velvet cushions. Some of the chairs were occupied by women, juggling sketch pads and coffee mugs, and chatting nervously to each other.

Peggy turned to look at Ros, who appeared to be blushing, unless she was already feeling the effects of the electric fire closest to them. She was about to speak, but was interrupted by a large woman in a long flowery dress and voluminous blue dyed hair, who pushed past them and took her place at one of the chairs,

'Hi everyone, I'm Maddie. I'll get the best view here I reckon!'

'What have you brought me to Ros?'

But before Ros could answer, Peter returned and ushered them to the circle of seats,

'Sit anywhere girls, make yourselves comfortable. There's drinks on the table in the corner and we'll have cake in the interval, made by our own Shirley over there. Jam what is it Shirley? Jam sponge, yes, lovely, always popular. Now get settled everyone – we'll get started in about five minutes.'

Peggy tried to get Ros's attention as they took their seats, but Ros was looking straight ahead, eyes fixed on the seat in the centre of the room. There was nothing for it but to get her sketch pad out, select a few pencils that might do the job, and wait for whatever was about to happen, to start.

Five long minutes later, they heard a door behind them open and close, and heard footsteps, presumably Peter, walking back into the room. He seemed to be heading for the chair in the centre.

Sure enough, when Peggy looked up from her pencil selection, there was Peter standing by the chaise longue in a flimsy, knee length dressing gown. As she watched, eyes widening, he untied the loose knot around his waist and slipped the gown off his shoulders, kicking trainers under the seat. With horror, she saw the gown fall to the floor and there was Peter, stark naked, standing in front of them.

As she watched, memories of the term 'Life Drawing' returned to her from somewhere deep in her sub-conscious. How could she have been so stupid? She had other things on her mind, that was it. She had never allowed herself to be this daft before. What now?

She couldn't look at Ros, but fixed her gaze squarely on Peter's face – eyes, that's where she should concentrate her focus. Eyes.

He was speaking, she must concentrate.

'Now, we'll have a few two-minute-ers first, then move on to a couple of five-minute sessions, and after a break we'll crack on with a full 30-minute job. Is that OK with everyone? No judgements here. Just draw – none of us are Picassos are we? Just here to learn.'

No-one was laughing. Did she want to laugh? Was she the only one who could see the absurdity of the situation? This naked man was just standing chatting as if there was nothing unusual going on. A man who had, she could see, recently shaved his nether regions, leaving the skin red and pimply. It all looked very sore. Could she run out and leave Ros to get on with it? It was her fault they were there after all. No. She had to stay and see it through.

Suddenly Peter threw himself into a flamboyant and revealing pose on the chaise longue – one arm raised above head, and the other resting on his chest. His legs were slightly parted and he was obviously not feeling the full benefit of all the heaters.

'OK, first two-minute sketch, starting now.'

This was going to be a long two minutes.

Peggy took hold of a 4B pencil – it didn't seem quite right to use any of the H's under the circumstances. She started with his head, hoping that the two minutes would be up before she'd reached his navel.

'OK, let me shift positions.'

Was that two minutes? It didn't feel like it.

Peter adjusted himself into another position, the other arm raised above his head this time, and his legs bent at the knees. From where she sat, his knees were covering anything she was reluctant to concentrate on, and she was already sketching before Peter announced that it was time to start the second two minute-er.

The time flew. She had forgotten that Ros was there, she was so engrossed, and Peter had just become one with the furniture. Her awkwardness was evaporating.

It returned slightly for the third short session, as he re-positioned himself to face her directly, elbows resting on his knees and his hands dangling somewhere in between, not disguising the area normally covered in polite society by clothing. This was awkward. His hunched position meant there was precious little to draw above his waist and before she knew where she was, she had formed a perfect likeness of Peter's genitalia on the fifth page of her new sketch pad.

Thankfully, Peter's 'OK' drew that session to a close and she was able to turn the page before anyone could see.

'Do you practise these poses in the bathroom Peter?'

A man opposite Peggy was laughing.

'Of course', Peggy thought. 'This man has thought to himself, 'how can I expose myself to women, and men maybe, without being arrested? I know! I'll set up an innocent sounding Life Drawing

Class, where I'll even charge people to come and look at me stark naked. It's a win-win.'

'Yes, I take this seriously Jeff – you need to be able to look at different muscle groups and know how the body is made up, before you can start drawing people with their clothes on.'

Peggy felt slightly embarrassed that she had not taken Peter seriously, although to be honest she had seen quite enough of certain of his muscle groups in this particular pose, which he was maintaining long after was necessary.

He suddenly swung his legs onto the seat, and found a position face-down where he actually looked as if he had died.

Peggy waited for a moment, but then heard him announce,

'Five minutes this time. I'll try not to doze off.'

No-one laughed and Peggy noticed that his bottom was dark pink where he had sat in the previous position for too long. There were small red circles on his buttocks where he had been resting on sequins from the fabric. Still she wasn't here to do any colouring in thankfully, and she set to work.

The next five-minute session saw Peter lying on his back, with the knee closest to her slightly raised, again affording her no view of anything she didn't want to even think about, let alone draw. The large woman with blue hair did at this point, have what she obviously considered to be the best view, and was flashing her pencils across the paper with relish, occasionally holding up her thumb to measure, god knows what, but she seemed to be enjoying herself anyway.

At the end of this session, Peter sat up, threw on his dressing gown and tied it round his middle.

'Cake anyone?'

Peggy was astonished to realise that she was more offended by him offering cake around, covered in his scanty robe, than she was when he was naked, and that thought struck her as funny.

'How did you get on Peggy?'

Ros was nervously holding out a cup of coffee on a plate, which was nudging beside a slice of dry Victoria Sponge.

'He's a bit creepy isn't he? Can I see your drawings?'

'No Ros! Maybe at home, over a nightcap, but not now. He looks very sore doesn't he?'

As she spoke, she sensed someone standing behind her, and found Peter smiling over her shoulder.

'How did you get on ladies? Enjoying it?'

Thankfully they were interrupted by the blue-haired woman brandishing a half-eaten slice of cake. Her face was covered in crumbs and she was struggling to wipe away some jam that had adhered to her cheek, just below her left eye.

Peggy and Ros took this opportunity to move away as Maddie was re-introducing herself to a reluctant Peter.

'That'll teach him.' Ros laughed as they finished their drinks and after returning the cups and plates to the kitchen hatch, they both took up their seats and resumed the 'don't look at me in case I laugh' position they had held during the first part of the evening.

For the final session, naked Peter threw himself across the chaise longue – his head almost touching the floor on one side, and his feet resting the other side of the seat. This position afforded Maddie a full view of Peter's legs and genitalia and allowed Peggy and Ros to concentrate on his head, shoulder blades and chest, while adding some of the seat and the folds of the additional fabrics. Their shoulders relaxed and they drew silently for 30 minutes. Both were surprised when he slowly drew himself up to a seating position and announced the time was up.

After performing some stretches and bends, which Maddie watched in their entirety, and Peggy ignored, Peter and his flimsy robe disappeared into the Gents and moments later he returned in his grey cover-all outfit.

The two women hastily gathered their belongings, but were prevented from leaving by a small wiry man who had been sitting at the foot end of the chaise longue, drawing silently all evening.

'Now we share our drawings, over there on the table where the cake was.'

He guided them to the table and gently took their sketch pads from them, flicking through the pages before laying them down, open for all to see, on the table.

Other people had their sketches taken from them and laid out in the same way, and there were general murmurings of 'oh that's good Dave', or 'Maddie, love the way you caught the light there'.

'Did you all enjoy the session? Great, same time next week? Ladies?'

'No,' Peggy blurted, 'I think it's too far for us to make it every week, but thank you, it's been great. Very relaxing.'

The wiry man, who now seemed to be familiar somehow, started,' But I thought..'

Peggy stopped him in his tracks,

'Sorry, we need to go.' And grabbing Ros's arm, she whisked her away through the main doors and out towards the cold dark night.

Neither of them spoke until they were around the corner, out of site of the Hall windows.

They faced each other and laughed until they were breathless.

'That Jeff,' Ros spluttered,' he lives up the road by the church! Too far to come! Oh my god, what fun! I'm assuming we're not going back.'

'Definitely not! But we'll chalk that one up won't we? I've just realised, Peter – with his normal clothes on, doesn't he work in the Co-op?'

'I think he does. I can never go in there again. Come on, I have a nice home-made Sloe Gin ready to be opened.'

Peggy lifted her sketch pad in its see-through V&A carrier bag, 'I'll show you mine if you show me yours!'

FOUR

'Blimey Peggy, who have you been entertaining here?'

Peggy hurried to clear away the remnants of the previous evening's Sloe Gin and snacks.

'I love the posh sofa! Whoever it was he left these'.

Joe had been hiding a bunch of limp chrysanthemums behind his back and he whipped them into view like a magician producing a rabbit from a hat. There's a little card sellotaped to the paper, it's a bit wet I'm afraid. Peter?'

Peggy snatched the flowers from him and put the whole sorry mess, including the unread card, into the bin. Who did these men think they were, sending her flowers, to her own property, in full sight of Derek, and now Joe? It was unforgiveable.

'I've always detested these flowers Joe. They remind me of harvest festivals at school.'

'I'll remember that then!' Joe laughed and the whole business was pushed to the back of her mind, in an instant.

Peggy laughed back, as she passed Joe a mug of tea, flinching at the heat while she waited for him to take the handle of the mug.

'Oh, sorry, I was engrossed in your drawing. Is that the bloke from the Co-op? I heard he offers himself out to merry widows.'

'Don't be cheeky or I'll call Security! Ros and I went to a Life Drawing Class in the Memorial Hall last night. Honestly, I didn't realise what we were going to or I would never have agreed, but actually after the initial embarrassment I enjoyed it, even if I didn't realise at the time what a creepy man he was.'

Peggy ignored Joe's expression of doubt and continued excusing herself,

'I'd probably have been happier if he'd had some clothes on, of course. I really enjoyed the drawing part but maybe I'm more of a portrait artist.'

Joe laughed, but she needed to explain.

'Unless you're going into Medicine with that as your specialism, I don't see the point, literally, of drawing shrivelled up genitalia. So much better to have a picture you can show off to people. And clothes are good to draw. My old Art teacher used to do still life arrangements for us, and there was always loads of draped fabric behind all the bowls of oranges and empty wine bottles. I loved that. She was the only decent teacher there. The rest were all just fire-fighters, going around breaking up playground battles and con- fiscating cigarettes.'

Convinced that Joe had been suitably persuaded about her innocence, and genuine interest in art, she finally stopped talking and waited for his opinion on her drawing. Finally he found the words he needed.

'It's good Peggy, really good. My Tracey used to work for an Art Dealer, just in the office like. We had to go to a few exhibitions before she got fed up with it and her legs got bad. It's as good as anything I saw there.'

'Get away.' Peggy batted away the compliment and gestured for Joe to sit down in her new chair.

'Help yourself to a biscuit. I made them first thing this morning, orange shortbreads, they're ok but probably won't last long. So, what do you think of the flat? Is it what you expected?'

'I'll be honest with you Peg..'

Joe caught the jerk of Peggy's head at the sound of her name being shortened, and quickly added

'gy, Peggy. I've been looking at this block since it was built, wondering what sort of people would want to live here, you know, perched up on the hill overlooking our little town. And I've wondered what a builder could put into a place to make people pay so much when they don't even own the ground under their feet. But...'

He rested his mug on a small glass coffee table and stood up, wandering around the large living area, and towards the kitchen,

'Do you mind if I..?'

'Please do. I'll give you a full tour if you'd like me to. Come on.'

Peggy set her mug down on the floor by her own large wooden chair, she was still in awe of its brightly coloured Orla Kiely upholstery, and began the tour of her new home with Joe following at a respectable distance.

Apart from a moment when Joe inadvertently trapped Peggy in her bedroom for what seemed longer than it really was, the tour went well and Joe was clearly impressed.

'Best bit,' he started as they returned to their seats, 'best bit for me is your en suite. I'd love something like that so I can get myself sorted without having to wait for the boys to finish whatever it is they get up to in there. They just dump wet towels on the floor and walk away, then moan when there's no fresh ones in the cupboard.

Sorry, listen to me ranting!

I think it's great Peggy. You've set yourself up really nicely in here. I suppose I can see the appeal now, now I've been inside. The views over the fields are great. I could see my house from the kitchen, and across the fields I spotted the snowdome at Milton Keynes from your bedroom balcony. Lovely.

Your friend Ros? She lives here too did you say?'

'Yes, I've known her for years but we've only just caught up again since Leonard died. She's on the ground floor so she gets a little bit of garden, but we meet up for a natter in the communal grounds at the front of the building, or in the graveyard. You know, just to catch up.'

Joe was enjoying his coffee and shortbreads and did not seem inclined to interrupt. Peggy was enjoying having someone to listen to her, and relished the opportunity to set her new life out in words, for herself as much as for Joe.

'I went to school with Ros, we lived a couple of streets apart and bussed over to a school in Leighton Buzzard. Not special friends back then, but being out of towners, and the school bus girls, well it forges some kind of bond. We rubbed along alright, we went to village hall discos together and such. I used to look at the lads from the boys' school but she was never that interested.'

Joe laughed again, 'I remember that old bus. That all stopped by the time I was due to go to senior school, mine was closer to home and we had to walk there. It must have been fun going on a bus every day, with your friends?'

'No Joe, not fun. I never really liked the girls I was at school with. They spent all their time hitching their skirts up on the way there, and rolling them back down on the way home. Applying make-up in the mornings and wiping it off in the afternoons. The bus always smelt of cigarette smoke and chewing gum. I wondered if they wouldn't have been better buying menthol cigarettes and cutting down on the cost. A bit like buying washing powder with the fabric conditioner already in. They can't have enjoyed their cigarettes – rushing to take a few drags before they were seen. Smoking should be enjoyable, relaxing, or what's the point?'

Joe shook his head in agreement at the pointlessness of teenage smoking, while remembering his own rushed roll ups behind the bike sheds.

'You a recent smoker then Peggy?'

'I started just after I got married. Leonard hated women smoking so that's what spurred me on to get used to it. Now I just enjoy an occasional celebratory puff – I'm not addicted or anything, just, it kind of reminds me I can make my own decisions now.'

'What did you do after school then? College? University?'

Peggy shook her head.

'No, nothing like that. I wasn't interested in any of the careers they pushed at us; didn't want to be a teacher or a nurse. No-one in my family had ever been to university, so that was never an option, and if you didn't want to go to university the school didn't care what you did. But local companies used to come in for Open Days, recruiting for staff. Ros and I were in the same queue at one of those and we both ended up getting jobs at an insurance place in Bletchley and went in together on the bus. I think the money lured us in. That's how I met Leonard, on the bus.'

'Oh, nice. Love at first sight eh? I can't imagine Leonard as a young lad, flirting on the bus.'

You can't imagine it Joe, because he was never like that. Of course he wasn't.'

They both laughed, but in different ways. Joe was chucking at the thought of the old man who criticised his hedge cutting being young and frivolous. Peggy felt bitter about how she had let herself be drawn in by Leonard. How different her life might have been if she had gone into a different queue at the Open Day. If she hadn't had a minor fall out with Ros that lasted only a week but was long enough for their separate seats on the bus to provide Leonard with an opportunity to hook her into his dreary world.

'He paid my bus fare a couple of times. I didn't ask him to, but he was insistent. Then one morning he said I could pay him back at the end of the month. I was a bit surprised by that. He sat next to me on the bus for a few days and we started talking, and that was that. The end of my life as I knew it. We were married within a year or so, and Leonard said married women didn't work. Bit old fashioned but I didn't like my job so I agreed in the end. Anyway, I lost touch with Ros by then. I lost touch with *everyone* actually. Family, friends, the lot. I believed every bad thing he said about them all.'

'That's terrible! There's a name for that isn't there? I think there's been stuff about it in Tracey's soaps. Gaslighting I think they call it. I can't really imagine you being treated like that though. Wouldn't have thought you were the type.'

The silence between them was not awkward. It was a comfortable, reflective pause in a difficult conversation.

'That's interesting. Gaslighting – what an odd expression. So it wasn't just me then? Even if that is a thing Joe, there was something more about him, some imbalance in his head, something not quite right about him.

Maybe Ros suffered from that too. Anyway, whatever it was, she cut herself off she says. She had her mum to look after. Miserable old woman she was, made Ros's life hell. She died a year or so before Leonard and I bumped into her at the cemetery at the back of the Church, Ros – not her mum. You know, the overspill bit? I was looking for somewhere dismal to bury his ashes after the funeral and she was putting flowers on a grim looking grave beside the stone wall. I never did bury his ashes; I've still got them here. Anyway, we got talking, she told me about this place and there you are. She's been a good friend, although there's something wrong with me I think because I'd find it hard to tell her that!'

'I'm pleased for you.'

After another few minutes of silence while they both sipped too hot tea and pretended to be comfortable with it, Peggy was the first to speak.

'Well, you know you're always welcome to visit Joe, but I sense there was a purpose this time. Do you want to tell me, or do I have to ply you with alcohol to get you to talk?'

'Ooh, no, too early for that! Actually you're right. I, um I wanted to see you, to ask you something.'

'This sounds ominous. Shall we carry on with the tea? Or .....?'

'Tea! Tea's fine, thank you. Honestly, it's too early for me, and I'm seeing my boys in The Three Cups later – don't want to turn up squiffy do I?'

'Don't worry Joe, I've taken a step back from whisky now. Ros has got me on the Prosecco. It's rather lovely. But go on, How can I help?'

'Well it's awkward really because I don't know if you know, you know.'

'I know nothing Joe, rest assured. Just tell me.'

'Well it was my Tracey, she was talking to your tenant at number 45, your old house, you know, the Cliftons.'

Peggy nodded patiently, and waited.

'Apparently, he's lost his job and her mother has asked them if they'd like to go and live with her. See, they can't afford the rent. They might get back on their feet I spose if John gets his job back. He's been working up at the Abbey, a maintenance man, but they've laid him off. Between you and me I don't think he was very good. They don't lay people off up there for no reason. Anyway, they're in a bit of a scrape now with no money coming in and their second on the way any time.'

'They haven't approached me Joe. I might be able to help them, do you want me to talk to them? I could have a word with Melanie, John wouldn't have to know. Is that what you're asking?'

'No, no not at all.'

Joe reached out and took another shortbread biscuit, and crunched while Peggy watched him.

Joe's shorts and legs were covered in paint splashes, some blue and some green. She realised for the first time that he was a handsome man in a rugged way and Peggy briefly imagined herself drawing him, with clothes on of course. She followed the pencil line from his sand-coloured workman's boots, crumpled grey marl woollen socks and up across his shin towards the kneecap, and then skipped up to his wide shoulders, the fabric of his checked shirt stretched at that point, to almost bursting. He had let his hair grow recently and it was obvious he hadn't shaved for some time. She noticed a few white hairs in among the blond and brown stubble on his cheeks and chin. New dark lines had appeared under ice-blue eyes, that were framed by long black lashes.

'So what do you think?'

'Sorry, what do I think about what?'

Peggy gathered herself. What had she missed?

'Sorry, I was thinking about something else, start again.'

Joe shuffled in his seat and began again.

'Well, me and Tracey, we're not getting on that well at the minute and she's suggested I move out for a while. She wanted me to go and stay with one of my mates, but I wouldn't have anywhere safe to park the van, with all the decorating gear in. You know it was broken into a few years ago? Well I lost everything, all the tools, everything. I was insured so I replaced it all eventually, but I lost weeks of work. I can't have that again.

Anyway, I won a bit of money last year and I tucked it away for a rainy day and now it seems like the clouds are gathering. So I wondered if I could take on your old house for a few months. If the Cliftons sort themselves out and want it back, I'd just move out, but if not, well I could stay and look after the place.'

He sat back in his chair, took another swig of his tea, and sat cradling the warm cup in his hands.

'I'm so sorry, I had no idea things were bad between you and Tracey. And here's me whining on about Leonard.'

'I don't know if it's permanent. It's since her legs got bad, she's just bitter I think. Jealous of anyone who's not suffering like she is.

Anyway, she says she gets more attention from the man who comes to change her bandages every week than she does from me. Maybe she's right, I don't know. But I do know I make her miserable and she says she'd rather I wasn't there, "messing the place up all the time."'

His impersonation of Tracey's midlands accent was accurate, his pinched face while he spoke her words made Peggy feel that the woman was in the room with them, and she laughed.

'Sorry! It's not funny, it's just, well you did look and sound a lot like Tracey when you did that.'

'It's alright.'

Joe ran his hand through his paint splattered hair, making the front stick up and for a moment he resembled an ageing Tintin, but he quickly restored his hairstyle and looked up at Peggy with such sadness she felt ashamed for laughing.

'Honestly, I am sorry Joe. I had no idea. Your boys are always so cheerful, you are too! I just assumed everything in your world was good. That's terrible of me, not to have seen.'

'She's always thought I cared about her being older than me, but I don't. I didn't when we met and I don't now. But recently she's got old, well I mean old in her head. She won't go out anywhere – we used to go for walks through the woods, before the boys were born, then when they were nippers. But now they don't come with us, she says what's the point of the two of us going wandering about in the woods on our own. Her sister bought us tickets to the theatre last month, to see Cilla the Musical. She loved Cilla when we were younger, used to sing like her if there was Karaoke on at the pub.

But she gave them back to her. Said she might as well sit at home and listen to a CD of the real thing.'

'That's a shame.' Peggy did think it was a shame to have returned a gift, but had some sympathies with Tracey about people making a living from impersonating someone else. After all, if you can sing, go sing your own stuff. Well that was her opinion anyway but even she could see that would be no help to Joe right now.

'Yes, her sister was a bit put out – she hates Cilla so didn't want to go herself. Still, I think she sold them on.'

'Well Joe, I've no objection to you taking over the house if that's what you want, you'll need to talk to the estate agents office to finalise everything. Tell John to come and talk to me himself sometime. I am sorry about you and Tracey – maybe a break will do you both good.'

'Yeah, maybe. I don't think so though.

Realising it was probably time to go, he finished his tea, put the cup on the table and stood up slowly.

'OK, well I'll go and have a chat with John before I go to the pub in case I forget eh? I'll tell him to give you a call. And don't worry about Leonard's ghost – I don't think he'll bother me.'

Peggy was startled, had she mentioned the banging and knocking to Joe? She didn't think so.

'I heard you talking to him, telling him to clear off.'

Joe smiled,

'I think he's probably gone now – gone to find someone else to annoy.'

He spoke in such a matter-of-fact way about listening to her private conversations with her dead husband, Peggy wasn't sure how to respond.

Joe stood to leave and walked towards the door.

'I'll be able to get out won't I? I mean the doors are all locked from the outside, but I'll be able to leave won't I?'

Peggy opened her front door and pointed him towards the stairwell, smiling.

'You'll be fine, but if you have any problems, Derek is usually around to help out.'

She watched him walk along the corridor but as she turned back towards her flat, she realised he was speaking again,

'By the way, your friend, did he find you?'

'Friend? What friend?'

'Colin he said his name was. Colin Rothwell? Came to your old house looking for you. John wouldn't give him your new address, and the bloke wouldn't leave a number, but he said he'd come back sometime if he hadn't found you. Said he knew Leonard.'

'No, he didn't find me and no, I don't know who he is. But I'd like to know who's poking about asking for me. Don't tell him where I live will you? Tell John not to.'

Then,

'If he comes back, can you get some more information about him please Joe? I'd like to know who he is, at least.'

Joe gave a thumbs up and disappeared through the door to the stairwell. Moments later, Peggy stood at her kitchen window and watched as a tiny Joe made his way across the fields, stopping briefly at Peggy and Leonard's house, presumably to speak to the financially embarrassed John and Melanie. A few moments later he re-appeared and set off towards the pub, finally disappearing between the rows of houses. His drooping shoulders seemed to carry such a weight on them and she was sad she hadn't noticed that before. Maybe some time apart would help him sort things out with his Tracey, or maybe it would seal their fate in another way. Who could tell?

She cleared the cups away and picked up the Book Club latest. Why had she committed herself to reading this tripe? And did she really care 'Who Killed Sam Sword?'?

She poured flat prosecco into a tall glass and carried the book through to her bedroom where, lying diagonally across crisp white sheets, and wrapped in her new turquoise velvet throw, she would be able to admire the distant views while reading nonsense and dozing her way through the afternoon.

The book was dull. Her mind was on something else but she couldn't think what it was. Not until one of the suspects in the book arrived in a taxi at Stansted Airport in an attempt to 'escape justice' – so corny. She realised what had been troubling her. The unopened email from Stacey at the travel agents.

Peggy knew the email contained confirmation of her travel plans to Bulgaria and she also knew that she couldn't go through with it. She had caught Stacey rolling her eyes on her last visit to re-arrange the plans for a second time, and the glances between her and her two colleagues made it clear Peggy had been a topic of their tea-break conversations.

She sneezed, four times. This was unusual for Peggy and was probably due to her using too much of her new fabric conditioner.

'Constitution of an ox or a bull, and the looks to match.'

That was one of Leonard's often-repeated declarations. His tone would be that of someone paying a compliment. Maybe that was how he had got away with his cruelty for so long; making her believe she was the one who was slightly unhinged. When they were first married, she would retaliate against some of his jibes, but he would carry on as if she hadn't spoken, or accuse her of being the one who had caused any tensions,

'Ooh touchy', 'hit a nerve there' or 'someone's been on the bottle last night'.

So she stopped responding to his nasty remarks until in the fashion of osmosis the comments seeped into her sub-conscious and became facts. Without even thinking about it, she had for many years accepted she was useless, ugly, and a secret alcoholic.

'Leonard's dead.' She was speaking aloud. Alone in her own beautiful apartment, she had allowed the memory of Leonard to creep in and taint the air.

'He's dead. You've rented your house out, bought a property, furnished it with lovely things, and you're out meeting people. And you can't be that ugly or these men at Ros's groups wouldn't be talking to you like they do, and sending their wretched flowers.'

She reached for her personalised Zoflora spray bottle (a house-warming gift from Ros), and within a few minutes an aroma of Midnight Bloom filled the air. Leonard was gone.

But the sneeze had given her an idea. She reached for her new mobile phone in its mock snakeskin case and called Stacey direct. Illness, that would be her reason for cancellation – Stacey couldn't argue with that.

She didn't argue, and the plans were once again put on hold. That's what Peggy had told her although even without a view of Stacey's face she could imagine the eye-rolling and gestures towards her colleagues as she mouthed,

'Her again! Cancelling again. Time waster.'

Peggy didn't care. When she ended the call a weight had lifted and she returned to the search for Sam Sword's killer with fresh eyes.

FIVE

'I'm feeling bored Ros. All these classes are great. I am looking forward to Stitch-along next month, and if I find a suitable choir I would still like to join, but I'm feeling like there's something missing. Now I could be going out every day to do something meaningful, I'm spending even more time on my own with no intellectual conversation – no offence. Shortbread?'

'Ooh, very orangey. None taken. Did you make these? Nice – I bet they were lovely yesterday, a bit soft for dunking this morning.'

15-ALL.

'Yes, you know I've been wondering about looking for a little job,' Ros continued, the minor victory behind her,

'Maybe in the shop at the Abbey, or perhaps volunteering in one of the charity shops on the High Street. If I always washed my clothes when I got home, I imagine the musty smell would fade pretty quickly. Mother always said I should have followed a career in retail, although if I was out of the house for more than an hour she'd be calling WPC McMichael to come and bring me home so how she'd have coped with me being out all day, who knows?'

'We're thinking along the same lines Ros. I was wondering about one of the smarter charity shops. Not the dog charity ones – I wonder what the stuff is like if it's come from houses full of dogs or cats – it would take more than a squirt of fab-con to get your work clothes back to normal. I might be wrong there of course, it's been known. I suppose the money *goes* to animal charities – that doesn't necessarily mean the stuff comes from houses with animals in.'

'Well, pop your cup in my bag and let's have a wander along the High Street. I'll drop our flasks and bits in through my door – you can collect your tin of biscuits and your flask when we come back. It looks as if the sun's coming out, it might be nice to have a stroll – maybe you'll find someone to exchange a few intellectual words with.'

Said with a smile, but Ros knew Peggy wouldn't be able to come back from this surprise attack while she was busy screwing the lid on her flask. Ros knew she had game set and match, and due to her well-honed skills of timing, she was probably winning the tournament, even without Peggy's acerbic vocabulary.

Twenty minutes later, the two women were peering through the window of a tired looking charity shop, analysing the goods for sale. The hand-made posters stuck to the door advertised past events, and a faded pink sheet headed 'Thank you Boys and Girls', pronounced sums raised of £90.81 from a long-ago Scout Car Wash.

'Which of these did you imagine were the smarter ones?'

'Well, the Hospice ones – we might all need a hospice one day – that's the charity I will always give to. Some of these others, I wonder what they do with the money. I imagine some of it gets spent on the annual party for the volunteers. I'm not prepared to hand over cash so a lot of home knitted woman can sit sipping sherry at my expense.'

'I assure you madam,'

Peggy and Ros spun round to face a large woman in a tight magenta business suit, with jacket buttons straining across the middle, wrinkling the emerald green sateen blouse beneath. The magenta trousers were at least six inches from the floor and revealed not only the top of some American Tan ankle pops, but a pair of diamond studded, black patent sandals with kitten heels.

'Yes you. I assure you that all the proceeds from this establishment are poured straight into our central fund. We pay for our own Christmas dinner, which we take at The Three Cups over the road if you must know.

What are you looking for anyway, peering in like that? You're unsettling my regulars.'

The women glanced through the now open door and could see a few elderly customers staring their way. One man was holding a bundle of video cassettes in one hand, and a brown teapot in the other.

'Come on, come in and have a proper look. Our stuff doesn't smell if that's what you're worried about. Millie and I give everything a run through in our own washing machines before it gets put on a rail.'

As she spoke, she tapped her name badge 'FIONA' with pride, emphasising the personal pride they took with the goods for sale.

'You won't find the pages of our books sticking together either. Come on.'

She steered the two bemused women in through the door of the shop and they were greeted by the regulars.

They both spotted the 'Staff Wanted' sign at the same time.

'I say', Ros was the first to speak,

'You say Staff Wanted – but how many people are you looking for? And is it paid or voluntary?'

Fiona laughed.

'You two? Ha! I've never met a more unlikely duo for working in here! I've seen the pair of you wandering up and down the High Street with your noses in the air. You,' she jabbed an arthritic finger towards Ros, 'you weren't so snooty when your mum was alive were you? Coming in here looking for Mills and Boons to keep her busy so you could have a bit of peace and quiet.'

The regulars shuffled into the corner of the shop where worn shoes and hats were piled on every shelf – all eyes on the three women. Peggy, more offended by the choice of literature than by Fiona's outburst, broke the silence.

'Mills and Boon? Really?'

'Yes, she liked them. Fiona, that was quite rude. We're wondering about working for your charity.'

'Yes, Fiona,' a mumble from Hat Corner, 'what's come over you? I've never heard you speaking like that before.'

The video man broke away from the huddle and walked towards Fiona with his free hand outstretched. He ushered her into the back room of the shop and there were the sounds of a kettle being filled.

'Should we go Peggy? I feel a bit awkward in here now, what with her abusing me and mother, and now this private situation going on.'

'Leave? No way – this is the best entertainment we've had in weeks!'

The bell rang out from the doorway as a new customer entered. Not put off by the huddle of regulars in one corner, and the two women standing by the till, all facing him and all staring, he adjusted his hat so it covered his eyes and continued towards the china and glassware shelves. He began scrutinising a set of coffee cups, picking each cup and saucer up and replacing it carefully. Without revealing his face, the stranger scoured the shelves as if looking for something specific and after a few minutes of carrying out his search in silence, he turned and left the shop.

Peggy turned to Ros,

'Isn't that the chap who fell over outside the coffee shop?'

Before Ros could answer, they were interrupted by a red-faced Fiona appearing from the back room, accompanied by the video man, still clutching his collection of old films.

'I'm so sorry Ros. I've no idea what came over me. It's all getting a bit much in here. Just take those videos Frank, settle up tomorrow. You lot, can you go now? Change the sign to CLOSED as you leave will you?'

Fiona turned to the two women and rolled her eyes.

'They treat this place like a meeting place, hardly ever buy anything, they just stand by the window and gossip. I guess I've given them something to gossip about now haven't I? Look, there they go, straight into Dolly's Tea Shop. That should keep them busy for an hour or so.'

Peggy's recently acquired make up knowledge had made her more observant about how other women maintained an appearance of youth, and she was always ready with some advice for anyone falling short of normal standards,

'You might want to check your eyebrows in a mirror Fiona. One of them has moved a bit – you look furious.'

Fiona grabbed out at a circular vanity mirror, and sweeping the price tag out of the way, proceeded to rub at her eyebrows.

'I'll rub them both off and even it up. There.'

She returned the mirror to the shelf and faced the two women, who stared at the transformation. Fiona appeared to have aged 20 years, and her face seemed wider without the definition of the jet-black brows. Her cheeks were red and puffy and strands of hair had loosened from the tight bun, revealing streaks of white among the black.

'Shall I make us all a cup of tea while you straighten yourself up Fiona? I have a comb if you'd like to borrow it. Ros? Tea?'

Ros nodded and Peggy retreated into the back room of the shop, clattering cups into a washing up bowl and tutting loudly as she retrieved tea and sugar caddies from a grubby shelf above the sink.

Fiona slumped into a shabby chic chalk painted chair, and rummaged in her handbag, pulling out lipstick, comb and a tin labelled *Feathered and Full Brows*. Her hands moved quickly from tin to face, lipstick was applied and dabbed, then tweaking stray white hairs into place she took a final satisfied glance into her compact mirror and returned all the equipment to her bag.

'There – normal service resumed. Do you still have all those Mills and Boons Ros? I'll take them off you if they're in your way.'

'No, they went to the tip with all her other stuff, when I moved. I don't have room for bookcases in my new place.'

Then seeing the look of disappointment cloud the newly pampered face of Fiona, she added,

'Sorry.'

'Such a waste. My ladies love reading those.'

The two women then settled into an uncomfortable silence, while they listened to Peggy moving around the back room and both greeted her with relieved smiles when she appeared carrying three cups in her slender, but rather large hands.

'Tea, no sugar – OK? So Fiona, how many vacancies do you have for the shop here?'

'Well, three really. I know I was a bit unkind earlier, but do you two honestly think this is something you want to be doing? I mean, we do get some odd customers, and they have to be handled sensitively. Could you do that? And to be honest with you, some of the stuff that comes in is a bit, you know, grubby.'

'Definitely we want to do it, don't we Ros?'

Not stopping for confirmation or otherwise, Peggy continued, 'We could work together on shifts, or fill in separately – it's up to you. Is it paid? Or voluntary?'

'It's voluntary, to start with anyway. If you want to give it a go, do a couple of shifts – separately at first might be best so you get proper training. How about Ros you come along on Monday morning, and you,' pointing at Peggy, 'a few days later? That'll give us time to size each other up and see what we think.'

'We'll do it, won't we Ros? Come on it'll be fun. Have you finished with your cups; I'll wash them up? First thing I'm going to do when I get here is sort out that back room – it's grimy! Fiona? Finished?'

Peggy carried the cups out to the back room and there was more tutting and splashing before she reappeared behind the cash desk.

'What time do you want Ros on Monday? 9?'

'9 is fine with me. I'll see you then Ros.'

With that, Fiona stood up, set the re-vamped chair back in its place and moved towards the shop front, opening the door for the two women, beckoning them to leave.

'Thank you Fiona, it's been an interesting morning. We'll bring ID and stuff with us won't we Ros – you need to know who you've got working in there I suppose. We'll see you next week. I hope you have a good day. Bye.'

As Fiona Mayhew closed the door on her visitors she wondered what on earth had just happened to her. Hurling abuse at that poor woman. She'd had enough problems looking after that awful mother of hers and there she was compounding the misery by humiliating her in front of a shop full of onlookers. She seemed to have made matters worse for herself by chumming up with that Peggy, Fiona knew all about her. There was talk she'd done for her husband and covered it up, but nothing was ever proved. Then she'd broken down in front of Frank – what would he want in return for his private chat and sympathy? She shuddered at the thought. And now she'd got talked into those two coming in to work with her. What would Millie say?

She left the Closed sign on the shop door, turned the lock, and headed for her handbag where she found a welcoming miniature of brandy. She unscrewed the top and downed the lot, closed her eyes, and stayed there for a few minutes, feeling the warming liquid move down her throat, soothing her jangling nerves. Then, ignoring the peering eyes of customers at the window, she went into the back room and settled down on her comfy chair for a doze. She deserved it.

Meanwhile, Peggy was ushering Ros away from the shop in the direction of The Three Cups.

'Cause for celebration I think, don't you?'

Ros finally spoke,

'I haven't even agreed to it yet! You've just got me talked into a job, and neither of you even asked if I wanted it.'

Peggy, ignoring the protests, headed straight for the bar.

'A bottle of your cheapest Prosecco please Mark. We're celebrating.'

'Ooh – have your numbers come up?'

Joe's eldest son Mark turned and reached into the tall chillers behind the bar to retrieve a bottle of Prosecco and began filling a metal bucket with ice.

'Go and sit down ladies, I'll bring it over. Two glasses?'

Peggy nodded, set a £20 note on the bar, and moved Ros towards a table in the large bay window with views of the High Street, and their new workplace, the charity shop.

The two sat in silence until Mark appeared with the ice bucket containing the Prosecco, and two tall champagne flutes. He set them on the table and with a flourish more in line with a waiter at The Ritz, removed the bottle from the ice. Once he had dried it on the black bar towel, he began to unscrew the wire around the cork, popping it discreetly and pouring cold fizzy wine into the two glasses.

'There you are ladies, complimentary peanuts. Enjoy.'

Then bending towards Peggy, whispered 'I just need another £3 for the bottle, when you're ready, no rush.'

'Here, I'll pay it. My contribution.'

Ros reached into her pocket, produced three one-pound coins, and set them on the table.

'Well that shows how long it is since I had something to celebrate – I was expecting change that I could go to the Coop with!'

The women laughed, chinked their glasses, and drank their fizz.

'Lovely, very civilised. Listen, do I have to go in first for my shift? I know she was having a bad day, but she's obviously not keen on either of us and she was quite rude about Mother. Were we at school with her? I don't recognise her at all.'

As they spoke, Fiona, wearing her coat and hat, could be seen arguing with two young women, both trying to push buggies into the shop past her as she was trying to leave. She was successfully blocking their way and eventually she managed to shut the door behind her, lock it and walk away from them, heading for the bus stop. The young women were laughing, impersonating Fiona's shuffling steps and eventually they headed off towards another charity shop where they managed to gain entry without any trouble.

'Sad case isn't she? Well maybe you and I can cheer her up. She looks older than us so even if she went to our school we wouldn't have known her. I don't recognise her, but she's obviously had her eyes on us for a while. I'm glad she thought we had our noses in the air – that's just the image I want us to portray. You're in first. You're less likely to upset her than me.'

'Anyway,'

Ros bent close to Peggy, whispering,

'I have to ask you – are you a regular in here? You seem to know your way around. What would Leonard say?'

'What Leonard would say is "where's my dinner woman? why haven't you starched my shirts?" That's what Leonard would say. Anyway, he knew Mark. He didn't like him; always said he was a layabout, but he's a good lad. He works on one of the farms on the road out of town, but when they're not busy he does a few shifts in here. I used to walk into town with him when Leonard was alive, when I was going to the Library and he'd be coming here. Nice lad, but he needs a haircut. I don't think his mum pays him much attention – or anyone else for that matter.'

'Are you about to gossip Peggy?'

'I was! But I won't, not now you've noticed.'

The women laughed and carried on topping up their glasses until the bottle was empty, then carrying the ice bucket and glasses back to the bar, they shouted cheerful farewells to Mark, and to all the other afternoon drinkers, and headed back out into the festive lights of the High Street.

'You go home Ros; I've got a couple of jobs I want to do first. Honestly, I'll be fine. I'll see you later, or tomorrow, or whenever. Go on, off you go.'

Confused, Ros turned towards home, dabbing her hot cheeks with a tissue she had found in her handbag, hoping no-one had seen her spilling out of the pub, and praying that her mother wasn't looking down on her, willing some form of retribution to befall her for straying from the straight path she had always insisted on.

Peggy, however, had a spring in her step. She had made a decision. She was going to un-cancel, if that was a thing, her big trip. She'd been in a pub. She had drunk Prosecco during the day. She had a job, albeit unpaid at the moment but she could see herself taking over from that ludicrous Fiona, and managing the place within a few months. Her confidence was high. She could do anything. She would travel.

SIX

'Are you having a laugh?'

Peggy recoiled at the hostility from Stacey in the Travel Agents.

'I only cancelled it this morning Mrs Thomas. I managed to get you your money back, but there's admin fees to pay every time you change your plans. Mr Borthwick hasn't passed these on to you yet because he says he was a friend of Mr Thomas, but it's the third time you've done this now. How do I know you won't be back in tomorrow cancelling it again? We're not here to be picking up the pieces every time you change your mind.'

How dare this slip of a girl speak like that? To her? Peggy.

'I would say, young woman, that that is exactly what you are here for, and I have never asked to be spared admin charges – if that's the price of having some flexibility with my life, then it's worth paying.

Please ask Mr Borthwick not to intervene on my behalf again. He owes me nothing.'

At the sound of raised voices, a gentleman with a mop of carrot red hair and skin the colour of self-raising flour appeared behind Stacey. He was buttoning his pale grey suit jacket and adjusting his matching tie. If it hadn't been for the colour of his hair, Peggy thought he might not have been visible against the fashionably muted shades of the office walls.

'Mrs Thomas,' the pale man thrust a hand towards Peggy. He had a firmer grip than his appearance might suggest.

'How can we help? Come through to my office. Stacey, two coffees in here please.'

Stacey glared in Peggy's direction and scraped her chair back, tutting as she headed for the coffee capsule machine.

'Mericano OK?'

Peggy ignored her and walked into the back office with Mr Borthwick, taking the chair he offered her.

'Sorry about that Mrs Thomas. Stacey's one of my most experienced agents and I assure you she's normally very patient and professional.'

He paused suddenly and Peggy realised Stacey had appeared at the door, a china cup and saucer in each hand. She glared again at Peggy, then at Mr Borthwick, placed the cups in the centre of the desk and left, closing the door behind her.

'As I was saying, she's a very experienced agent, but I think she has been confused by your plans changing so often. Are you really sure you want to travel to Bulgaria? Away from the normal tourist sites? Alone?'

'Yes Mr Borthwick, I do want to travel to Bulgaria, and yes I would rather be alone than be irritated by an unsuitable companion. Before you say it, I would consider any companion to be unsuitable. I am a person who prefers to be alone. It's what I am accustomed to.'

'But the language Mrs Thomas. It can be challenging; how will you get around?'

'Please call me Peggy. Thomas reminds me of my deceased husband. I have been learning the language Mr Borthwick and while I appreciate I am probably not as fluent as a native speaker; I would imagine I could find my way around and order a meal for myself. How hard can it be? I am sure the local people will be as friendly and welcoming as they appear to be in the books and tapes I have been borrowing from the library.'

Mr Borthwick shuffled some papers on his desk while he considered a suitable response.

'Of course, Peggy, you must bear in mind that the people who make the books and videos you have been using to learn the language, will always, how shall I say this? They will always be careful when selecting the characters to portray a specific friendly and welcoming nature. That might not always be the case when tourists arrive in the country and meet with ordinary, non-acting people going about their everyday lives.'

'Are you trying to put me off? Mericano – is that black coffee?'

Peggy picked up one of the cups and drained the coffee in one gulp.

'Sorry, I was parched. Is it really your job to deter your customers from travelling?'

'All I'm trying to say is that if you are nervous about travelling, and that is why you often, always, cancel your plans, maybe you could try somewhere closer to home for your first trip. Maybe somewhere where they speak English, or even an area in Bulgaria where they are more accustomed to English tourists. Perhaps you would be more comfortable with somewhere less challenging, yes, that's what I'm trying to say.'

'Well what would be the point of that Mr Borthwick? What would be the point of travelling somewhere to practise my languages, where everyone speaks English? I might as well go into Bletchley for a couple of weeks!'

Peggy reached out for her coffee, but seeing that the cup was empty, and remembering how quickly she had finished it, she reached instead for the other cup, and drank from there. Well, he wasn't drinking it.

'I'll tell you what we'll do Peggy. I'll ask one of the girls to reinstate your previous booking, on a 48-hour reservation – we don't offer that for all our customers, but I did find your Leonard very helpful early on in my career in the town, you know, with the Lodge and all. You go home and have a good think about the trip and then you let me know in two days' time if you want to go ahead and finalise everything. How's that?'

Peggy didn't know about the Lodge and all, she had never before heard of Leonard being helpful to anyone in his whole life, and was not aware that anyone had feelings other than dislike for him. But Mr Borthwick's plan made sense. She was starting to worry that once the effect of the Prosecco had worn off, she might be finding the whole idea of going to remote parts of Bulgaria a bit worrying.

'Agreed. Thank you. And thank you for the coffees. Stay there, I'll see myself out. And I'll talk to you in two days' time. You've been most helpful.'

She stood and walked away from Mr Borthwick and for the second time in the day, a High Street trader was left wondering what on earth had just happened.

Stacey was standing on the pavement holding a metal smoking device to her face when Peggy left the shop. She took a drag on it and her face disappeared in a cloud of smoke. Peggy coughed and walked away, knowing Stacey's eyes would be rolling skyward again, and she wondered if the woman had any other expressions, or was that just how she was.

When she got back to Sovereign Court, Joe was waiting for her by the front door.

'Ros said you'd be along shortly. Hope you don't mind me waiting. There's something I need to talk to you about.'

'That's fine Joe. Come up, I'll pour us a drink.'

She pushed open the large doors and he followed, gasping again at the size and opulence of the hallway. The freshly polished black and white tiles sparkled from the twinkling bulbs of a large chandelier hanging over their heads, high above the sweeping staircase.

They both nodded at Derek the caretaker with his large shiny name badge proclaiming he should be addressed as Mr Lewis. He stood in judgement of all visitors, behind a large mahogany reception desk, complete with bell for any times when he might be briefly absent from duty. Peggy ignored him and headed for the staircase.

'He can think what he likes.' Peggy announced while they were still in earshot.

Joe lowered his eyes, feeling heat rising in his face.

'Silly old sod likes to think he offers moral guidance to all of us single women, but we know what his true motives are, don't we?'

She winked at Joe and again he felt colour and heat rise in his cheeks.

'Do you have many visitors Peggy?'

The words were out before he had time to think.

'Hah! No I don't actually, but I play a game with him where I hint that my visitors arrive and depart while he's off on one of his errands around the building. He's not sure about me and that's how I like it. Are you OK for another two flights?'

Joe's breathing was heavy by the time they reached the top floor, but Peggy was clearly accustomed to the climb.

'This must be what keeps you fit Peggy – saves on a gym I suppose.'

'Yes, I tell Ros she should visit me more, but even when she does she's in the lift – she'll be sorry when her knees pack up through lack of use. Here we are.'

The air in Peggy's flat was cool, and Joe was pleased when she suggested he sit himself down while she made them a drink.

'I've been enjoying Vodka Martinis this week Joe. Would you like one?'

She waved away his protests about the time of day and took two cocktail glasses from a shiny red cabinet, stocked with pairs of glasses in all shapes and sizes, and began her preparations.

He watched, fascinated, as she poured liberal amounts of vodka and another liquid he couldn't identify into a cocktail shaker. She removed ice from a bag in her new American freezer and put the lid back on to the shaker.

'The first time I did this I forgot to put the lid and the strainer on! What a mess there was, and what a waste!'

Joe smiled in sympathy as if this was a familiar situation for him, in a 'we've all done it' way, but he had no idea what she was talking about. He'd watched the Tom Cruise film years ago when Tom became a super cocktail barman, but he had no idea this went on in people's homes. This was far removed from his preference for a nice pint of beer on a Saturday night.

Finally she poured the clear liquid into the two glasses, and dropped an olive into each.

'There, shaken not stirred.'

'Oh yes, James Bond, right?'

'Certainly, James Bond Joe, now – cheers.'

She chinked her glass with his and took a large sip, nodding at him to do the same.

'I don't really like the taste, but I feel it's something I should persist with. When I'm on my travels, I may encounter a cocktail bar and I think it's important that I know what I'm doing. Don't you agree?'

Joe nodded, wincing at the sharp taste of his drink, and confused about why there was an olive in his glass. Was he supposed to eat it? He decided he would watch and see what Peggy did, and follow suit, although he wasn't confident that she knew much more than him.

Now, what did you want to see me about?'

Joe had forgotten that he was the one who had initiated the meeting, and for a few moments he struggled to remember what it was he needed to see her about. He had been distracted by wondering how she would get on in another country when she seemed so unfamiliar with normal social behaviour. She would be sure to upset someone. How would she survive, miles from home and not having anyone around to help her out.

'Oh, yes, sorry. Well you had a visitor, again, at the cottage. The same man asking after you. He asked about Leonard first, but he knew he had passed on, er, died. Said he was a friend of the family, and was asking where you were living now.

I didn't tell him your address, obviously, said his name again, Colin. Colin Rothwell.'

'What did he want? We didn't have any friends of the family. What did he look like?'

'He was a smart bloke, well dressed, sort of greying hair. Maybe your age or a bit older. He was wearing a brown coat and he had a hat on, like my dad used to wear – trilby he called it but I don't know if that's its proper name. Seemed nice enough, but you never know do you? Seemed a bit edgy to me, you know.'

She didn't know.

'What did you tell him then?' Peggy had no interest in the details, she just wanted more information than Joe appeared to have, and he was waffling.

'Well I said you'd moved out, into your own place like, not far away. And I said you were doing OK. He did seem like he was pleased to hear that. Don't you recognise his name?'

'No, but there was a man in the charity shop earlier in a brown coat, and he had a trilby on, pulled down over his face – it looked a bit odd actually. I thought that might be him. And what's he up to?'

'Did Leonard have any other family do you know? Like cousins or anything?'

Peggy was staring out of the window, into a dark sky. What did she know about Leonard? Not much as it turned out. Only as much as he had told her, and only then when she asked questions. He seemed not to want to talk about his past and she hadn't pressed him – not interested she supposed. She thought about how much she pressed Ros, even now, about her life. She recognised she was quite a nosy person – never wanting to give much away about herself, but keen to know all the ins and outs of other people's backgrounds. She liked to know what made people tick, but as she gazed into the world beyond her window she realised that not only did she know nothing about what made Leonard tick, she had never tried to work it out, and never really cared. She took a sip of her Martini before answering,

'No.' She took another sip and looked up at Joe, who appeared to want a more detailed response.

'He said his parents had died a long time before he met me. He never mentioned any family, and I never asked. I wonder who this man is. How can we find out?'

'Well I said I'd talk to you and he said he'd come back to the cottage in a day or so to see if you wanted to see him.'

'Well I want to know who he is but I don't really want him coming here.'

'Leave it with me, I'll try to find out a bit more about him. I could suggest you meet up in Dolly's, then I could be in there as well – at another table of course – and keep an eye. You know, make sure he's not an axe murderer.'

'You're watching too much TV Joe. How are you getting on anyway, now you're living the single life? Cottage OK?'

'The cottage is great, thank you, yes. Lovely. Incredibly quiet, and no sign of Leonard roaming around. I can still hear all the sounds from the soaps coming through the walls when Tracey's watching her TV. Well, she doesn't do much else actually, apart from bang on the wall when there's a spider or a mouse in the kitchen. Then I have to go round and sort it out. But still, I get time on my own. I've got the spare remote for her TV and it works through the window, so when I think she's probably fallen asleep I go and zap the sound off.'

Joe laughed, and Peggy appeared shocked but when she visualised the reality of what was going on in her and Leonard's old home, she laughed too – like she never had when she lived there.

'What?' Peggy had caught Joe looking at her in an odd way. He had finished his drink, leaving the olive in the bottom of the glass, and was staring at her.

'I, it's just that I don't think I've ever seen you laugh like that. You know, if you don't mind me saying, but your face changes when you laugh – you look, you know, different.'

He supposed he had gone too far, so tried to change the direction of what he was saying, knowing that if he had any sense at all he would just shut up. But still, he felt unusually jovial, and very friendly towards this woman who he had known for a long time, but not really known at all. And she did look younger when she laughed, and rather lovely. He carried on,

'All the time you lived next door, I never heard any laughter and I know how much voices can be heard through those walls now. I hear my name being mentioned in a bad way, even though I'm not in there anymore. I don't think I ever even heard voices when you two were living there. Nothing. You were quiet neighbours. Now I'm wondering what you heard from us! And I'm worrying!'

'You shouldn't worry Joe. Having you and your family as neighbours was a bit like having The Archers on a low volume all the time. I knew it didn't matter if I missed a few episodes because nothing much was going on, but occasionally something would make me smile, then I'd listen in for a few minutes until I realised the story wasn't going anywhere then I'd go about my business again. I do like The Archers by the way, it's sort of a compliment.'

There were a few moments of awkward silence while Joe continued to stare at Peggy, his cheeks flushed and warm, until Peggy's clock chimed seven o'clock and he was jolted back into the real world. He stood, and started to put his jacket and scarf on – the scarf took longer to arrange than it probably had earlier in the day, and he had buttoned his coat so that there was an extra button on one side at the top, and on the opposite side near his waist. Peggy decided not to embarrass him by mentioning it – he would find out soon enough and would imagine she hadn't noticed.

He reached out to shake Peggy's hand, but by the time she had put her glass down on the table, he had returned his hand to his jacket pocket, and the awkwardness made them both smile.

'Olive?' Peggy took her olive and popped it into her mouth, feeling the pimento stuffing ooze onto her tongue.

'The best bit of a Martini as far as I can see.'

Joe watched the olive being chewed up and swallowed, but wasn't keen.

'Not my cup of tea to be honest – you have mine.'

The pair moved towards the door and eventually agreed that it should be Peggy who dealt with the locks and bolts, standing back once the door was open to allow Joe to pass.

'I'll see what I can find out for you and I'll see if I can get a phone number from him, then you can make your own arrangements, I think that's best. Then if you want me to hang around I will. OK?'

Peggy smiled at Joe's obvious concern for her and nodded in agreement, watching him weave his way along the corridor to the lifts.

A few minutes later she was at the window, watching him in the warm glow of the streetlights. He negotiated his way through the Kissing Gate at the edge of the field, and wandered along the pathway towards the cottages.

'Nice man,' she found herself thinking, as she hummed a tune from Madam Butterfly, washing their glasses, and placing them neatly back in the cabinet.

'Yes, a nice man.'

SEVEN

Peggy's introduction to the Choir Set had not started well. She had already approached several community choirs in the area, but they had not welcomed her repertoire suggestions and had not agreed that only people who sang well should be choir members.

Explaining her predicament to Ros over coffee one morning, on their favourite bench in the churchyard, Peggy was giving a clear indication that Ros's idea of joining the local choir group might not be a good one.

'Why are you bringing up a choir again now? I tried that when you mentioned it before and those people don't like me. Anyway I was never sure whether you originally suggested it to be kind, or if you'd heard me singing along to Handel's Messiah and realised I needed help. I've always loved that piece so much – Leonard hated music – said it was heathen.'

Ros passed Peggy a steaming coffee from the flask, and waited for her to place the cup on the floor at her feet before passing her a home-made brownie.

'These are vegan. But they are lovely. A friend from Book Club is coming round for a coffee tomorrow morning and she's plant-based so I had to rummage through some magazines for a recipe. They're alright.'

Ros took a bite from her brownie and began chewing, finally resorting to swilling her mouth round with hot coffee to unstick her teeth and tongue.

'Well here's the name of the man who runs the local choir, Laurence. He's a bit of a dish apparently – if you like that sort of thing. He'll be down there later tonight – go and have a chat. He sets up from 6.30. If you like the idea, I'll come with you to the singing sessions, but there's no point me vetting it – my standards aren't as high as yours are they?'

The two women sat in silence as they chewed their brownies, helped down with the coffee.

Relieved to be rid of the plant-based treat, Peggy was keen to know about Ros's first shift at the charity shop. Ros was cagey.

'Fine', and 'Quiet' were the answers.

'Did you have a sort out in that back room? Was Fiona there? Did you have to wash your clothes when you got home?'

The back room had been left for Peggy apparently, Fiona was there and was quite irritating with her constant chatter and yes when she got home her clothes smelt of damp, cheap perfume, and body odour, mainly from Fiona – the stuff in the shop was definitely clean and smelt fine. She wasn't sure if it was for her, but she'd offered to give it another go. Fiona was apparently not desperate to arrange another shift. She was gloomy about the festive season and was not expecting a huge pre-Christmas rush.

Ros was pre-occupied with her visit from the Book Club person who turned out to be Jean, the woman in the charity shop cashmere cardigan, who had been so annoying at their first shared visit.

'How was that arranged then? I expect she came into the shop to buy more second-hand clothes did she?'

Tired of the questioning, Ros explained that yes, Jean had come into the shop, seemed to know Fiona well, but it wasn't clear how, and had bought several second-hand designer label outfits. Ros had watched her go straight into the Dry Cleaners with them and had bumped into her in the Co-op while Ros was buying some cat food for a hedgehog that had started visiting her garden. She'd named it Spike and was speaking about it as if it was a domestic pet.

'So you're paying for cat food and what? She just says she's coming round for coffee and vegan chewing gum?'

'We got chatting outside, that's all. She said she finds her days a bit lonely and I said I felt the same. We both like the same books, and films actually, and we both knit and crochet and stuff. I just invited her round, that's all. She was pleasant.'

Peggy was rattled by Ros's new friendship and she couldn't understand why. She didn't think she felt jealous. They hardly lived in each other's pockets, but Peggy liked how close they had become, how they shared little snippets about their lives and seemed to trust each other with secrets they hadn't shared with another person. Well that's how Peggy saw it anyway.

This Jean, she seemed odd. She'd flirted with Mikey, but it was half-hearted – as if it was all for show, and he certainly didn't appear to be comfortable flirting back. Oh well, maybe it would be one visit and they'd realise they didn't have that much in common after all.

Peggy hadn't finished her coffee when Ros started to pack away the flask and she held her hand out for Peggy's cup, forcing her to down it in one. It was still quite hot and it was a flushed Peggy that wished Ros well as they parted that morning.

Maybe out of spite, or maybe because she genuinely wanted to sing with other people, not just in the shower, Peggy did want to join a choir and had been trying to find something suitable for so long. She really felt that this might be the place she could meet a long-term companion. Not necessarily a new husband – actually she couldn't imagine anything worse – but maybe someone to arrange trips to museums or galleries with, or exchange intelligent conversation.

Whatever the motivation, at 6.30 that evening Peggy was hovering outside the Memorial Hall, waiting for Laurence to appear.

She was adjusting her hand painted silk scarf for the fourth time when the tall, willowy and handsome figure of Laurence unfolded itself from a new white Audi TT, positioned many spaces away from all the other cars in the parking area. The car had pulled in as Peggy had arrived on the High Street, pop music blaring through the open windows, with the driver singing along and thumping the steering wheel in time with the simple, monotonous beat. Peggy had raised her eyebrows at the spectacle, muttering 'Moron' under her breath. Well if this was the leader of this local group of no-hopers, he was clearly trying to use the choir as a way to enhance his own career.

He bounded across the car park, carrying folders stashed full of loose papers under one arm and holding the other aloft in greeting.

'Peggy?'

Peggy nodded, taken aback that this man knew her name.

'Hi! Ros said you would be joining us tonight. Welcome to our merry band of songsters.'

'Oh did she now? Well I wasn't sure I'd be joining you, Laurence and I've a few questions to clear up before I agree to any sort of commitment.'

Laurence was better at hiding his surprise than Peggy, and merely laid his free hand on her back, guiding her into the hall.

'Here, take a seat while I switch lights on and get rid of all this stuff. OK with you?'

Peggy took the offered seat, adjusting her scarf again and smoothing her new striped top. She was so pleased she hadn't been persuaded into the one with all the flowers over the shoulder. So limiting when it came to accessories and the sales assistant had been right, horizontal stripes were indeed very flattering – how had they gained their reputation for increasing body size was a mystery.

Laurence, moved effortlessly around the hall, like a two-legged gazelle, flinging chairs into a horseshoe shape in the centre of the room, and placing two sheets of printed paper onto each seat. He set out a tray of glasses with three jugs of water and left them on a side table.

'There, they can help themselves then, and hopefully we won't all get our sheet music soaked by Shaun when he forgets himself and starts dancing in the middle of the group.

Now then. Experience?'

The lift in his voice implied a question, but Peggy wasn't sure what the question referred to.

'Of singing? None in public since our school performances of Messiah every Christmas in the big church. Such happy memories. Is that a problem?'

Laurence shook his head vigorously, holding his hands up to repel the very idea.

'Not at all,' he shouted, 'not at all. This is a friendly group of both guys and gals.'

He laughed,

'That's what I call them, my guys and gals.'

He shook his head, smiling as he remembered all their happy times together, while Peggy looked on; her face displaying obvious concern at just how much fun she might be expected to join in with, and her lip curling just slightly upwards as she mentally invented excuses not to take part.

'I like to encourage a fun environment, even', he flicked a look at Peggy and continued, 'onto the reluctant choir members who don't really want to bring in mince pies at Christmas, or think about a Treasure Hunt on Easter Monday.

At the sessions I let the guys sing along and I join in sometimes, in the middle of a song if I think it needs a bit of oomph
added – especially with the high notes! Then there's the concerts
– we have two a year – ticket only, so you'll have to get your
friends and family along to watch.'

Peggy listened patiently to this diatribe of unwanted fun. She
noticed a glint in the choir leader's eye when he mentioned
friends and family. Did he already know she had none – of
either? She realised it was time to set some ground rules.

The thing is, Laurence, I don't know what type of people
actually come to your sessions, but as I said to that clingy Victor
chap at the Community Choir, I really believe that if people
can't sing, they shouldn't. He wasn't clingy after that – obviously couldn't take a bit of honest feedback.

You see I'm off on a big trip shortly so if I join now I'd miss a
few sessions, or maybe I should leave it until I get back. And I'm
an Alto, although as I am sure you are aware, that section does
seem to attract a few oddities from our society. And I wouldn't
want to be with all women – I find I can't tolerate their prattle.
I'm not keen on men either to be honest with you. Still I'm
prepared to give your choir a shot if we can agree on times and
dates that would suit me. What do you think?'

'What a rude man. Surely, I would be paying him to be in the choir so it's reasonable for me to have a say in when I was willing to go along.'

Mark was polishing a tray of champagne flutes when Peggy arrived at The Three Cups and he had gestured for her to take a seat at the bar. Without being asked he served her a glass of Prosecco and set it down on the bar near her, along with a saucer of small Japanese crackers.

'I've heard it's easy enough to get into his choir gang. Mum had a go once but she said there was too much standing. You know, tough on her knees. She said he was a bit of a dish, but Dad said he thought he was a bit of a smoothie. That's an insult from him. What did he say then?'

'Yes he is quite attractive in an obvious, kind of catalogue model style, but not my cup of tea and he has no empathy with other people's feelings at all.'

Mark turned towards the back of the bar, unable to hide his smile at the irony of Peggy, who he had known all his life, complaining about someone else not understanding other people's feelings. She was staring at him when he turned back to return her card, and managed to mumble,

'Dreadful', before averting his gaze and concentrating more than was necessary on polishing the already sparkling glasses.

'What did he say?'

'He was abrupt. He said the meeting times were already in place he wasn't prepared to be flexible at all. Anyway, he said his guys and gals wouldn't be up to the Hallelujah Chorus, they do more popular stuff so I might want to look elsewhere.

I didn't say anything to him, obviously, but there are no choirs left I haven't tried. I know it's not me, but you know how it is, people are all right to start with, then they start asking questions about your personal life, and worse still are the ones who want to share the minutiae of their dull existences – as if that's all part of the whole choir business. Anyway, I said I would turn up next week and join in – see what I think. He gave me these songs so I could have a practice at home. I mean, honestly – Abba! And a senile lower member of the Royal Family I believe – Lady GaGa, who on earth is she? Everyone in there looked ancient. Made me feel quite young, but will they be up to jigging about to that stuff?'

Mark continued polishing and re-polishing the glasses on his tray. He served two regulars who had taken their beers to a nearby seat and without any embarrassment listened to Peggy's review of Laurence's choir evening, pouring himself a small malt whisky – he deserved it.

Peggy talked until she had finished her Prosecco and surprisingly pleasant dish of snacks. She said her goodbyes to Mark, such a lovely boy, and nodded politely to the beer drinkers, who returned her nod with wide grins.

Out on the High Street, the combination of Christmas lights and the brightly lit front window of the Co-op were still illuminating the pavements. The cold breeze made her think about Mark's malt whisky, so she set off to see what the friendly little shop had to offer.

She had no idea there were so many different malts and found it difficult to select just the right one. The assistant was no help, just shrugging her shoulders in response to Peggy's questions about flavour and notes – this is an expression she had heard on Saturday Kitchen while Leonard was having his regular Saturday soak, she was keen to understand its meaning.

Aghast at the cost of the bottle, she finally paid for a carrier bag to hold her new purchase and a few extra treats for her night in with Wolf Hall in paperback. She left the shop assistant a little wiser about customer service, and as she walked through the automatic doors of the Coop she spotted Laurence with his guys and gals. They were spilling out of the Memorial Hall, chattering, and laughing, and hugging each other – what an awful display of over-exuberant intimacy.

She walked past them, clutching her purchases close to her chest, and managed not to look at all interested although she noticed they all had an odd expression on their faces.

They looked … happy maybe.

LEONARD

I have often wondered why Pegbag agreed to marry me. Wondered too why I asked her. Maybe I was caught up on the romance of the firm's bus trip to the Cotswolds, snaking through the countryside, knees briefly touching as we bumped through the winding lanes.

She hardly spoke on that journey. Had her nose in a book the whole time. Cider with Rosie. She said she thought it would be relevant to the day, and seemed to think I might be impressed at her literary knowledge. I have no idea how a book could be relevant to a trip on a coach into the middle of the countryside but back then she still had a strong will. That had to stop once we were married, no time for books.

Laying on the bathroom floor I can't help thinking about Peggy and our life together. I know she heard me fall because she stopped whatever she was doing down there. Sounded like she walked to the bottom of the stairs, but then everything went quiet. Without instruction she wouldn't have the gumption to phone for an ambulance but I can't make any sound come out of my mouth. Has she gone to fetch that oaf from next door? Has she ever been happy in our time together? I've never asked. Is it my job to care about that? Not sure on either count.

She has certainly been more thoughtful since the first stroke, filling the fridge with my favourite foods against the doctor's orders. Dr Matthews had recommended a diet of plain chicken and vegetables, no alcohol and no chocolate. Peggy knows me better than that. She hadn't let me down – regular steaks, quarter pounder burgers, those lovely chocolates in the gold wrappers with the nut in the middle, and my favourite choux buns, filled with cream and iced with coffee and chocolate. Delicious.

The buns were from the new bakery on the corner, 'Nice Buns' it's called. The young woman seemed nice enough, but she hadn't been keen on feedback about her business name. It was the right thing to do, to let her know it's short sighted to limit yourself to advertising yourself as selling just one product. Still what do I know? Just years of experience in business compared to her youth and 'new approach' – that's what she called it. She'd soon learn – there might be queues outside her shop now, the novelty factor, but that won't last. Now the butcher, he's a different story. Proper history Bill has; own family farm, his father was the town butcher, his father before him and so on. Striped aprons covered in blood – that's what a man expects to see in a butchers shop. You know what you're getting and what Peggy gets is great big juicy steaks, marbled with fat. On Mondays, Pork Chops, Bill keeps those with the kidneys attached, lovely fried up with onions.

Can I smell cooking now? Probably not. She's not a proper cook like mum was. Always the smell of baking, a pan of soup simmering on the hob.

Mum, Dad, Daisy and me living in that house together all those years ago.

Daisy, she was a funny one, married off at 17 to that boy with the noisy scooter and the greasy hair.

Dad hated his new son in law but then dad had hated everyone. Thinking about it, all the arguments with neighbours, or shopkeepers, or his own family even, I just assumed he was always right. He was Dad, he must be right. But we never gave a thought to what other people were thinking about him. There was that dog, the one that bit him but really did it bite him? Just a scratch on his hand when he pulled it away, but he made next doors have the dog put down. No wonder they didn't like him. But when you're a child, you think your parents are like gods.

We were all frightened of him.

Mum was probably glad she went first, but 34 that's no age is it? Seemed old to me when I was ten, but she had her whole life ahead of her. Maybe if she'd lived longer Daisy and I wouldn't have needed to get married and move out so young. Go our separate ways. I just wanted to get away from him. I think I told Peggy he was dead; he probably is now. I wonder what happened to Daisy. Is she still with her husband? He was a funny one too – didn't like me contacting Daisy, told me to clear off and leave them alone, said they didn't need anyone else. I wrote so many letters but she never replied. I wonder if she even got them.

Maybe I have grandchildren. No, that's not right. Nieces and nephews. I was spared the idea of grandchildren. Peggy wanted children but she understood why it was a bad idea, eventually anyway. She wanted a job too. It didn't take so long for me to talk her out of that one. That's odd now I think about it – she wanted children more than she wanted a job. She's clever. No doubt about that. And she played instruments when I met her, piano and some stringed abomination – no room for them in our little house. Why anyone wants to waste their time listening to music I don't know.

This shivering is worrying but that's Peggy lighting a fire now. Good old girl. She knows what to do in an emergency. We've talked about heating. She agrees with me – no need to heat a house when I'm out at work and she's generating her own heat with housework, but this morning it's different. This morning something big has happened. Funny how you know isn't it? No sirens yet but perhaps they don't like to make a noisy approach when it's a serious case. That's what I think I am now, a serious case. What day is it? Cotton, a work shirt? Is it a weekday?

It was a Monday when Miss Roskins called me out of class and took me down to the Head's office. It was Art. I had red paint all over my dad's old nylon shirt. There's red on this shirt too. What was I painting? I can't remember. That's annoying.

She said she was sorry but she wasn't – I knew that even then. Sorry she had to be the one to tell me I suppose, but she didn't even know my mum so why would she care? Anyway I thought she's probably got this wrong, but they told me to go home. Miss Roskins said I shouldn't have to walk. I didn't care, I just wanted to get out of that office, get away from her lies about my mum, get home and see she was OK, then I could come back and finish painting my post box, yes post box. That's what it was, Santa's post box. There was a bit of an argument but she must have won because next minute she's driving me home in her big car and we were singing hymns together. Onward Christian Soldiers – that was it – marching as to war, with the cross of Jesus going on before. Heading home to prove that woman wrong.

'My mum wouldn't leave me Miss Roskins; I know she wouldn't.'

Miss Roskins had kept on driving, through the high street and through the level crossing. There were no trains on the line but people were milling about as normal. That wouldn't be right either. If anything had happened to my mum, they would all be at home, with their curtains closed. Everyone loved my mum, everyone except my dad.

He was standing at the front door with Daisy. She had been sick all night and hadn't been at school. He looked so angry and I couldn't understand why. I wasn't expecting him to be angry. Then I thought maybe he was cross that they had taken me out of school for a made-up reason. That would be it.

Miss Roskins stayed in her car and I got out after thanking her for the ride home, and assuring her everything was OK, it was just a mix up. She put her hand on my arm and squeezed. I remember that.

I waved as she drove off and I walked towards the house. As soon as we got inside the door I could see how dark it was. Our curtains were closed. I'd just adjusted my eyes to the dark when I heard a crack, and felt a massive pain in the back of my head. I saw the carpet coming up towards me and landed on my face.

'She was clearing up *her* sick, coming down the stairs with a bowl of water and tripped on *your* marbles.'

He glared and jabbed a bony finger at us both as he spoke. His face was white. I'd seen him angry before, but not like this. He hardly spoke to us after that, ever. The blood dried up on my head and after a few days in my room he let me go back to school. People visited, uncles and neighbours but he never let me see them. Then mum didn't come back and it was just the three of us. OK he fed us and we weren't ever taken away like Peter in my class had been – whisked off to a new family in Stevenage people said. But Dad had an edge of cruelty about him, we knew it was our fault that mum had gone and I knew that if my father was like that, then that's the sort of father I would be and I knew having children wouldn't suit me. They would never live up to my high standards of behaviour and they would just irritate me.

Funny, I never told Pegbag why I didn't want children and she never asked. Just accepted it. Like she just accepted living in this damp cold old house, and accepted me not really giving her enough money. Those saps at work give their women too much money. Always having their hair done or going out 'window shopping'. To my mind if it's real window shopping you don't have to get a taxi home because of all the bags you're carrying. That's wanton waste and not something I ever allowed.

Funny to think about Peggy down there, probably worried sick about me, daren't come upstairs I suppose for fear of what she'll find. She'll leave it to the experts, that's what I've always told her to do. She knows her limits, knows her limits. Her mum and dad had tried to give her ideas above her station, about a career and such like but I could see she had potential as a proper wife and she became my project I suppose, someone I could improve, shape into someone more suited to me and my life.

It's been good. I think she would agree, a quiet life here with no-one intruding onto my way of things. There was a friend of hers used to pop round, but she soon got the message, we didn't want her here and she finally stopped troubling us. What was she called now? Rachel? Rebecca? Peggy said they'd made friends at school because no-one else liked them and I can't disagree with that! I don't think there was any bullying or anything – was there? I don't know if she said there was; don't know if I asked. Now I've made myself laugh but no noise came out. That was a funny feeling. Laughing without making a noise. Even laughing is unusual for me. Now I've made myself laugh again, silently.

Funny when I think about Mum again, I can see her face, looking at me, smiling.

She makes me feel I could run and run and run, like we used to run through the cornfields in summer, skin golden brown in the light of the late afternoon sun. Running and laughing til we reached the other side where Dad would be waiting with a picnic, all spread out on the red and white rug, the old Ford Popular parked at the side of the road. Daisy sat on the rug, her face covered in jelly and she would be laughing too.

They were happy times. Have I had happy times since then? Have I made Peggy happy? I haven't have I? Did I ever try?

Leonard looked closely at the artexed ceiling, stained from many water leaks and never repainted.

He understood.

I am disappointed with my life. Could I do it differently? Can I do it differently? Can I try again? Have some fun?

Too late?

I need to talk to Peggy. She needs to know I was right and it was her fault we weren't happy, not mine, her fault that we didn't have fun. We could have had good times here if she'd just settled down and forgotten her past and her dreadful brother dying in that motorbike accident that was probably his own fault. Her fault, not mine. Hers.

NINE

Derek Lewis tried hard to see what was in Peggy's carrier bag when she eventually managed to heave the doors open with her shoulders.

'You might have helped an old lady Derek. I'm struggling a bit here after hefting these bags up the hill.'

Derek stood firm behind the reception desk.

'Never seen you struggle Mrs Thomas, you manage alright.'

'Unbelievable! Well while you're not busy, I need the key for downstairs, in the storage room – can you at least help me with that?'

While walking up the long climb towards Sovereign Court, Peggy had remembered an old box of papers and photos she had kept back from the bonfire when she had cleared Leonard's stuff out of the cottage. This stranger was unnerving her; she had no idea who he was. Maybe there would be something in the box that might throw some light on who this man was.

'Want me to hold your bag for you?'

Peggy had almost snatched her Co-op carrier bag out of Derek's hand. That was the last thing she wanted, for the old man to be spreading the word that she was a secret alcoholic, which she most certainly was not, and Ros hearing the gossip.

'I can manage this thank you. Are you free now to venture into the storage room?'

Derek discovered after checking his desk and phone, that he was indeed free and available to assist with the storage room adventure, so they set off, through a warren of doors and corridors, all dark and stacked with empty paint pots, ladders, and containers of fuel.

Peggy tried to take everything in so she could repeat it all to Ros, but remembered that she was not to be included in the coffee and plant-based snacks the next day. She was surprised at how much this affected her, but wasn't sure what the emotion was – was she jealous, or annoyed? Her automatic reaction might have been to sneer at Ros's new friendship, but Ros had seemed defensive of this woman. She would make sure she was available for the following morning – there would be much to talk about then, she was sure.

'Here we are – what are you after in particular?'

Peggy knew what the box looked like but couldn't remember which container she had stuffed it into. She looked around at the mountain of stored rubbish, some covered in dust and cobwebs. Derek saw the confusion,

'Your stuff's over there, behind those garden benches, that's it.'

He had guided her to a particularly dark corner of the room and shone his torch into the space, so she could clearly see her three large yellow plastic containers.

'I can move 'em so you can get into the top of each if you want, then maybe you'll remember which one you want. Don't want to be down here long or the rats'll get used to us and start coming out to investigate.'

Peggy was not prepared to allow him to see her fear, so she stood back while he clicked the tops open on the containers and she peered into each one, finally identifying the box beneath some old magazines and newspapers – why had she kept them? For packaging purposes only, surely.

'That's the box, can you get it out for me please? I'll take the newspapers and magazines too – they probably just need chucking out.'

The caretaker made a meal of fetching the box and papers out of the container, sealed all three back up and they made their way back up to the reception area, Peggy brushing cobwebs off her jacket as they walked. She found herself thinking he is caretaker here, why isn't he down here with a brush?

'People have no pride in their work anymore do they?'

'What's that?'

Peggy hadn't realised she was speaking out loud.

'Oh you know, I was just thinking about life.'

She wasn't embarrassed because she felt she had highlighted an obvious flaw in his character that he should be aware of, and he wasn't embarrassed because he had no idea she was talking about him, so no-one was harmed in the discourse.

She took the lift up to her flat. Stairs would have been difficult while juggling the box of photos, the newspapers and magazines, and her precious cargo of malt whisky and snacks.

Her flat seemed more empty than normal, even when she flicked on the succession of lamps around her sparsely furnished Living Room. Dark clouds were gathering over the woods and she snapped the curtains shut in the arched windows hoping the expanse of ethnic colours in the fabric would brighten her mood.

She wandered around the space, gathering a good crystal glass, and bowls for her snacks. She rummaged in her shopper and found Wolf Hall, the pages showing little sign of use, and dumped that on the table with the glass. Finally she topped up the bowls with nuts and Chipotle savouries and only then did she feel warm enough to remove her coat and scarf, depositing them in the hallway cupboard with her boots.

Her slippers, leopard skin effect with a little black velvet bow on the top, were waiting for her by the sofa where she had left the boxes from the basement.

The clock chimed eight times, or was it nine? Either way it surely was a perfect time to open the malt.

The first sip was always a shock. So sharp, but a little ice cube in the shape of a skull (from a plastic tray; another little flat- warming present from Ros) was enough. That's better, just a hint of water – not too much so it dilutes the flavour, but just enough to take the edge off. Peggy took a chilli curl crisp and lay it on her tongue, letting the spice fill her mouth as she rested her head on the back of her sofa, feeling the warmth from the chilli and the heat of the whisky move down her throat, filling her with a welcome glow.

She was startled awake at the sound of the clock chiming again – an hour! She'd dozed for an hour with the crystal glass still resting on her chest, thankfully.

The box.

There it was, full of her own memories and hopefully information about dead Leonard. Her curiosity about him had been growing over the past few weeks, as she realised how little she knew about his life before he met her. She knew nothing about his parents, what they had been like, how they had died, presumably in a tragic accident. She knew nothing about what sort of a boy he had been.

She had often wondered if he had been a homosexual – she couldn't bring herself to think of him as gay – there was nothing gay about that dreary man, no rainbows in his life that hadn't been destroyed by gathering black clouds. No, even if he was unaware of his true sexuality, no-one would ever describe him as gay.

She picked up the pile of newspapers and magazines and watched as a photograph fell to the floor from within the sheets of paper. A large photo with familiar writing on the back.

It was her mother's hand and she knew without looking exactly what the photo would be – an image she hadn't seen for many years.

The group of smiling faces were standing outside a dark bricked house, in front of a large bay window, swathed in lace curtains.

There in the centre were her parents, with her mother proudly holding a baby, barely visible among the handmade shawl that had occupied her time while she had been pregnant.

This then was her younger brother's Christening day, her father wearing a cap to hide his bald head, and her grandfather resplendent in dark suit and white arran jumper – he never saw the sense in shirts and ties, but wore the suit as a nod to the occasion.

Peggy's brother Ray was in the front of the group, sitting cross-legged on the floor, wearing his school uniform. And there, standing in front of her grandmother, was the young Peggy, her curly dark hair scraped up into a high ponytail, revealing an oversized forehead and large dark eyes. She remembered the scratchy wool suit her mother had only finished stitching together the night before. It was a dark turquoise colour, with flecks of black and had what looked like a pleated skirt, the jacket buttoned to the neck with a large collar. So unfashionable but this younger self didn't seem to mind, her face was beaming with joy and anticipation of the huge table of food she knew was just inside that window.

The day hadn't ended well. As usual alcohol had played its part in the celebrations and an overindulgence by her grandfather had led to disagreements with uncles, and tears from her mother and aunts. These rows were always patched up within a few days, but the thought of them always hung over any family event like a black cloud, with everyone underneath just waiting for the storm to break.

She and Ray were mainly oblivious to the goings on until the big eruption and her abiding memory of that day was that there were small yellow onions on the buffet table.

'She's coloured her silverskins! Caroline, have you dyed your onions luv? Is that strictly Mrs Beeton?'

Her mother and the aunts always gathered in the kitchen, sitting around the table drinking pots of tea, buttering bread for endless piles of sandwiches, jiggling babies and children on their laps and laughing.

Her dad and the uncles would gather on the driveway, comparing cars, and journeys,

'You came up the A5? Are you mad? I never touch that road, no if you take the first right off the .....' and so it would go on, offering each other shortcuts and tips for getting from A to B and back in the shortest possible time. They never tired of these conversations, and while they talked they drank beer. It was when the talk turned to politics, religion, or football that things would turn nasty and soon all the guests would be ushered out, leaving Peggy's mother to set the house back to normal, pack away the bread and butter and cover the cooked ham in foil. Then Dad would fall asleep on the sofa, and the children would be scuttled off to bed.

In this photo, uncles and aunts were scattered around the central family, smiling, and laughing, dressed up as if at a wedding, aunts in hats, and uncles awkward in suits, with shirts and poorly constructed ties. Cousins of various ages being held in place with their parents' hands on their shoulders.

If she could just go back and talk to them all one more time. What would she say? Would she listen more carefully to their warnings about Leonard? Probably not.

Ray had died in his twenties, a month before he was due to finally marry his childhood sweetheart Moira. Moira had tried to contact Peggy after the funeral, but Leonard had sent her packing and she had never heard from her again.

Post-Leonard Peggy sipped her whisky and wondered how she had let that happen, but at the time it had been easier to let him have his way. He was persuasive, convincing her that she agreed with him and she had just gone along with it. She had allowed him to remove her family from the life she shared with him, so she had been alone. Alone with her own thoughts and plans, even distant from Leonard who she had grown to hate with such a passion.

She and Moira had never been the best of friends, but they had shared memories of Ray and she had let her down, badly. Where was Moira now she wondered, and how had her life panned out?

So many times her mother had reached out to her, inviting her out for shopping days, or to meet up for tea, coffee or even wine, but each time Leonard had been adamant that he needed her more on that particular day. The last conversation she had with her mother was the evening before she had collapsed with a fatal brain haemorrhage while working in the family café. The family had money worries and she was sure the business would have to close, but Leonard had come home from work during the call and she had rushed her mum off the phone.

They had both gone to the funeral but Leonard had made it clear he wasn't prepared for her to become her father's carer, had argued with him and they had left early. When Leonard had gone off to fetch the Astra, she had held her father tight, promising to visit.

To her surprise, Leonard whisked Peggy away for a holiday on the morning after the funeral. He said he had been planning it for some time, but she realised that was unlikely. Three weeks in a cold damp caravan at Skegness, with windows facing onto the brown sands and flat sea would not be anyone's idea of a good time, but she had taken books with her, books that would not alarm Leonard – just some modern fiction she had found in a bundle for sale at the library. Leonard had taken a chess set with him, hoping to teach his silly wife how to play, but she had beaten him twice so the board and plastic pieces were pushed back into a carrier bag in the boot of the car and chess was never mentioned again.

There were no phones on the camp site and while Peggy read and grieved for her mother, Leonard busied himself with his binoculars, facing out to sea. She had assumed he wanted to be the first to spot an invasion but now, she realised she had no idea what he was looking at and had never thought to ask.

Three weeks of misery, so bad that she was glad to be home in their bleak cottage and desperate to speak to her father.

Leonard had let himself into the house first and bent to collect the mail.

He tossed all the leaflets in the bin, kept a couple of official brown envelopes to one side and passed her a small white handwritten envelope.

Three weeks had gone by, she hadn't visited, and her father had collapsed and died while working on his allotment. Doctors said he had been drinking solidly since the funeral and had been inconsolable. She hadn't even spoken to him. Leonard had said he probably had stuff to do and she should leave him alone. How pathetic she felt for listening to him.

Guilt. That's what Peggy felt. Her lovely happy family, smiling out of the photograph had been shattered and she hadn't been there to hold them together – surely that was the job of the only girl in a family and she hadn't even been able to do that.

She put the photograph on the table, promising herself to find a frame and display it somewhere where she could see it every day, and remember them all.

Could she promise herself to get in touch with some of them? Her younger brother had settled down and had a family. She knew he had at least one child, because she had bumped into one of his schoolfriends who had congratulated her on her new nephew but she knew nothing more. How old would he be now? Her little brother, peeping out from that shawl, in his mother's arms.

Perplexed about why this photograph was in a box of Leonard's stuff, she laid the precious image carefully beside her on the sofa and returned to the box.

There were old tobacco tins that rattled when she shook them, but thoughts of child Leonard's milk teeth popped into her head and she quickly set the tins to one side. The old Sellotape on a small cardboard box was well past its sell by date and lifted off as Peggy touched it. The lid popped open and inside were six old Bakelite plugs, each with an inch of yellowing cord flex protruding from the back.

'Who cuts off plugs?' she said out loud, 'you mean old sod.'

She picked up her new iPad, checked an online auction site, and with a smile on her face chucked the six plugs into the 'SELL' box.

'Vintage!'

There were faded packets of Kodak prints, bulging with images of scenery and distant birds including a few that seemed to be just of the sky until closer inspection revealed the silhouette of some bird or other. Some had Leonard's spidery writing on the back to indicate that the invisible creature was a Kestrel over Dunstable Downs, or an Owl in flight, Ashridge, November 1967.

In 1967 Leonard would have been nine years old; would he have been wandering about those places on his own? How had he got there; whose camera was he using? There were no more after 1967, and Peggy wondered why. Had he lost his interest in feathered birds? Nine was a bit early to be taking an interest in girls, but maybe something else had come along to fill his time – something more normal for a boy of his age maybe. But he'd kept these photographs for all his life, odd.

Peggy was flicking through the last pack, about to stash the whole lot in the 'rubbish' box, when she noticed a couple sticking out of the back of the packet. They were a different size to the rest and were of people. At last! Something of interest.

The first was of a small boy, maybe six or seven years old – but what, she wondered, did she know? The last time she had mixed with young children she had been one. Still this boy looked about the age of someone who hadn't been at school for long, so that made her guess about right she thought.

This was probably Leonard the boy. And the woman whose hand he was holding was probably his mother. Mother of Leonard. This was someone she hadn't thought about for years, not since Leonard's awful reaction when she had brought the subject of his parents up in one of their early 'let's get to know each other' conversations. Well, she had wanted to get to know him but he hadn't wanted her to know anything, and he had expressed no interest in her family, other than criticising them when they had met, and wanting them to play no part in the new Mr and Mrs Thomas's lives.

She looked hard into Mother of Leonard's eyes. Were they cruel eyes? Is that why Leonard was so cold, why he appeared to have no heart or soul? She actually looked kind, that was a surprise for Peggy. She was smiling into the camera, a little nervously maybe, but smiling nonetheless, and holding tightly onto her son's hand. Who took the photo she wondered, who had hold of the camera?

Was this definitely Leonard? Peggy peered into his face and yes, there was the same cruel little mouth – not looking as cruel as she remembered it, but still thin-lipped and turned down giving him the appearance, as he always had, of someone who disapproved of what he was seeing. Those piggy little eyes could only be Leonard's too, and even at that age he appeared to have the same fifty-year-old man's hairline – greased back, even at that age.

There was no scar on this young boy's face though, the scar that she knew had troubled Leonard all his life, particularly on cold days. So that had happened after his birdwatching days. She picked up the photo packets and put them in a LEONARD – KEEP box, feeling suddenly sentimental about this young boy with his innocent hobby.

Setting the mother and son photograph to one side, she could see another image of the two, but this time Leonard was slightly older, and there was a girl holding his mother's hand. A girl with blond curly hair to her shoulders, pigeon-toed in shiny black shoes and wearing a white frilly party dress. Both children wore excited expressions, but the mother appeared to be subdued, peering at the camera through her fringe, Princess Di-style. There was something about her haunted expression that Peggy found unsettling. It was as if this young woman was appealing to her, while shrinking back into herself.

Trying to tuck the photograph behind the others, she discovered that there was another image stuck to the back, a picture smaller than the others of four people this time. Presumably, the stern looking man at the centre of the group, with his arm resting on the woman's shoulder, was Leonard's father but it could be Leonard she was staring at. Even in the monochrome image she could see his skin was pale like his son's, and the dark hair slicked back, away from his face. Like Leonard, the tiny knot in his tie was worn just a bit too close to the collar of his white shirt, and the too-small, knitted waistcoat strained across his bony chest.

There was writing on the back and Peggy could just make out 'the seafront, October 1967, Works Outing'. October? Just a month before the final bird had been captured on film. There was a stamp in the corner of the image and Peggy had to turn the photograph around to read 'Hawkins Studios, Gt Yarmouth'.

Frustrated that she couldn't use her finger and thumb to zoom in on the picture, she finally fetched her magnifying glass from a drawer in the sideboard to see the four windswept people in close up. Leonard looking happy – well, happy for Leonard anyway. He was wearing the same awkward clothes as his father and proudly clutching a soft toy presumably won in an arcade. He hated arcades! The young girl was wearing a beautiful double-breasted coat with a white fur collar, but her gloved hands were empty. She was not smiling, and maybe she had been crying – so hard to tell. Again the mother appeared distracted, looking beyond the camera and off into the distance. She wasn't smiling, and if she had spoken, might have said,

'Can we just get this over with please, I'm late for my root canal treatment at the dentist.'

Well that's how it seemed anyway.

132

So, Leonard had a sister. She had never known. Maybe they could have been friends. A sister-in-law, she liked how that sounded.

'Yes we have my sister-in-law coming round on Christmas Day with her children, it'll be such fun.'

And maybe it would have been fun. They might have gone on days out together. She could have been Auntie Peggy to a brood of nephews and nieces – all the fun with none of the responsibilities of parenthood. How they would have loved to read with their aunt, visit galleries and museums – Tring Museum with its stuffed animals, the lions, tigers, and monkeys with their pink bottoms. That would have been a nice life.

Peggy wondered if Sister of Leonard was still alive – no reason to think she wasn't – Leonard had died at a fairly young age and the girl was clearly younger than him.

Social media was beckoning to her. Ros kept telling her to keep up with the new technologies but she had no interest in other people and they would have little interest in her so what was the point? But Ros badgered her to join in, she had found people they were at school with and had shown her the fat, old and balding versions of boys they had played with on the green – as if that would be an encouragement. Peggy found it all a bit disgusting, but maybe she could trace down some of her own family and Leonard's too. Ros might help her – if she could face the smug expression of 'I knew you would', from her friend. She picked up her phone and sent a brief text – 'what information would you need if I was to let you try to find some of my family on social media?' Perfect, making it sound as if she was doing Ros a favour.

She stood and stretched. She had been sitting hunched over the musty box of Leonard's life for too long and it was very dark outside. She realised she hadn't eaten since lunch and declared,

'Woman cannot live by whisky and snack items alone.'

Wandering about her kitchen wiping smears from the glossy cupboards along the way, she picked eggs from the ridiculous ceramic chicken pot Ros had presented her with for no reason at all, and moved on to the American double fronted fridge, something Leonard would have found too indulgent. There she found mushrooms, cheese, and butter. Another omelette, her fourth that week. With half a bag of pre-washed rocket scattered alongside it on the plate, and some parsley snipped from her windowsill herb garden, she felt this represented a good, nutritious meal, and was ready to argue with anyone who disagreed.

'I'll eat what and when I bloody well like Leonard. I don't have to listen to you anymore, and yes, that was lemon and garlic-infused olive oil I drizzled over the greenery – not a spec of budget salad cream in sight. What are you going to do about it?'

'Alexa, play me some Mozart.'

Without argument, Alexa produced some Mozart after an initial announcement, and Peggy settled on the empty armchair, placing a large glass of Argentinian Malbec on the side table. She ate the omelette slowly, savouring the slightly undercooked eggs mixed with the salty cheese and the mushrooms, finally using her fingers to wipe the last of the rocket around the plate, mopping up every remaining drop of the dressing.

'Delicious.'

She liked to speak to herself, out loud. She was reassured to hear her own voice, a voice that had been silent for so many years. Speaking to herself offered no opportunity for correction, she could say what she liked without fear of judgement or idiotic countered opinions. She spoke to Leonard as often as she liked, telling him what she was doing, and hoping he was spinning in his urn at some of the apparently unnecessary household items she had purchased. Especially the white goods from John Lewis of all places, where Leonard knew for a fact people only visited to show off.

'More money than sense.'

That was his mantra for anyone who fancied the idea of a fridge that someone else hadn't used before. She laughed at the memory of his rage when finding out that Joe and Tracey had bought themselves a drinks chiller.

He had stood and watched the delivery van reversing up the lane and had been straight out, pretending to sort the rubbish, so he could ask what had been delivered. Poor Joe caught between the aspirations of his wife, and the Scrooge next door.

He'd come rushing back into the house, apoplectic,

'Who do they think they are for heavens' sake? The man is a painter and decorator! What is he doing even buying wine or beer? They've got ideas above their station those two.'

Peggy had smiled and nodded, thinking of the warm Liebfraumilch she endured every Christmas Day, wondering what it would be like to drink good quality chilled wine, maybe at a table in one of the cafes around St Mark's Square in Venice. She had looked at Leonard then and wondered how long he had got. How long could his weak heart and thickened arteries last before they gave out. She remembered thinking it wouldn't be long, and she'd been right because under a year after their last Christmas together, she had found herself in John Lewis, choosing her American Fridge – the property would come later, and would need to be big enough to house the fridge because that was her priority.

A fridge with an icemaker and its own separate section to be filled with white wine that had been purchased from a person who knew his wine - an expert.

She had found that she had a particular liking for the Viognier variety of grape, which when made well produced, so she had been told, delicate aromas of apricot, peach, honeysuckle, and gingerbread. She wasn't so sure about that, but she enjoyed it anyway, particularly when chilled to perfection.

TEN

The word 'hangover' was in Peggy's mind as she opened the front door of Sovereign Court to be greeted by a chilly breeze that blew through the trees and smacked her in the face. She wasn't sure what a hangover might be, never having experienced one before, but there was the word, buzzing around her painful temples. She felt a bit like a celebrity emerging from an underground night club and facing camera flashes of paparazzi as she blinked into the watery winter sun and considered her walk down to the High Street for her first shift in Fiona's shop.

The thin brown trousers might have been a mistake. Stylish yes, and most certainly flattering but the wind was cutting through the flimsy fabric and she might need to invest in some boots with thicker soles to give her more protection from the frosty pathway than these ballet pumps were offering. She pulled her coat around her, tying a knot in the belt to prevent it flying open as she walked, adjusting her scarf up to cover her mouth and cheeks, leaving just eyes visible under the fake fur Russian hat.

There were two freshly dug graves in the churchyard with floral displays, one spelling out DAD. The other was a large red and white shield, with the letters MUFC in white chrysanthemums, cutting diagonally across the mass of red roses. She'd heard those initials before but could not remember where. Was it something to do with non-uniform day at school? She had read about that ridiculous phenomenon in the papers – what a nonsense. As far as she could see when she watched the school bus emptying its unenthusiastic contents onto the Market Square, the children wore more identical clothing on non-uniform day than when they were personalising their designated school clothing. Very odd.

She passed the porchway of the old church, and glanced in to see the wooden slatted bench where she and Ros often sat for a last chat before parting after a trip into town. They would pause to chew over who they had seen, what bargains they had discovered and to check over a new outfit they had bought from the little boutique favoured by the modern over fifties woman about town. So many times they had discovered in their little sanctuary, that although maybe a lime green dress had appeared to enhance older skin in the lights of the shop, in broad daylight the colour drained all life from the face of the new owner – it wasn't too late then to trot back into town to the ever-patient Della and request an exchange or refund. And not too late, she had realised, for Ros to have popped into Nice Buns the bakery and acquire a box full of sweet treats, not appreciating that by that time Peggy was already home and peering out of her bathroom window to witness Ros's return.

Something caught her eye under the bench, glinting in the weak morning sun, and she took a detour to check what it might be.

Bottles, and cans. Empty of course, their alcohol contents having been consumed in the early hours by some hoodlums who couldn't be bothered to take their litter away with them. They had even left the blue carrier bag they had presumably used to drag the haul up the hill to the church. So lazy. She immediately set about filling the bag with the cans and bottles, together with a few crisp bags she found on the floor, gave the bench a wipe with her gloved hand and headed back for the path into town, trying not to notice the endless graves of people who had died at her own age or younger, leaving a host of mourning family and friends, indirectly listed on the headstones.

Deeply missed mother, aunt, friend, grandmother etc etc. Even in death she thought to herself, it was all about someone else – so it seemed anyway. What would her gravestone read? Just name and dates, that's all. Apart from Ros who seemed now to have found another source of entertainment in that wretchedly common Jean, who else would even realise Peggy had gone, let alone spill tears over her departure? Something she had in common with Leonard then, what a depressing thought.

She was just about to leave the churchyard when she heard a voice from behind her,

'Morning Mrs T – taking your empties into town?'

139

She spun round to see Derek, red faced, and slightly breathless from the effort of walking and shouting. He was bowling down the hill towards her, taking little care to avoid the ancient overgrown graves.

'They're not mine Derek – I found them in the porch over there.'

'Yeah, whatever!'

Derek seemed unable to halt his large body from careering past her, but he turned and beamed at Peggy, delighted no doubt with his supposed discovery, his laughter producing clouds of icy mist around his head.

'Derek, why would I be drinking lager and cider in the church-yard, when I have a perfectly good, high quality drinks selection at home?'

'Methinks the lady does protest too much, ha! Isn't that what the big man said?'

Realising that further denials would only exaggerate her guilt in this idiotic man's eyes, Peggy turned away, knotted the blue carrier bag, and remained silent, watching the bulk of Derek hurtle towards the lychgate, his legs barely able to keep up with the upper part of his body, and unable to arrest his own speedy descent.

She thrust the bag into the first bin she found on the High Street, looking furtively around to make sure there were no witnesses, and set off again for Fiona's shop, slightly nervous but with her head feeling better for a few minutes of walking in the December air.

All the lights were on in the shop as she pushed the door open and heard the bell tinkle her arrival. She could hear noises in the back room but there was no sign of Fiona which was irritating – how could the woman expect to sell anything if she didn't instantly respond to an incoming customer. There were so many obvious improvements that could be made in the area of customer service and Peggy felt excited to get started if she could only find Fiona.

She ventured further into the shop, brushing aside rails of creased jumpers in gaudy shades of purple and green. The sight of two shoed feet sticking out from behind the counter was her first glimpse of another human presence in the building, and as the feet were twitching rhythmically she was not too fearful of venturing closer. On closer inspection, it became clear that the bulky frame of Fiona was lying in a tight space, wedged between carrier bags bulging with clothing and books, and the thankfully dormant electric fire.

Without warning, the two shoed feet and legs were raised at right angles to the floor, and slowly lowered again, stopping just inches from the lino.

Fiona exhaled and once again the legs were drawn up so the toes of her shoes were pointing at the ceiling. Seconds later they were lowered to a few inches above the floor where they stayed until Peggy heard Fiona exhale again and the whole process began once more.

Peggy watched for a few routines of this awkward exercise and when she realised Fiona had no idea she was not alone, she decided to let this strange woman know she was there.

'Fiona.'

'Oh my god, who?'

Fiona scrambled to her feet, pulling her sparkly black jumper down over her stomach and thighs, leaving just her curvaceous legs visible. Peggy could see that the leopard skin lycra had been stretched pale, well beyond normal expectations. As usual, there was a black, lace topped ankle pop sock peeping over the top of black sling back shoes with just a centimetre of skin visible before the ascent of the leggings.

'I didn't hear you come in.'

Fiona's tone was accusing, but `Peggy simply smiled. This must be what the podcast she had been listening to the previous week had meant about making concessions for less bright colleagues in the workplace.

Lindy and Morag were a delight. Their irreverent look at office life was revealing. Just 15 minutes a week of 'You Don't Have to Be Mad to Work Here, but...' made Peggy laugh out loud, or LOL as Ros would now say. If work could be so much fun why hadn't she kicked up more of a fuss when Leonard said the workplace wasn't any place for a woman? When Leonard spoke about his office, it was of a dark atmosphere where masculine superiority ruled, and although his colleagues appeared to have enjoyed a good relationship outside working hours, Leonard was never included in that world.

He had once spent a weekend away from home, saying he was going to a hotel in Leeds with some workmates – even the word was alien to him – and appeared to have been wrenched from somewhere deep inside his intestines. She remembered trying to halt her lip from curling at the thought that someone had sought his company when they weren't being paid to do so, but was so looking forward to a weekend without him that she hadn't asked any questions. She had later discovered the trip had involved a visit to a consultant specialising in halting the onset of male pattern baldness, and a night in a cheap B&B close to the railway station. Receipts for the consultation – £150 (half an hour maybe?) and the B&B – £24 (candlewick bedspread and greasy bacon) had been found in his weekend Sports Jacket, but no evidence of any spend on enjoyment. No drinking, no fancy meals out, no workmates, no mates at all. His hairline never changed so she had assumed he had been horror-struck by the cost of treatment, or it hadn't worked.

Peggy was still smiling at the thought of friendless, balding Leonard, while Fiona brushed at her jumper, flicking balls of fluff and scraps of paper from her chest and arms.

'I forgot it was you today. Thought I was here on my own.'

Disappointment was tinged with annoyance in her expression as she looked Peggy up and down, trying to gauge what use the woman might be to her, without causing more trouble than she was worth.

'Used a till before?'

'Never.'

'Stocktaking experience?'

'None. I could clear up the back room for you if you'd like me to. I have my own rubber gloves and 500ml bottle of Lavender Zoflora I can donate to the cause.'

Peggy's encouraging smile was received with obvious relief from the sparkle-clad Fiona and she stepped back to allow Peggy to walk through the doorway into the 'STAFF ONLY' section of the shop.

The floor was filthy, strewn with torn carrier bags, the sink was full of plates marinating in greasy water, and the worktops around the sink area were covered with dirty cups and spoons, occasional clumps of half dissolved instant coffee and dried out teabags.

'Sorry if it's a bit of a mess out there love, the cleaner walked out on me last week. We had a bit of a row when I asked her what exactly she did in the hour I paid her for every week, and she told me I could 'stick my job where the sun don't shine'. Haven't seen her since. I think her Bob had a bit of a win on the horses last weekend and the money's gone to her head. She'll be back. 'A fool and his money..' that's what my old mam used to say. And there's no bigger fool than Susan's Bob.'

Fiona, absorbed in her memories of her mam and foolish Bob, smiled insanely towards the door of the shop, twiddling at the various rings adorning both hands.

Peggy took this as her opportunity to get to work on clearing out the filth that was the back room. As she pushed the sleeves of her oldest jumper up beyond her elbows she vowed this would be her last shift in the shop. She had no wish to become Fiona's unpaid skivvy and having heard her speak in a more unguarded way, she realised they had nothing in common, and she had no desire to allow Fiona into her new world.

She cleaned cupboards – no point putting clean cups and plates onto those sticky shelves, or clean forks into a crumb filled drawer. She washed every item of crockery and cutlery, carefully putting them away into the newly fragrant storage areas. Then she washed and disinfected every surface, swept and cleaned the floor, and finally sorted a few bags of donations into what appeared to her to be an orderly fashion.

As the church clock struck 12, she was handing Fiona a cup of tea, and a plate of her own home baked cookies – a little stale for Ros, but she was sure this would be the best thing to pass Fiona's Hollywood pink lips in a long time.

'Thanks Peg.' Fiona took the cup and plate without acknowledging Peggy's 'don't call me Peg' look.

'How have you got on? It's been quiet out here I must say. Just a couple of the regulars in here to get warm while they wait for Dolly's to open. Still, I sold that old fur coat – it's been in here for months and I started to think it was putting people off coming in – you know some folk can be a bit funny about fur and most of them don't know how to tell if it's real or not. I told the woman it was Faux Fur and she bought it. But it was real alright.'

She tapped the side of her nose conspiratorially, and winked.

'Who's to know eh?'

'That's dreadful!' The words were out before Peggy realised, and as Fiona was between Peggy and the door, this was no time for a confrontation. A brief memory of Fiona slapping some girl in the Memorial Hall toilets because she'd flirted with a boy she'd set her mind on popped into Peggy's mind. That, together with the fact that her coat was still hanging on an otherwise empty clothes rail in the store cupboard, made this a bad time to start an argument.

'I mean that's dreadful that someone wouldn't come in the shop just because there's a coat in here that might, or might not, be fur.'

She laughed her fake laugh,

'People, they're all mad aren't they? Anyway, I've had a good old clean up out there, and put everything away, so I'll be on my way if that's all right with you Fiona. Lots to do today, you know how it is. I won't be able to do any more shifts I'm afraid – I've got some overseas trips lined up and lots to prepare.'

She retrieved her coat as she spoke, and pointed at some of the areas she had cleaned, indicating where crockery had been stashed, and opened drawers to show where the tea towels lay neatly folded beside a box of batteries and light bulbs.

Finally flinging her handbag over her head and across her chest, she pushed past Fiona and headed for the door, pleased finally to be nearer to safety than danger.

'Thanks Peg. That's great, and I can see you're a busy woman with not much shop experience, so it's probably best all round if we call it a day. Good luck with everything, and Bon Voyage eh?'

As Peggy closed the shop door behind her, she had the feeling she had been sacked, but it was she who had quit. She who had decided not to go back into the shop. What had happened there?

She was still frowning when she called into the Dry Cleaners to collect her favourite mustard coloured wool coat, the one with the three enormous brown buttons down the front. She wasn't going to let Ros's description of her as a yellow snowman put her off, and had decided to get it cleaned so she could start wearing it more often.

'Morning Mrs T. All ready for you, it's come up lovely. Everything alright? You look a bit cross.'

'I'm fine Sanjeev, I think I just came off worse in a conversation with Fiona from the charity shop up the road, that's all. Do you know her?'

Sanjeev shook his head,

'No she never comes in here. My wife won't go in there anymore. She said she thinks the woman is a bit of a drinker – you know all happy and laughing one minute and abusive or falling asleep the next. The other charity shop people are regulars in here – bringing in stuff that just needs freshening up, but that one – she's never brought anything in. She tells people everything is washed and pressed before it goes on the rails, but my wife says it smells in there. Anyway last time she went in, the woman was throwing someone out for trying on shoes. No customer service skills eh? You're best keeping away I reckon.'

Sanjeev had an infectious laugh, throwing his head back and roaring at his own joke. Peggy had never been able to feel miserable around this man, and he had once again worked magic on her mood.

'You should go and treat yourself to a little glass of something Mrs T. Here, leave that coat with me and put your lovely woollen coat on – that'll cheer you up. There was a beautiful cerise scarf in the pocket so I cleaned that too – you'll look like Joan Collins.'

He pointed behind him to a large poster of the actress, in her role as Alexis Colby, wearing an aqua blue sequined off the shoulder dress and holding a long cigarette holder to her lips, eyes smouldering at the camera.

'What a woman eh Mrs T?'

Sanjeev had moved around the counter and was removing Peggy's mac, holding out the scarf for her to put on before helping her into the newly refreshed wool coat.

'Gorgeous autumn gold goes so well with the scarf, that's what my wife said anyway. Myra knows her colours you know, she's well known with the women in our family for putting colours together that no-one else had thought of, and looking so beautiful, always.'

It was true, Sanjeev's wife cut a striking figure marching their three children along the High Street on the way to or from school, never hiding behind the black, grey, and navy shades more familiar in the town.

Peggy caught a glimpse of herself in the shop window and found herself agreeing with Sanjeev – this was a good colour combination. Maybe the scarf was missing when Ros had last seen her in this coat.

'Premium clean?' Sanjeev was holding Peggy's navy waterproof coat up with his left hand while the right hand was writing on the small yellow ticket he would pin to the lapel.

'Yes, premium please – I need to wash that woman and her ghastly shop out of my clothes.'

The two laughed together and Peggy left the shop feeling much better. She headed straight for Lounge Bar of The Three Cups where she knew Mark Field would be doing his afternoon shift. She fancied a cider and some peanuts in her autumn gold coat – not looking at all like a yellow snowman.

ELEVEN

As Peggy pushed the pub door closed behind her, she heard Mark's distinctive Bedfordshire drawl,

'Well, here she is now, you can ask her yourself mate.'

As she turned around, she was faced with a familiar sight – a tall man in a pale mac, wearing a brown trilby. Only his head moved in her direction and she recognised the man who had fallen in the street outside Dolly's and had touched her arm as she had walked past him.

'Well, well, we meet at last. Peggy.'

He held out his hand towards her.

'I'm Colin, Colin Rothwell. Brother-in-law you might say.'

Peggy's eyes flashed towards Mark who shrugged and held up a champagne flute as his question.

'Or something stronger? Single malt Mrs T? One ice cube?'

'I'll join her – could you bring them over to the table in the window please?'

Peggy allowed herself to be steered towards the table she usually shared with Ros. Where was Ros when she was needed? Nowhere to be seen, that's where.

'Beautiful coat Peggy. The colour really suits you.'

'I'm sorry Mr Rothwell. There has been some confusion. I do not have any brothers in law – for that I would need a sister I think, unless...'

Her voice trailed, and she pondered for a few seconds.

Colin Rothwell spoke again, his facial expression offering assurance. He did not believe there had been any confusion. He knew what was what.

'Your Leonard, god rest his troubled soul, had a sister. Daisy, my Daisy, my wife of 38 years. You knew about Daisy, surely?'

When Mark appeared with the drinks, she looked up to thank him and saw Joe at the bar, out of breath and with his face still red from the bitter cold. He nodded to her, and made an odd gesture of pointing two fingers at his own eyes, then pointing just his index finger towards her. He made these movements a few times, then nodded again.

Mark saw the gesture and laughed, gently thumping his father on the arm before heading off to serve a group of raucous women who had burst into the public bar wearing party hats and sequined outfits.

Colin continued to wait patiently for a response, but Peggy had no idea what to say. Not usually one to be lost for words, this was a troubling reaction. Was it more troubling than learning that after all there had really been a sister-in-law she could have had a relationship with? Did they have children – could she truly be someone's Auntie Peggy – the thought was so appealing, and the words had such a fine ring to them.

'I've seen a photo, only recently. There were parents, with a young boy who was unmistakably Leonard – exactly the same but younger, and smiling. There was a young girl in the picture too, blond. I wondered if this could be a sister but no, I knew nothing about Leonard's family, apart from the fact that his parents were both dead long before I met him.'

Colin Rothwell whistled through his teeth and sat back in his chair, knocking his trilby to the floor.

Like lightning, Joe appeared by their side, and swooped the hat into the air, returning it to its position on top of a folded beige mac.

'Everything alright Mrs T?'

He turned and nodded to a bemused Colin Rothwell.

'We've met before mate – I'm Joe Field. Old friend of the family you might say. Very old friend.'

Joe stuck out his hand to be shaken and Peggy was relieved to see her new brother-in-law respond in a friendly way to Joe's ninja tactics.

'Yes, hello Joe, I remember. I seem to have met all your lovely family now. Did you wish to join us?'

'No he doesn't, do you Joe?'

Peggy glared towards Joe. She wanted to find out what this man had to say about Leonard, and Leonard's family. She wanted to know when she could meet her sister-in-law and organise theatre trips, or days out. She wanted to know when her nieces and nephews' birthdays were – Ros would be able to help her select an appropriate gift. Where was that woman?

'Well I'll just be over there if, you know if you need anything. And Mark – my boy Mark behind the bar there, he's very fond of Peggy and he's working through til closing so... Well we're here if you want anything. Anything at all.'

'Thank you Joe.' Peggy's mix of embarrassment and sympathy for this man, out of his depth in the company of her sophisticated new brother-in-law, leant her voice a kinder edge, and she smiled as she raised her hand to dismiss him.

Mark was shaking his head as he handed his father a freshly pulled pint of Doombar and pushed an open bag of pork scratchings towards him. They began to speak quietly.

'Sorry Colin. Joe's a bit protective I think. He's looked after me since Leonard died, and he and his boys have been great company for me, helping me move and such.'

'No need to apologise Peggy. I realise you must miss Leonard terribly – grief is an awful thing isn't it?'

Peggy stared at Colin. Of course, he wouldn't know she wasn't in widow's weeds, although her freshly dry-cleaned autumn gold coat with the cerise silk scarf should have been an indicator.

'Why are you laughing Peggy? Have I made a mistake – you did say Leonard had died didn't you? I read about it in the paper too – have I made a horrible mistake?'

Peggy was trying to stifle her laughter, holding one hand on her chest to calm her breathing, and the other hand over her mouth – years of missed check-ups had meant her only visits to the dentist involved emergency appointments and the loss of yet another molar. She knew a close up of the inside of her mouth was not to everyone's taste.

'Oh I'm sorry Colin, I'm not the average grieving widow. I hated him. He was a vile man. Vile. I'm glad he's gone.'

There, she had said it out loud and if ghost of Leonard had followed her into The Three Cups that winter afternoon, he knew it now, for sure.

Peggy knocked back the last of her whisky and beckoned to Mark for refills.

Was she drunk? She wasn't sure and by the look on Colin's face he wasn't sure either.

He took a crisp, clean hanky from his trouser pocket and, after removing his glasses, dabbed at his eyes.

'Oh God, Colin I am sorry. Have I offended you? He was your wife's brother after all. I am so rude at times aren't I Mark?'

She lay her hand on Mark's arm as he placed two new glasses of whisky, each with just one ice cube in, onto the table, reaching to retrieve the empties.

'Not rude Mrs T, never rude. Overly honest sometimes maybe, but rude? No.'

He moved away and hurried back behind the bar where he began to relay the conversation to Joe, now on his third pint.

Colin wiped his glasses with the hanky and then replaced it into his trouser pocket, he took a sip from his glass and set it carefully back onto the card coaster.

'My Daisy died earlier this year. I thought I knew about her parents, but it turns out I only knew what she wanted me to know. Come on drink up, I'll walk you up the hill. I have to meet up with some old work chums later, for our monthly get together – shouldn't turn up squiffy should I? Some fresh air will do me good and we can talk on the way.'

Colin Rothwell brushed aside Peggy's attempts to pay for their drinks and settled Joe's bill too. This seemed to persuade Joe that this stranger wasn't all bad and the pair shook hands for some time before Colin was able to remove himself from Joe's grip and follow Peggy out of the pub onto the pavement.

'It's getting dark, but the days will soon be getting longer and we're heading for Spring – my favourite time of year. Are you warm enough Peggy? Do you have any gloves?'

She realised she had left the gloves in her mac. Well at least they would be cleaned and there would be no trace of Fiona on them.

'I'm fine, thank you. I can stick my hands in my pockets and it's just a fifteen-minute walk up here, behind the Church.'

They set off, along the High Street, walking in an amicable silence past shops full of pre-Christmas Sale posters and bright lights. Peggy always felt there was something magically Victorian about her town in December, and she never minded a walk in the cold air among the Christmas trees and twinkling decorations.

As they turned up the hill and into the Churchyard, Colin stopped and turned towards her, his breath freezing in the air around him as he spoke,

'Did he treat you badly Peggy?'

'He never hit me.' She realised this sounded as if she was recommending Leonard for a job in the caring profession, as if this was the highest accolade that could be bestowed upon a person.

Peggy guided Colin Rothwell towards a bench at the side of the path and they sat down to face each other on the damp wooden slats, keeping a discreet distance between them.

She could see the shadow of Joe lurking behind one of the larger gravestones and felt comforted that he was following. She had no idea who this Colin was and although she did want to talk to him alone, there is a difference between being alone with a stranger, and being *completely* alone with a stranger.

'Leonard wasn't a violent man. Just unkind, unfeeling, mean, selfish. He was all the opposites of what a mother might tell her daughter to look for in a husband. But when I met him he hadn't displayed any of those characteristics. Well not in an obvious way – I look back now and can see all his vile ways peeping through the façade he built around himself, but they weren't visible then. I think

I just suited the image of a wife he thought he should have – nothing I could ever have done would have made him like me. I think he only liked himself, and even then not all of the time.'

Colin was nodding, understanding, and surprised Peggy when he said,

'And if someone tells you often enough how useless you'd be without them, you begin to believe it's true, don't you?'

'Yes! How do you know? Are you a psychiatrist?'

'No,' Colin laughed and Peggy saw that he laughed as much with his eyes as with the rest of his face. And he had huge eyes, chocolate brown like Maltesers.

'I am, or rather I was, a Senior Tax Manager in an international accounting firm. Rather dull to you I imagine, but I always enjoyed it, and I worked with some lovely people. I took my pension just after Daisy died, a pension she didn't know I had by the way.'

Colin laughed again in a way that made Peggy slightly uneasy. Leonard had hidden finances away from her in the same way. Why would a man have done that?

'So no, I have no experience of psychiatry, but I confided in a friend about ten years ago and he told me to look a word up in the dictionary – I don't have a dictionary but I have the internet. Goodness me he was right. I realised that I was married to a narcissist, and so were you I think. Like you, I think I suited Daisy's image of who she should be seen with. She wanted the big double fronted house, she wanted the Land Rover and two expensive dogs and me going off to the office every day to bring in the money to pay for it. I wanted children but she never did.'

The nieces and nephews floated away like ghosts into the night.

Colin Rothwell shrugged.

'That's me anyway. She died quite suddenly last year, some congenital heart thing – I didn't hang around the hospital for long enough to hear many details. What remains of her is buried just over there by the wall, where the holly bushes are. I hope she's enjoying the prickly company.'

They both looked over towards the ancient wall, mostly covered with berried ivy and holly. Leonard's sister was buried close to Ros's mother – another viper in the grass. They had probably never met in life, but would be enjoying each other's nasty company now.

After a few moments of contemplation Colin continued,

'Anyway, when I no longer had a reason to be out of the house every day, I discovered I didn't want, or need, to work anymore so I told them I wanted to retire. It all happened quite quickly. Then I found out she had stashed money away; in the house I had paid for. I was older than her so I imagine she thought I'd go first then she could lead the life of the merry widow. No offence.'

'None taken Colin, none taken. I *am* the merry widow and it sounds like brother and sister were mirror images of each other.'

'Yes, not a nice pair but I bet we have a lot to talk about. Come on, let's get you home and we can resume this another day.

As they stood up from the memorial bench, Peggy watched a couple stride arm in arm past the church towards Sovereign Court.

They were laughing, high pitched laughter, two women's voices. And one of them looked very much like Ros.

Before Peggy and Colin parted with awkward handshakes, he had passed her his business card,

'Obviously I don't work there anymore, but my mobile number is on the back. Call me. Or text me – whichever you're more comfortable with. It would be nice to have a coffee, or something stronger if you prefer, before Christmas maybe. Anyway, I'll leave it to you, and if you decide you don't want to, then that's fine. I would understand.'

Peggy had been distracted by the 'something stronger' remark – did everyone think she was an alcoholic for heaven's sake? She was new to this drinking business, which was all it was, just enjoying herself.

'Really,' Colin continued, taking Peggy's silence as reluctance to meet again, 'really it's OK if you would rather not. I know this has all been a bit strange.'

'No, sorry, I was thinking about something else. That would be lovely, tomorrow afternoon?'

Was she too eager? She had been too long away from people, had no idea what the norms were when making future plans for social events.

'Tomorrow is perfect – Dolly's? I owe them a visit for looking after me when I fell. 3 o'clock?'

Time and place agreed, the two shook hands again and parted. Peggy setting off up the hill towards her flat and Colin heading down the hill towards town, and where? Hopefully he wouldn't pass Joe in his hiding place. She hadn't even asked where he lived, and he seemed to know so much about her.

Then there was the Ros situation. She paused at another memorial bench – dedicated to someone who's name had been masked by a passing gull, but who apparently had spent a lot of time sitting there, admiring the view. Peggy had often wondered where this person had sat, to admire the view – now just rows of twinkling lights in the distance. Was there a seat there before the death, or had they brought their own collapsible seat? Something to ponder at another time.

She pulled her phone out of her handbag and with one finger typed a text to Ros.

'Sorry not been in touch. Coffee tomorrow morning? 10 in the church porch?'

She didn't want Ros thinking she'd been pining away waiting for her – always better to sound as if she had been too busy to care that she'd obviously found someone else to entertain.

There was another, more pressing reason for the catch up. Peggy wanted to know if Ros had found anything out about her family. She would have been straight to work on this new project and she knew Ros was one to stay up all night investigating something if she had a lead or two.

As she pushed open the front door of Sovereign Court, her phone pinged in her hand,

'10 perfect. CU there. Lots to talk about.'

Peggy rolled her eyes – CU there indeed, and yes – lots for them both to talk about hopefully.

TWELVE

Peggy dropped the two letters from her pigeonhole onto her hall table and headed for the kitchen. Without taking off her coat, she flicked the oven on and began searching in her fridge and freezer for something to tempt her palette. She harvested leftover smoked salmon, a lemon, and a half empty jar of that nice dill dressing from Ikea, assembling her meal onto one of her new moroccan plates, purchased from the China seconds shop in the High Street – a pre-Christmas treat for herself.

The blue and white symmetrical patterns were pleasing against the bright orange and yellow of her food, the dressing was splodged in the centre, and some still-green fronds of dill were plucked from the otherwise dead greenery, and placed on top. There were two slices of granary bread left in the bread box, bearing no signs of mould. These were buttered, quartered, and added to the plate.

Barely any pattern was visible by the time she carried the plate and cutlery through to the warmth of her living room where she discarded the autumn gold coat and cerise scarf – pleased at the sight of them against the grey of the evening.

'There Leonard – I left the fire on all day and survived! Now I'm going to have wine with my meal, chilled white wine. If I'd buried you, I bet you'd be spinning in your grave at the very thought.'

Peggy caught up with the Archers while she ate – she hadn't realised so many days had gone by since listening to the podcast and things were certainly moving along with the Canterbury Tales.

She was woken sometime later by heat in her ankles and she realised she had stretched out too far from her sofa in her sleep. Her feet were red, like spam her mum would have said, while warning of chilblains and other dreadful, yet unexplained illnesses.

Stacking her plate and glass, now warm, she wandered into the kitchen to discover the oven on and smelling vaguely of chips from a previous meal – there must be a loose one stuck in there somewhere, but she could sort that out another time. She needed to get some proper sleep before she could face Ros and listen to what fun she was having with her new friend, and she needed to be able to concentrate, without looking too eager, in case she had unearthed any news about her family.

'Alright, alright. Even I don't think leaving the oven on all evening when I hadn't even used it was a good thing. That was a mistake Leonard – even you made those. Lots of them.'

She spoke towards the drawer where ashes of Leonard lay, in a sturdy box provided at no charge by the funeral directors. Constantly delighted whenever she thought of how she had rejected the offer to buy a superior container for him, she was beginning to wonder when this bio-degradable box would start to disintegrate and realised he would need to be disposed of at some point. But where? Something else to think about in the new year.

'It's Autumn Gold Ros, not mustard.'

'Yes, it's lovely Peggy – suits you, and I love the scarf. Did I buy you that?'

The two had poured coffees from their own flasks and Ros was offering a small tin of chocolate brownies. Peggy took one and gladly accepted the accompanying paper napkin, decorated with a large rosy faced Santa.

'Plant based brownies Peggy – you'd never have known if I didn't tell you. I've used flaxseed and agave as substitutes.'

'Substitutes for what Ros?'

'Not sure, but they are delicious. I make them for, for my friend, for Jean. She has a plant-based diet and it's such a healthy way of eating. I'm thinking about it.'

Peggy watched as Ros sealed the lid back onto the double cream she had added to her coffee, tucking it into her leather tote bag, unaware of Peggy's ironic gaze.

'OK – you first. What's your news? How was your shift yesterday with Fiona? Everything OK? I looked through the window when we, I, passed the shop, but didn't see you. Just Fiona re-arranging the DVD basket. Did you actually go?'

Peggy realised the reason she had been so keen on working in the back room at the charity shop. She had no desire to be seen working in there, not by Ros, not by Ros's friend, not by anyone else either. She was relieved that there would be no repeat of the experience.

'I cleared up the back room. It was filthy and I had to put my coat into the dry cleaners straight after. The place stinks. I told her I didn't want to go back, but she spoke as if she was getting rid of me. Dreadful woman. I don't think I want a job you know. I think I'm happier not getting involved with all that.'

Ros was laughing.

'She did that to me! I said I'd be back for another shift and she said there weren't any more shifts available – talked like she was running some big business, and I was some snotty nosed kid trying to get in on the bottom rung of some highly-desirable ladder. She's had us Peggy, got the back room cleared up, she had me ironing some of the more creased clothes and now she can carry on just bossing that poor Millie about – she knows no better.'

The two laughed and chinked flask cups in celebration.

'We tried Ros, we tried. What other news do you have then?'

Peggy waited, tense with anticipation and worry about how to form her features into the correct expression to greet Ros's bomb-shell news.

'No, you first. I saw you heading into The Three Cups, just after that stranger had gone in there, and it was ages before you came out – together!'

'Were you following me? Where were you?'

'I saw you come out of the dry cleaners in your mustard, er autumn gold coat. You looked in a bit of a flap so I watched to see if you were heading home, then I would have walked with you, but you went into the pub. I thought you'd be OK having a chat with Mark in there, I thought he'd be able to calm you down, so I carried on and went into the Black Horse. I had my tea in there – very lovely pie and chips, but posh – you know, a tiny amount of gravy in a little jug, served on a piece of slate, with chips in a basket lined with newspaper. Anyway, enough about that – who is he?'

'He's my brother-in-law.'

Peggy let that sink in.

'Leonard had a sister, Daisy. He, Colin Rothwell, was her husband.'

'Was? Is she dead too?'

'Yes. And that's not all she has in common with Leonard. She sounds like she was just as vile as him. Colin Rothwell, such a nice man, he called her a narcissist, said that's what Leonard was too. We're meeting again today, this afternoon, in Dolly's, so I'll find out more then. Don't you go turning up will you? I think Colin Rothwell would be less talkative if someone else was there.'

'Why do you keep calling him Colin Rothwell?'

Peggy knew she was including his surname every time she thought about him. This, along with how he knew so much about Leonard's life before she met him, had been troubling her all night and was the reason she had not been able to sleep, and therefore why she was now wearing so much concealer and foundation. The last thing she wanted was to hear from Ros about how peaky she was looking, or to have her questioning about why she wasn't sleeping. Ros was someone else who probably gave more than a passing thought to her recent foray into alcohol.

'Is it too intimate if you just use his first name? Do you think that's what it is? Like when suddenly an uncle tells you to just use his first name, and drop the uncle bit?'

Undeterred by Peggy's horrified expression, Ros continued with her psychoanalysis.

'Like he might have more up his sleeve if you're on first name terms?'

'Ros, where do you get this stuff from? What sort of uncles did you have? I didn't have any like that. There were a couple who were a bit clingy at home time, but I don't think they had evil on their minds. That's a whole new topic for another day.'

She realised that Ros wanted to change the subject and start spilling her own beans. This uncle business was a distraction, a vehicle for moving the subject round to herself, and Peggy was pleased to do as Ros wanted, for today anyway.

If Ros didn't offer up any family news, Peggy would have to ask for it and she didn't really want to do that.

'Come on, enough about me, what's your news – and can you keep it clean for heaven's sake?'

No further encouragement was required.

Though never specifically described a relationship, one had clearly developed. So the groping about with boys behind the Village Hall had been experimental, and found to be wanting. What Ros wanted was girls, not boys, and she had apparently never before found anyone prepared to enter into reciprocal arrangements with her, until now.

'Jean from the Book Club?'

Ros nodded.

'Jean who we have recently discovered went to our school, and was engaged to Stuart Bickerstaffe for three years before he ran off to Australia with Marcia from Woolworths?'

'The very Jean, yes.'

'But you complained about how common she was when we were at the Book Club.'

'No I didn't Peggy, you did. I thought she was a breath of fresh air, knowledgeable but not snooty, beautifully dressed without shoving it in your face, and an enthusiastic drinker of cheap wine. What more would I look for in..'

Ros's voice trailed and Peggy offered to fill in the gap,

'In a friend?' she offered.

'No, I knew you would take this personally. Not in a friend – that's you. I want more. I want someone to spend lots of time with, no that sounds wrong. I've got you as a friend, but I have never had a relationship with another person who thinks only I am marvellous, who wants the best for me, who lights up when I walk in a room, and someone who makes me feel like I light up when I see them.

You must have felt like that about Leonard at one time, surely? Whatever you grew to feel about him, there must have been a time when he made you feel like that, wasn't there?'

Peggy shook her head. There wasn't, not one time.

'I think about her all the time, and she thinks about me all the time.'

As if by magic, Ros's phone pinged and she reached for it. The text made her smile, but she simply returned the phone to her pocket, saying nothing.

'Jean would like to meet you. Properly, not at the Book Club. I've told her all about you, and about Leonard – not too much detail, obviously. Just that he's dead, and you're glad.'

'Well you seem to have summed it all up perfectly Ros! What else is there to say? Anyway I have met her and I wasn't keen, I'll be honest. What do you have in mind anyway? Plant based Christmas Lunch with recycled paper crackers and tofu surprise instead of a pudding?'

'Actually yes. Christmas Lunch, at mine. You me and Jean. Please say you'll join us. I know you're not doing anything.'

Peggy took some time to drain the dregs of her coffee, replacing the cup onto the flask slowly before lowering it into her carrier bag.

'I'll see. Seems people around here know more about me than I know about myself, and I don't know how I feel about that. How would that be I wonder, playing gooseberry to you and Jean around your dining table. Just the three of us, red faced and bloated from too many brussels.'

She pushed her glasses onto the top of her head and gazed unseeing out of the church porch, her ageing eyes able to focus only on the assembled graves of those who would never again receive an invitation to Christmas Lunch.

'Go on,' Ros nudged her on the arm, 'say yes. You can leave before Jean gets her karaoke machine going – if you want to that is.'

'And you won't try to make me stay a minute longer than I want to?'

Ros held out her hand to shake on the deal, beaming.

'OK, and I suppose I should say thank you.'

'You should, but you don't have to and I doubt if you will. Come to mine at 12. We'll have a couple of cocktails, and eat at two. Queen's speech – Jean's a bit of a fan, then Karaoke or home after that. You've made my day Peggy.'

Peggy recoiled at Ros squeezing her arm.

'Enough woman. I don't want to see you lurking about outside Dolly's later – I'll see you tomorrow at 12 to let you have all the detail, then we can get on with Christmas and get that out of the way.'

As Peggy turned towards the main door of the building, leaving her friend to turn right towards her own ground floor flat, Ros whispered,

'And a Merry Christmas to you too', but punched the air with delight and returned Jean's text, 'She said yes.'

THIRTEEN

The time had not been right to chase Ros up about her social media investigations, that could wait. She had obviously been too busy with other pursuits. She wondered if she could master social media herself, she had some time on her hands and surely if Ros could work these things out then so could she. She would try her hand at this new technology and see how she got on.

Was she surprised to hear Ros's news? No, she was not. Although she had never voiced the words in her head, Peggy always knew that Ros had made a choice not to pursue relationships with any of the local boys who had tried to force a solitaire onto her hand. She was never short of male attention as a young girl, indeed many of the more attractive lads at the insurance company had favoured her with their energetic efforts. So it wasn't just caring for her mother that had kept her from socialising for all these years then. Peggy felt pleased for her friend that she had found someone to share some time with. In fact, it was with some relief that she realised she wouldn't be the one to be pressured into the action-packed city breaks Ros had been chattering about for the few weeks. The very idea of being herded around popular tourist attractions with a bunch of noisy strangers, hearing about their big houses, golf handicaps and hordes of ghastly grandchildren was appalling to her.

This friendship Ros had struck up with the awful Jean gave her some assurance that her status as sole traveller to non-touristy sites was still in place – even though she hadn't actually been anywhere yet.

As she wandered around her glossy kitchen, compiling a healthy lunch, with Earl Grey tea (no wine), she remembered the envelopes that had arrived the previous evening. They remained, unopened, on the hall table and although she assumed they would contain only generic offers and information about bin collection dates, she decided to check – just in case there was a Christmas card or some other sign that someone remembered she existed.

Sure enough, the first provided information about when the rubbish and recycling bins would be collected. Why Derek continued to put that into her pigeonhole she had no idea – bins were his business not hers. The second was an official looking letter, addressed to her personally. Intriguing – not a bill hopefully. She reached into the drawer and pulled out Leonard's old letter opener – sharp and pointed with a bone handle. The weapon sliced through the envelope like a knife through soft butter.

She saw the signature first, clearly written, Adrian Borthwick. The letterhead 'CAMERONS – We Plan You Travel' emblazoned across the top of the handwritten letter.

Dear Mrs Thomas

Following your visit to Camerons recently, we have not heard from you so we are assuming you wish to proceed with your forthcoming trip on 4th March 2019. If this is not correct, please call me on my personal mobile number above to discuss further.

Kindest Regards

Adrian Borthwick

Peggy felt her heart race, a feeling of cold rushed up her back and into her neck, but her cheeks burned. She dropped the letter and sank onto her pine bench. Weakness in her hands and feet meant she could not bend to pick up the letter. Her head rested against the cold wall and she raised her eyes to the ceiling, certain that death was close.

She stayed in that position for many minutes, waiting for chest pain or blinding headaches to begin – this was how she imagined Leonard must have spent his few minutes – was this his revenge? Was he meting out the same end for her that she had left him to? No chest pain came, and no blinding headache. She reached up and felt her cheeks, cooler now, but the skin on her arms was cold, almost clammy. She checked her appearance in the mirror opposite where she sat, and forced a smile – no downward tilt of the mouth and both arms were moving up and down OK. Not a stroke then.

Was this a reaction to the letter? Surely not.

Did she want to go travelling to Eastern Europe in just under three months' time? No she did not – there was too much to plan, too much organising to be done before she could embark on a trip like that. What had she been thinking?

Her handbag was resting beside her on the bench. Ros was always telling her to take her bag into the bedroom with her, in case anyone broke in. But in her mind if someone broke in she would be happy for them to have the contents of her bag – a lipstick and a purse with nothing but £20 and a bank card in. Better that than waking to find a masked, weapon wielding intruder staring down at her in the middle of the night.

She reached in and took out her phone. Ignoring the red dots on the message icon, she dialled Mr Borthwick's number, and as instructed left a message, which after the normal introductions and pleasantries ran along the lines of: -

'There is no way I can consider taking a holiday in March of 2019 Mr Borthwick. This must be postponed immediately. Please transfer my deposit to the same trip, to take place at a later date this year, or early next year. I will call in to discuss the detail. To my way of thinking, 2020 feels like a much better time for me to be travelling. Thank you and season's greetings to you and your staff.'

She didn't feel very seasonal towards him, or his staff, but she did not want to lose that deposit so it was probably best to be civil. Feeling much better, she began pulling clothes out of her wardrobe and choosing just the right outfit for her meeting at three. She would wear a different coat, maybe the black astrakhan she had found in an

Antiques shop in Ampthill, with the moss green silk scarf. Layers were a perfect foil for the varying temperatures in Dolly's – if they sat too near the door she would freeze, but the steam that often billowed from the kitchen meant sitting at that end of the tearoom was uncomfortably warm, even on the coldest of days.

She found a thin grey mohair jumper and added a coordinating cardigan in the same wool, but in a shade closer to her green scarf. Delighted with how she looked, she set about tweaking her hair and adding a light pink lipstick – she knew now that red lipstick had aged her horribly, making her skin appear corpse-like, and highlighting the natural wrinkling around the mouth which was standard for a woman her age who had decided against the use of Botox.

The church clock struck two. She had lunch to eat, then she had to get herself down to Dolly's by three – lunch would need to be even lighter now or she wouldn't be able to cram in any cake and she didn't want to appear rude in front of Colin Rothwell, Colin. If Colin was eating cake she would need to join him.

She ate just the lettuce and cucumber from her plate and removed the smoked salmon quiche – an individual tart from Nice Buns that was close to its sell by date. The tart was placed back into the fridge, an ideal early supper this evening before the festive feast she had foolishly agreed to at Ros's the following day.

They may not be flattering to the calves, or very glamourous, but Peggy was thrilled she had decided to wear her new winter boots for her trip into town. The graveyard was covered in a light frosting of snow, turning into slush where people had walked. The High Street was no better, muddy, and wet, with deep puddles in the pavement where slabs had moved and tilted over time.

As she turned the corner she saw Colin, looking dapper in a dark tweed coat, and black trilby hat, his trousers tucked firmly into a pair of long wellington boots.

'They were just shutting the doors as I got here. Early closing for Christmas Eve.'

'Oh of course. I don't really celebrate Christmas I'm afraid so I lose track of all the days. I didn't think.'

'It's OK Peggy, we're sorted.'

Colin held out a bag with two disposable coffee cups in, and a plate covered in foil.

'She's given me a take-out. We just need to work out where to sit.'

They looked around. The High Street was bereft of seating – she thought the local council had removed benches to prevent teenage drinking in town. Daft really because all they did was head for the graveyards and alleyways – in her experience a lack of seating never stopped a determined teenager from swigging cider.

'My house is just up the road.' Colin began,

'I wouldn't want you to feel awkward. I've lit a fire in the front room, it should be nicely established by now. You're welcome to come back to my home and have tea. If you'd like to. I'd understand if you didn't feel it was right, but it would certainly be warmer than sitting on your bench halfway up the hill.'

Peggy returned Colin's smile. This did feel right. He dressed like a gentleman, and appeared to be well-mannered. He'd used his initia-

178

tive to acquire the cake and tea/coffee and seemed so eager to please. Leonard would just have been delighted to get out of spending any money in that situation, well he would never be in that situation – he would never have agreed to go anywhere like a tearoom with her, or anywhere else. She could feel Leonard's disapproving breath on the back of her neck.

'That sounds perfect, thank you. I would like that.'

Colin's house was huge. She had passed by a few times on the bus, but it was just further along the High Street than the territory where she and Ros shopped. There were two gates, one either side of a brick wall spilling over with holly and berberis glowing with their bright berries in red and orange. The whole hedge appeared to be lit by Christmas lights.

They crunched across the gravel driveway and Peggy noticed two cars parked in front of a double garage, one a big jeep type of vehicle and the other a red mini with the union flag on the top.

'The mini belongs to my neighbour's boy – there are five drivers in their house and their driveway was starting to look like a used car lot so I offered Ned some space here. He comes and goes at funny hours, but I think it makes the house look more lived in so I don't mind.'

Peggy joined Colin's laughter, thinking what a friendly and helpful man he was, although he offered no explanation for the other vehicle so she assumed that must be his.

When he opened his front door, warm lighting and the smell of wood polish mixed with burning logs wafted over her.

'Lily, my cleaning lady has been today. She insisted I had a pre-Christmas clean up, even though I told her I wouldn't be having any visitors. She polishes everything to within an inch of its life – I keep telling her there won't be any banisters left soon. I think she enjoys it. It's beyond me.'

Peggy gazed ahead at the staircase set in the centre of the hallway, its polished wooden banisters were gleaming and the patterned red carpet – wool, she could tell – was spotless, disappearing up onto a landing where a portrait of a stern man in a judge's wig and robe stared down at her.

'My great grandfather on my father's side – Thomas Rothwell. Quite the character by all accounts. Here, let me take your coat – I'll hook it here by the front door in case you find me dull and want a quick getaway.'

They both laughed again, less nervously this time, and Colin guided Peggy through a door on the right where a fire was glowing behind a tall iron guard. The mantelpiece was covered in greenery, from the hedge in the front of the house presumably. Tall white pillar candles in black holders, the sides uneven and gnarled were arranged amid the greenery and around the fireplace. She was impressed although she wasn't sure why, but these were candles that were used for lighting purposes, not just for show and that pleased her.

'Take a seat, I'll get plates and proper cups. She gave me coffee in these cups – is that alright for you or would you prefer tea? I think I would prefer tea.'

'Yes, me too, thank you.'

Peggy settled herself in an armchair beside the fire – although the sofa looked tempting she was conscious of the social difficulties if Colin joined her on there, maybe sitting too close, or worse still, straining to sit as far away as he could.

She looked around the room, taking in the small paintings of local scenery, the piano with sheet music propped up against the stand, the artefacts scattered around shelves and hanging from walls; hints of global travel with one wall presided over by a large stuffed fish in a glass case. There was writing on a gold label probably heralding the fisherman who had caught the enormous beast and wrestled it from the water, but Peggy did not have her distance glasses with her so the important detail would remain a mystery for now. The fire, hypnotic, crackled with new logs spitting sparks against the guard, tiny blue flames turning white, then yellow and orange.

Peggy's mind wandered to Colin and something niggling at the back of her mind. The house was prepared for a visitor, but he would surely not have known that Dolly's would be closed. She wondered if he had another visitor due later in the evening. Something felt not quite right. Even Fiona, who from her shop window had an eagle eye on everyone in the town, had described him as a stranger. She had never seen him before and nor had Ros. Joe, whose family had been in the town since its days of being populated only by landowners, agricultural labourers, and a few tradespeople, had no knowledge of him. Yet, he lived on the High Street, had a cleaning lady and a job –

this house was lived in but no-one had seen him coming and going in all this time.

Had her years with Leonard made her cynical and suspicious, or merely wise?

She accepted the china cup and saucer graciously, resting it on her knee while she nibbled at the carrot cake, served on a matching plate. The cups were delicate, but there was no sign of femininity in the decoration, just rigidly symmetrical rectangular patterns in a deep burgundy and navy, trimmed with gold.

She registered that this had all been washed by hand – there were no signs that a dishwasher had ever been involved. Or maybe, she wondered, had it never been used before. Should she be flattered that he was quite literally fetching out the best china for her?

Colin had settled himself on the sofa, apparently oblivious to her analysis of his home and domestic arrangements. He had his legs outstretched and ankles crossed, his body involuntarily pointing itself at a large TV beside the fireplace.

'Your TV makes mine seem ridiculously small – do you watch sport? Or nature programmes? Films?'

She felt awkward in his company now they were no longer on neutral territory. If she needed to escape in a hurry, she would have to step over his legs and, she noticed, exceptionally large feet – or large shoes anyway. She smiled at the thought of a tall man with tiny feet inside huge shoes walking, clown-like up, and down the High Street, waving manically at shop-owners on either side of the road.

Receiving no response to the viewing question, she pursued a more direct line of enquiry.

'Have you lived here long?'

Colin held her gaze while he considered his answer. Embarrassed, Peggy's eyes scanned the room for signs of a female presence. There were none. She wasn't sure how a female presence might manifest itself and thought of her own minimal living space – was there evidence of femininity in her home? She wasn't sure.

'This was my father's home. He and his father were both reclusive collectors. My parents split up shortly after I was born. My mother and I went to live with her parents in Norfolk, so I haven't spent any time here, until recently.'

This explained a great deal about the decoration of the place.

'That's a shame. Did you have a happy childhood?'

She hoped she wasn't coming across as interviewing him, but there were great chunks of information missing about him, and consequently about Daisy. Peggy knew her time with him would be limited and needed to get as much out of him as possible.

'Yes,' he continued, 'my grandparents were quite young and good fun. I didn't miss my dad at all. I'm not sure why, but we always spent Christmas with an aunt in Leighton Buzzard. That's how I met Daisy. She and Leonard were at a school disco my cousins dragged me to. I don't remember having much to do with her on the night, but she got hold of my address and we exchanged letters for a few months and then when we met up, she proposed.'

Peggy gasped, surprised, hot from the fire and struggling with the crumbs caught at the back of her throat. A coughing fit took her for several minutes. Colin waited patiently at first, then when he realised this could be a serious attack, fetched a glass of water and a box of tissues. Peace was eventually restored.

He continued, without any break in the story, anxious to tell his tale.

'I know, looking back there were so many signs I should have seen; should have listened to my own unease about how desperate she was to get away from her father. I think I knew it wasn't me she wanted, but just the freedom she thought I offered her. Freedom at a price – a price I paid. Not her.

I invited my father to the wedding, against my mother's wishes and as she predicted he found a reason not to turn up on the day and we never communicated again. He died shortly before Daisy. His solicitors contacted me and I had to arrange the funeral for a virtual stranger. He left me this house and quite a bit of money, then Daisy died and I did the same all over again. She had money I knew nothing about and I have no idea where she got it from.'

He laughed, looking up from his cup and saucer, staring straight into Peggy's eyes,

'I waited for the third thing – they say good fortune – or bad – comes in threes, but nothing else happened, until now.'

Colin reached forward and poured more tea into Peggy's cup, adding a tiny amount of milk and one eighth of a spoon of sugar – just as she had, and just as she liked it. How observant and attentive he was, even in the middle of this strange tale. She wondered at how alike they appeared to be.

After a few moments he continued without appearing to break his chain of thought.

'I should have tried harder with my father. I never heard his side of the story back then but since moving in here I have found his journals and obviously there were two sides. It's made me feel quite ashamed'.

'But even journals only tell one side. You would have to balance them against anything your mother told you. Did you have other family who shared information with you?'

Peggy had been reading Psychology magazines. She knew it was important to always get a few perspectives on family situations, and was pleased to be responding in a neutral, more advisory voice to Colin's outpouring.

'My aunt in Leighton Buzzard seemed to bear out my mother's side of things, but then she would, wouldn't she? My father had two brothers and I am in contact with my cousins but they know no more than me.

Anyway, here I am now, living in my father's home, finally able to get to know him through his possessions. Maybe I am turning into him, I don't know. Since retirement I have rarely been out – apart from my missions to try to find you that is. I've been quite solitary.'

Missions? How did she feel about being a mission? This wasn't Leonard, she told herself, Leonard wouldn't have made her a mission at all, not before their wedding, or at any time afterwards.

'How long have you lived here Colin? I saw you when you fell outside Dolly's, but I don't remember seeing you before that? Where were you living? Had you and Daisy been living with your mother in Norfolk?'

Colin laughed, a really head thrown back type of guffaw which took Peggy by surprise. Hoping her practised expression of indignation had registered with him, Peggy coughed, a fake cough that she hoped would stop this unnecessary laughter.

'Oh, if only you knew, you'd realise how funny that is.'

Peggy couldn't have known, and was sure she wouldn't find it that funny, even if she did have some historical information to hand.

'Go on.'

'Daisy and I were still living in Newport Pagnell. She and my mother hated each other. If I wanted to see my mother, I went alone. If I wanted to speak to her I had to use a call box, until the introduction of these little devices that is.'

He pointed to his mobile phone, resting on the tray beside the teapot. A visual reminder to an onlooker that this man had other business going on, probably more important that his current visitor.

'I had to spend a weekend in Norfolk persuading my mother she could master the new technology, and she was quick to pick it up. That's how we communicated – just calls and texts to start with but then she worked out how to send me photographs of her chickens, and what she was having for dinner. Then she discovered video calls, but we only did that when she'd texted first to tell me to go for a walk so I was away from Daisy.

Daisy said I was a Mummy's boy, like her brother had been, and it wasn't healthy. I always thought her brother must have come to a sticky end, caused by his mother – the way she talked, but that wasn't true was it? He survived and married you didn't he?'

Peggy was praying that this wasn't Colin's way of asking her to open up and spill her whole life into mid-air. The fire had mellowed to an orange glow, and the remaining tea in her cup was cold. She longed for the familiarity of her own sofa, her books, and her own drinks cupboard. She noticed that like her living space, there were no festive decorations in Colin's home, and this house just contained a collection of someone else's memories.

Colin sat watching her as she tried to analyse who his father might have been. Colin himself could not be examined in the company of someone else's possessions and she found this frustrating. She felt annoyed with him for making her examine who he might be, when all she knew of him was based on his appearance, and what he had told her about himself.

She had allowed herself to be carried away by the opulence of the double gated property, the shine on the wooden banisters and the glow from the fire.

'It's Christmas Eve, and it's late. I should be going.'

Peggy looked around for her coat, and stood up, placing her cup and saucer back onto the table and brushing crumbs from her clothes into her hand which she made into a ball and then opened again, dropping the contents into the pocket of her trousers.

'Of course, Christmas Eve! I need to get going. I've promised to help out at a Christingle Service not far from here. The vicar is a friend of mine and he is not great with children, finds them a bit irritating, so I usually help out when he is forced to include them in the services. Funny, he doesn't mind when they bring pets into the church, but children seem to bring out all his anxieties.'

FOURTEEN

'The man sounds like a saint Peg; I hope you're not being conned!'

Jean had won all the cracker pulls and was rummaging through the spoils to retrieve prizes which she was keeping for herself, and hats and jokes which she distributed between them.

'He can't be too dodgy can he? Must have been through a few checks before he's let loose on kiddies at church, surely?'

Jean was ploughing through her plant-based lunch, while Peggy and Ros shared the dry turkey meat from the overcooked and exposed carcass sitting on the worktop, the moisture from each breast evaporating onto the windows of Ros's cold apartment.

'You seeing him again?'

Jean shovelled a fork full of parsnips into her mouth and began chewing furiously, staring at Peggy, waiting for an answer.

Ros chose to ignore Peggy's pleading expression and was also shovelling food into her mouth. Her manners had taken a nosedive since embarking on this friendship, or relationship whatever it was, with this Jean.

Glad of the silence, Peggy took advantage of the moment to enjoy a large swig of the Malbec she had bought from the Off Licence on the way home from Colin's the previous evening. The feeding frenzy on the opposite side of the table continued, but Peggy had too much going on in her head to eat. She found turkey to be a tasteless meat and although Ros had a reputation for great curries and pastas, this meat/plant and two veg meal was beyond help.

Finally her two companions rested their cutlery back on their plates, and sat back, holding their stomachs, Jean was the first to regain her voice,

'Great meal Ros, Happy Christmas. Peg – you not eating yours?'

Peggy shifted her gaze to Ros and raised her glass,

'You've caught me on a not hungry day Ros, but that was a great effort, well done. And Happy Christmas to you both.'

There, surely they couldn't expect more accolades from her.

Ros had decided against Christmas pudding thankfully – partly because of the effort, and all that steaming, but mainly because it appeared that Jean did not like dried fruit.

'Dead flies', was how she described the currants and raisins in the mince pies that Peggy had taken as part of her contribution. Jean was not so reluctant with the Port and Brandy Peggy had brought with her, pouring huge servings into three tumblers, and chin-chinning her way through the port before the start of The Snowman and Snowdog at 5 o'clock. She then fell asleep and although her snoring was a distraction, she was quieter company in the land of nod.

If Ros was embarrassed by this display then she hid it well, but Jean's nap provided the two friends with some time to have a civilised conversation about Peggy's meeting with Colin. They put warm coats on, hats and gloves and carried mulled wine into Ros's little front garden area. Seated in comforting darkness on the bench with Ros, Peggy felt as if order had been restored to her life. A life that had taken too many turns in the last few weeks.

Ros had no recollection of Colin's father, although she knew exactly which house Peggy described because the front hedge had been a regular source of greenery for Ros's seasonal door wreaths for many years, berries in winter and lush foliage for the remainder of the year.

'I'm sure he wouldn't have minded. I kept it looking trim for him, without him knowing.'

Knowing the cost of a sprig of foliage at the florists, Peggy was sure Ros's benefits were greater than Colin's father's savings on the cost of a gardener.

'I never saw him though. We knew someone lived there, always. I used to peer in from the top deck of the bus but now there's only single deckers you don't get such a look into people's business now do you? I remember he had an old land rover jeep type thing – it would sit in the drive for months, then be gone for months. Never thought much about it really. You don't when you're younger do you?'

'The thing is Ros, he talked a lot about himself, like he was explaining it all, like he felt he needed to tell me something but I don't know what, or why. I just wanted to find out more about Leonard, but I'm not sure if he knows more about him than I do. And it was odd sitting in that house, like sitting in a museum after it's shut, with someone who has actually broken in to steal something but you've caught them red handed and they're trying to throw you off the scent.'

Peggy ignored Ros's apparent confusion, accepted that was probably taking the poor woman's imagination on a journey she couldn't cope with, and carried on before she could ask for an interpretation.

'There was just something not right in some ways, but in others – well I'm telling you he was a perfect gentleman. So beautifully dressed, and so well mannered, and such lovely china – although thinking about it, that was probably his father's.

Anyway – what about you? You and Jean. How's that going? She eats a lot doesn't she? Plant based people on TV seem to have small appetites, and they're delicate creatures – you wouldn't call Jean delicate would you?'

Ros's laughter was forced, and produced to placate Peggy. Her hurt was overwhelming although she wasn't clear whether this was due to Jean's disappointing behaviour, or the fact that Peggy had witnessed and commented. She was fond of them both, but they were both difficult characters, and too different, or maybe too alike, to ever get on well. Like women with awkward husbands and fun friends, she may need to keep these two parts of her world apart.

Not usually known for her sensitivity, Peggy felt a stirring of emotion for her friend. She seemed close to tears, gripping her mulled wine in one gloved hand while balling a tissue in the other. She bent to flick leaves and mud from her shoe, giving Ros the opportunity to discreetly dab at her eyes.

'Christmas is always a tough day Ros – people who aren't used to company all thrown together in one room, food that frankly no-one really wants. Then throw in a load of alcohol. It's a recipe for disaster. I'm not saying I wasn't grateful for the offer, I was, and your lunch was better than I'd have had at home by myself.'

'See Ros,' Peggy continued through her friend's tearful predicament,

'You and I have spent years having miserable Christmas holidays, gazing longingly through windows and TV ads at other people, thinking they were having a better time than us. They weren't – there were just more of them in the same room, and the TV ads aren't real people – just paid actors.'

In a ground-breaking move, possibly fuelled by an excess of festive booze, Peggy reached her arm around Ros.

'I want to thank you for including me in your day, but enough is enough. We can meet up another day and have a proper old chat. Like we used to before all this shop work and trying to find hobbies started interfering with our lives.'

She released her grip on the shorter woman, who moved away quickly, relieved that the unfamiliar display of friendship was over.

'Go back in, wake Jean up and have some peace and quiet together. I'm going to wander home and put my feet up with Wolf Hall for a few hours – see if I can get to grips with the storyline.'

Relief swept over Ros like a warm blanket,

'Thank you Peggy. I'll see you tomorrow maybe. I did find some information about your brother but now is not the time.'

She was right, she didn't want her brother introduced into the madness of this Christmas Day. He would keep for a quieter time. She had waited this long after all, another few days wouldn't do any harm.

As Peggy pulled her coat around her shoulders and walked away, Ros spoke quietly,

'Jean said we should have bought each other presents, but I didn't think you'd want to do that.'

Peggy turned to look at Ros, standing with shoulders drooping, hair still messed up from the unexpected and awkward show of affection,

'Maybe she was right, maybe that's what was missing.'

'Nothing was missing my friend, nothing at all. Go back in and see to your guest.'

Peggy let herself out of the small wrought iron gate at the front of Ros's garden, and wondered how many other people's Christmas Day had been a source of disappointment. How many visits to A&E had been made, how many arguments brought on by months of anguish spilling over on a day that should be relaxing and fun. She had spent a few hours in the company of a good friend who had tried her best. She had been introduced to that friend's significant other and did it really matter that she wasn't keen on this other person? No, not at all.

She realised at that moment, as she walked away from the well-lit and welcoming ground floor flat that she already had what she had wished for – someone who if they were upset, she would be upset for them, and she would care. Ros had been in her life for a long time, and however bruising Leonard's words had been throughout their marriage, this afternoon had proved to her that she was capable of having feelings for another person, and if it turned out that she wasn't guilty of all the failings he had accused her of – maybe it was him who was wrong. Maybe she could be a nice person, could have friends and maybe those friends would care about her too.

As she rounded the corner of the building, heading for the front doors, her attention was caught by movement by the car park. She quickened her pace slightly, but was too late to avoid the attention of very drunk Derek, approaching her at speed, waving a bottle above his head.

'Merry Christmas Mrs T? Been to see your girlfriend eh?'

She had to make a split-second decision regarding her reaction. Indignation, defence of Ros and whatever Derek thought was going on in her ground floor accommodation, fear – the man had clearly been drinking for most of the day – and annoyance that the person who was supposed to be protecting the residents was lying on frosty grass, drinking, instead of fending off unwanted visitors.

She chose an option that didn't occur to her until the very last minute. She ignored him and walked straight into the building, muttering all available responses under her breath.

'Unbelievable, the man is a moron. What did he mean, 'girl-friend'? Was there talk? Ros always said they should be attending the weekly coffee mornings he presided over, just to find out the latest gossip, but neither of them were really interested in the lives of their fellow residents and as Ros pointed out, they could choose to eat stale cake and drink cheap coffee elsewhere if that's what they wanted to do.'

Relieved to be inside the building, her thoughts were once again interrupted by another movement off to one side, and again this was movement that had a voice. Not a drunk voice and not the voice of derision.

'Peggy, Happy Christmas.'

'Colin? I, I wasn't expecting you. Was I? I've been out to lunch. My friend Ros invited me over.'

He was sitting on the large leather sofa in reception, perched on the edge of the seat, and nervously clutching a wine gift bag.

'No, we didn't have any arrangements but there's only so long you can make a turkey Dinner for One last, and there wasn't even any washing up to do. I was bored, came out for a walk, and found myself here. I hope you don't mind. I've brought wine. Derek let me in.'

Peggy looked him over. Smartly dressed, again, which was impressive for someone who had lunched alone. She imagined other people in his situation may have not bothered to dress up to microwave a ready meal – had he eaten out of the foil container, or decanted onto a plate. She might ask later, discreetly. This, she imagined, would tell her more about his character.

The front doors were rattling as Derek made an awkward attempt to enter the building. She had no desire for the two to meet while Derek was so drunk.

'Come up Colin, I'll find some glasses and we can share your wine.'

Concerned at the prospect of lift delay, she hurried him up the stairs, feeling slightly like she was confirming Derek's views that she was a member of the oldest profession, but certain that this was preferable to another encounter with him – caught in the act.

Was the mulled wine at Ros's responsible for this reckless abandon? Or the idea that yet another year of her life was about to come to an end, and all around her other people seemed to have a sense of direction that she was missing?

Colin kept pace with her as they marched up the three flights of stairs. He wasn't breathless and his face was no redder than normal. Again she was impressed by this man – her relative by marriage only.

She let them into her apartment and began switching on lamps, directing him where to abandon his coat and assuring him there was no need to remove his shoes. It was one thing drinking wine with a virtual stranger but the idea of seeing him in his socks felt like a step too far. What if there were holes in them or even worse if her home was filled with the aroma of cheesy feet. No, a little mud could always be brushed away in the morning but the mental scars of stinking feet would linger for a long time.

She returned from the kitchen with a tray containing glasses, a corkscrew (just in case he had pushed the boat out and not bought a screw cap bottle), and bowls containing cheese snacks and peanuts. She found him perched again on the edge of the sofa. Could the man not relax a little?

She was relieved to see he was sitting centrally which avoided any embarrassment about whether she should join him there or not. The message was clear – the sofa is mine; you can sit separately – this was an arrangement she felt comfortable with and as the vision of herself as a high-class hooker evaporated, she began to relax.

'So, you've had Christmas alone?'

She was annoyed with herself for falling into the modern way of unnecessarily starting every sentence with the word 'so', but she did feel that in these circumstances it aided the flow of conversation. Maybe she had been too harsh with the people being interviewed on local news or on quiz shows – perhaps there was a case for 'so', occasionally.

Colin had answered, but she hadn't been listening. Should she ask him to repeat his words or just smile and hope for the best?

'Oh I'm sorry, say that again.'

Awkward and clumsy.

'I was just saying that after so many miserable Christmases watching Daisy drink too much and fall asleep straight after she had eaten the lunch I'd made; I relish the solitude these days. I really don't mind being alone. I feel less lonely on my own, than in the company of someone I had grown to despise.'

He continued, again Peggy realised, talking about himself.

'It's always been my habit to take myself out for a walk on Christmas evening – walk off the dinner, clear my head and peek into the homes of families celebrating together and enjoying each other's company. The lights in the High Street are lovely too, especially when there's not much traffic. It's a magical time of year isn't it?'

Peggy wasn't sure how long she thought it might take to walk off a portion controlled ready meal, but at least she was concentrating on the flow of conversation now, and took the opportunity to contribute a little something of herself.

'Do you know, the last Christmas I think I enjoyed was when I was about 13 years old. My whole family under one roof. My eldest brother had a girlfriend and that meant there were nearly as many women in the house as men – that was unusual. But the women cooked together, laughing in Mum's steamy kitchen, we ate around two tables shoved together, on a collection of chairs from around the house, then the men all cleared up while we sat and played cards in front of the fire. Everyone kept their party hats on all day, even my dad when he fell asleep during the Queen's speech. No sooner had the washing up been put away than tea was piled up on the table and we started all over again, with cold meat and pickles followed by a sherry trifle. Such a happy day. The last one where we were all together. I could never reproduce a day like that so I've never bothered. After the first year we were married and I bought Leonard a fountain pen with his name engraved on it, and he bought me a carpet sweeper, I told him not to bother again, and he never did.'

Peggy checked that Colin was still listening and hadn't fallen asleep like Leonard might have done if she had spoken for this long. He was listening, and watching her. She continued, pleased to be talking about her family, something she had not been able to do for so long. Even Ros didn't really want to know, probably because any talk of someone else's happy family life made her childhood feel even more miserable.

'Leonard didn't like turkey, preferring pork, so Christmas Day was much like any Sunday really. He was of the opinion that if you'd had a decent lunch there was no need for anything else later on so we'd make do with a bit of cheese and crackers in the evening. Then he'd snore for a few hours and I could get my books out and read in peace.'

She was making herself depressed recounting life with Leonard.

'Not the sort of Christmas that would feature on the front cover of a glossy magazine is it?'

They both laughed and sipped their wine for a few minutes, then Colin spoke quietly.

'I wonder what Christmases were like for the younger brother and sister. Mine with Daisy were much like yours. I don't like turkey either but who does? It's just traditional isn't it? Daisy would at least let us have chicken at Christmas, and I always cooked so I tended to do the works – bread sauce, enough for eight people, pigs in blankets, home-made stuffing, the lot.

Maybe they had a bad time with their dad at Christmas, perhaps that's what put them off.'

At last it seemed that Colin was about to divulge some background information about Leonard, new information.

'What do you know about their childhood Colin? I know nothing, so anything you have will be news to me.'

'Wow, where do I start?'

He took a long swig of his wine, emptying the glass and as Peggy stood to offer a refill, they heard the sound of her intercom buzzing.

She walked over to investigate who the intruder might be, and Colin stood up,

'I'm sorry, are you expecting guests? I'll leave, get out of your way.'

'You'll do nothing of the kind, sit down.'

Surprised and embarrassed by the ferocity of her own response, Peggy tried to back track,

'I'm sorry, no, I'm not expecting anyone, please take your seat.'

She wasn't going to let him escape so easily when he was just about to spill the whole story.

'Yes. Who is it?'

A breathless Joe replied,

'It's me. I just wanted to you know, wish you a Happy Christmas. I've brought beer.'

Peggy's eyes rolled. A wisp of loyalty prevented her from dismissing the man who had been a good neighbour and a friend for so long, but she could barely hide her irritation. She couldn't send the man away – it was Christmas Day, if someone took the time out to visit a person on Christmas Day it surely couldn't be right to just respond with a 'not today thank you'.

She pressed the button allowing Joe entry to the front doors. She didn't have long to provide Colin with some background. By the sound of the already breathless Joe he would probably take the lift up to the third floor so unless it got stuck between floors he would be bursting through the door, beer in hand, within the next few minutes.

'Ah, Joe.'

Colin was smiling.

'Nice man. It will be good to see him, *again*.'

Peggy wasn't sure how to interpret Colin's emphasis on his final word, but there was no time for reflection. She fetched a pint glass from the kitchen and opened the door to await Joe's arrival, leaving Colin to move to one end of the sofa in preparation for their new guest.

Peeking through the peephole in her door, Peggy could see not one but two figures silhouetted against the bright lights in the hallway. Joe closest to the door and standing slightly behind him she could see the taller and slighter frame of his son Liam.

Empty-handed Joe walked through the door first, followed by a sheepish Liam clutching a four pack of Mexican Lager, and three limes.

Confused, Peggy showed them through to the Living Room, grabbing a chair from the hall as she went.

'Colin, you know Joe,' nods all round, 'and this is his son Liam – I'm not sure if you've met.'

Colin beamed, 'Yes, this is the young man who helped me tow my car out of a ditch in the ice last month after we had both been to a concert at The Stables. Hello Liam – I had no idea you were Joe's son. Happy Christmas both.'

Liam was delighted at the recognition, but Joe, still confused by Colin's presence, was suddenly unsure what to do with his hands, whether to take his coat off, or where he should sit.

He finally decided that he would simply unzip his new wax coat,

'It was a present to myself, after all, no other bugger will be buying me anything.'

He eventually sat next to Colin on the sofa, and Liam opened a couple of lagers, abandoning the ceremony of the limes. Finally, Joe turned to face Colin and returned the festive greeting that had lain over them all for almost seven minutes.

Liam raised his bottle with a 'Cheers, Happy Christmas everyone.'

Peggy responded by raising her wine glass and took her seat facing the three men.

'This feels a bit like Dragons Den!' She laughed.

'So,' she continued, to fill the void, 'how have you two spent your day? Together?'

'Yes, Dad and I were at Mum's for lunch. Mark was working and he's just turned up. She's microwaving his now so me and Dad thought we'd pop out for a walk. It was his idea, to pop up. You know, see how you were doing. I said I thought you might be busy.'

He nodded towards Colin who held his hands up in denial.

'No, I did just the same. I microwaved a ready meal and headed out for a walk too. Funny isn't it? Us all heading out for a walk on Christmas evening. Is that your normal festive routine Joe?'

Colin's attempt to share a joke with Joe failed miserably and Peggy felt sympathy for this genuine and simple man who was clearly feeling out of his depth.

'I was at Ros's Joe. I met her new 'other half', Jean. It was pleasant enough but turkey is a dry old meat isn't it? I think everyone will be glad that meal is over for another year, don't you?'

Poor Joe – Peggy had added to his confusion. He had too many questions to ask in response to this news, his brain was set to explode. Peggy continued,

'Yes, she has struck up a relationship with a lady called Jean. I met her at the Book Club in October although I hadn't seen her since. She is a vegan, and now Ros has begun fostering hedgehogs. I'm not sure if the two are related, that might be a coincidence. But anyway, they seem to be getting along very well.'

Joe was staring at Peggy, then at his beer, unsure when or how to contribute to the conversation,

'Anyway, Jean fell asleep straight after lunch and so I came away and left them to it. So that's a new coat Joe? It suits you.'

'I knew about the hedgehogs. She had me build a little house for them, well two houses actually. I don't know if they'd eat each other but she was told to keep them apart. They sleep most of the time now, you know, hibernating.'

He paused, but no-one seemed keen to join in the hedgehog chat.

'Yes, it's a new coat. I bought it for myself. I entered a competition in the local paper to win one, but I didn't win so I thought well I'd just buy one anyway.'

Liam butted in,

'No other bugger's going to buy me anything, eh Dad?'

They all laughed, and Colin responded quickly,

'That's your age Joe – no-one ever buys me anything either, they haven't for years. Still I don't have to buy anything either so it works both ways, and I no longer have a cupboard full of foul-smelling aftershaves and comedy socks that I'll never wear, so there's a bright side to it. At least you bought yourself a good coat that you like.'

There were general nods of agreement from the three older members of the soiree, but Liam just rolled his eyes before downing the remainder of his lager.

'Come on Dad, let's head home. We haven't brought a torch and it'll still be treacherous trying to get across that muddy field at this time of night, in the pitch dark.'

Joe reluctantly heaved himself out of the sofa, and began the awkward process of aligning his zips in order to seal himself back into his coat.

Watching him, Peggy felt a wave of something unidentifiable for this gentle man who had cared enough, presumably without a complicated agenda, to walk out in the cold on Christmas Day, to check she was OK.

'Come for lunch Joe, tomorrow, here.'

It was more of an instruction than an invitation, and it was accepted in the same way.

'Yes Mrs T – I have some rounds to do in the morning – I'm looking after Ben Tillett's pigs and sheep while him and his missus are away in Tenerife. Animals don't know it's the holidays, see.'

Pleased the transaction had been agreed quickly, Peggy responded with an unaccustomed level of cheer,

'That's great Joe. I'll make lunch for about 2. Just get here whenever you can.'

She would never have invited Joe or any other man for lunch if they had been alone, but with the protection of Colin and Liam, she felt sure that this invitation would not be taken in the wrong way and lead to any awkwardness. Her mind turned immediately to the menu which would need to be put together from the bottom of her fridge and freezer.

Once the father and son had taken their leave, Peggy decided it was time for Colin to prove himself useful and divulge some of the information he must have regarding Leonard's past. Easing him in gently she first topped up his glass, and fetched another assortment of seasonal snacks, making sure there were some left in the cupboard for her lunch with Joe. She felt sure Joe was a snacks before lunch type of person, and was pleased she had brought a full shopping trolley home with her from the Co-op the previous weekend.

'So Colin, what do you know about Leonard?'

If he was surprised by her abrupt questioning he did not allow her to see it. He paused for a few moments, took a sip of wine and a few cheesy footballs, placed his glass back on the table and began.

He quietly told her all her he knew. That Leonard and Daisy's father had apparently been fine until their mother's death when they were both quite young. That the father seems to have blamed the two children for his wife's death and treated them unkindly, particularly Leonard who he had humiliated, abused physically and mentally, and criticised constantly. When Leonard had left home, the father seemed to have turned his hatred fully onto Daisy and she had seen Colin as a route of escape from the house.

'She would have married Jack the Ripper I think, just to get away from him.'

Peggy reflected on how quickly Leonard had moved from being an acquaintance of hers, to a fiancé, all within a few months. She had been flattered; had seen him as reliable and solid – everything she thought she should look for in a husband. She had never loved him, and had grown to despise him. She was glad he was dead and it seemed Colin felt the same about his wife.

'Might Daisy and Leonard have been good people if their mother had lived longer do you think? Or were they born bad?' Peggy's interest in psychology was proving useful and she was asking from a research perspective; it shocked her to realise how distant she felt from a man she had been married to for 40 years.

Again Colin considered his answer for some time before speaking, and like her it seemed he thought about his wife from a distance, like an outsider speaking of a character from a book they had read. There was no trace of emotion in his voice, he was giving Peggy the facts, as he saw them.

'I have thought about this a great deal. I have wondered if their father was always a bad man, or did he seriously blame two small children for his wife's death? But they were her children and if he loved her that much would he really have treated them so badly? All I know is, I gave that woman everything she asked for, and she turned on me. Gave me nothing back.'

He returned to his wine, but there was something about the way he had referred to his wife as 'that woman' that had made Peggy uneasy. There was a deep hatred inside him, deeper than the resentment or dislike she felt for Leonard. Something, not quite right but she couldn't put her finger on what it was. Maybe there had been too much wine consumed, it had been an exceptionally long day.

She watched him swirl the remaining dregs around, staring just beyond the glass, deep in thought.

'I must go. I will leave you to your beauty sleep.'

Abruptly he stood, and smiled, but the expression did not make it to his eyes – only his mouth moved. Something had unnerved him, or a memory had stirred within him but Peggy felt too tired to worry much about it.

After so long living alone, not worrying about the feelings of anyone else, she was unprepared, and unwilling to take part in any psychological game this man might be playing. If he was looking for her sympathy or attention there were other ways of going about it. She now had some scraps of information about Leonard, and realised she had no interest in learning more.

Peggy watched as Colin reached out for his coat, spending time finding the armholes, dealing with all eight buttons, and then fastening the belt in an untidy off-centre knot. He patted the pockets to reassure himself that he was in possession of keys and phone, and finally looked up to meet her eyes.

'You have a visitor tomorrow – I was going to invite you out for lunch, but I am sure there will be other times for us to catch up again. I am going away to visit family for a few days, or weeks – depending on how we all get on.'

Again the mouth only smile.

'So I won't be around for a while.'

Was Peggy supposed to care? She wasn't sure how to react. She was almost sixty, too old to be involved in playground boy/girl games. She had no experience to call on for help. Did her face portray her confusion? She hoped not, that might be rude.

'Oh well, I hope you have a good time with your family. That will be nice. I am hoping to try to meet up with my brother and his wife soon, if I can find them.'

She laughed, but he would have no idea why that might be funny.

Colin pulled on his hat and gloves, signalling it really was time for him to leave.

'I would like to see you when I return Peggy. Perhaps we could meet for a coffee. Can I call you?'

The dark cloud had gone from his expression. His eyes were smiling again and he was once again speaking kindly, looking at her while he spoke.

'Yes, of course, coffee would be nice, thank you. I will wait to hear from you. And I do hope you have a nice break with your family. Perhaps some time in their company will do you good.'

She hadn't meant to imply that he needed the break, or help, and worried that he might take her words the wrong way. She also noticed that his suggestion for their meeting involved coffee, not alcohol. Was this intentional? Suddenly she was worrying about what other people thought again. When had that happened?

'Yes, I have spent too long in my father's house I think. I will enjoy some time away. Thank you for your hospitality Peggy, I have enjoyed your company.'

She watched him walk along the long corridor towards the stairs and returned his wave just before he disappeared from her view. It would take a few minutes for him to negotiate the stairs and get out of the front doors, but she collected her remaining wine and wandered over to the Lounge window to watch him walk down the driveway, towards the graveyard shortcut.

Only when she was sure he had left the grounds of Sovereign Court, did she feel able to begin clearing away glasses and snacks, carrying everything through to her kitchen. She scooped rubbish into the bin, emptied glasses down the sink and began to fill it with hot soapy water. While the bubbles grew in the water, she glanced out of the window towards the row of houses where she had lived for so many years with Leonard, lit now by four new lampposts – a part of the town's regeneration.

For so long she had lived in that tiny cottage, with no money of her own, no friends and no contact with her family, under the complete control of that insipid little man.

How had she let that happen?

She had spoken in more depth to Joe more in the last few months than she ever did when he was her neighbour – why? Because Leonard didn't like him. She had lost contact with her family – why? Because Leonard had persuaded her that she didn't need them in her life and after a while it became too difficult for her to contact them; too much time had passed and she knew Leonard wouldn't like it. He had persuaded her not to move her piano into the cottage, even though there was a perfect space for it in the Living Room, against an empty wall, and finally she had given up playing her violin because he didn't like music.

Even Ros had been ignored for so long – Ros who had struggled, sacrificing her own life to care for a mother who treated her with cruelty and had made her life a misery. If she had been a true friend she could have offered Ros some relief, kept her company in darker times and maybe between them they would have found a way to escape their respective imprisonments.

She was happy for Ros that she had found someone to share her life with. Jean wasn't an ideal companion, surely even Ros knew that, but if she made her friend happy, even if just for a short time, then good for her.

There now in that little row of cottages was Joe, living in her home. Sleeping in the room she had shared with Leonard, bathing in the bath where she had taken refuge behind a locked door, listening to the Archers, and reading, stashing her books behind the bath panel. She laughed, remembering how Leonard had complained at the amount of time she spent 'pampering herself' when really all she was doing was sitting on the hard toilet seat, learning to speak languages that he would never understand, muttering abuse at him in foreign tongues.

Before she went off to bed, she needed to make sure there was food for her lunch with Joe the following day. She removed salmon from the freezer, checked the veg box and found broccoli, potatoes, and a bunch of wilting dill. Joe would want a dessert; he would call it pudding. There was a strawberry cheesecake that was still within its sell-by date and there was no mould around the spout of the squirty cream.

Happy that the catering was in order, she swapped her day clothes for fleece pyjamas and finally sank into the luxury of fresh Egyptian cotton sheets for a dreamless, worry-free sleep.

FIFTEEN

'People call it Twixmas, Peggy. This time between Christmas and New Year, it's actually got a name. New Year didn't even used to be a thing did it? You had Christmas, then you went back to work and got on with your life back then. Now it's like a two-week holiday. Cheers.'

The two women chinked their flask cups. Both were wearing sunglasses to protect their eyes from the bright sun already melting snow from the paths in the churchyard, leaving only patches of white on shaded graves under the wide trunks of yew and oak.

'I had Joe round for lunch Ros.' Peggy felt it would be wise to get this topic dealt with early on. Much better than if Ros found out for herself, and started making more of it than she should.

'On Boxing Day. I know. Jean said she saw him walking up the driveway with a bulging blue carrier bag and a bunch of flowers. I wasn't sure if his visit was unsolicited or not, but we didn't see him leave for quite a while so we gathered he'd been invited.'

'Oh we did, did we? Can I have no privacy Ros? It wasn't a secret, don't look at me like that. It was nice, he's a nice man and he's a fearsome Scrabble player. Don't be sordid, this is no laughing matter.'

Ros continued to laugh, nervous that she was about to be told off, but surprised at how defensive Peggy was being about being caught lunching with this younger man.

After a few moments' silence, Ros made enquiries about the menu, nodding her approval.

'Good choices, everyone is sick of turkey at Christmas, a nice bit of salmon, that's good.'

Ros left a calculated pause before returning to her enquiries, no longer laughing,

'What did you talk about?

'We talked about everything Ros. I didn't ply him with whisky this time. He brought a few bottles of beer for himself and a nice bottle of white wine for me, but I only had a couple of glasses. He also brought me a present. A very pretty silk scarf. I was embarrassed not to have bought him anything, but he said not to worry, the lunch was better than a gift.

We talked about my plans to travel, about his plans for his future. He definitely doesn't want to stay with Tracey, but there was no awkwardness with him. He's just a really good friend.'

Peggy caught an odd look flash across Ros's face and reassured her, smiling,

'So I have two friends now.'

'Three if you include Jean!'

Peggy smiled but wasn't ready to get carried away with that idea. There would need to be a few conversations with Jean to establish whether she could ever consider her as a friend, but something had happened over the last few days and she realised the value of Ros's friendship. She wasn't prepared to lose that with a few unkind words, if only she could hold her tongue.

It was two hours later that the two women wandered back towards home, parting company in the driveway. Ros turning right towards her brightly lit kitchen where Jean had been preparing a late lunch of Leek and Potato Soup, and Peggy heading for the front door of the building, looking forward to lighting the fire, and enjoying her lunch of baked camembert with chunks of toasted ciabatta, and leaves soaked in balsamic dressing. She would never take for granted the ability to choose her own food, and eat whatever she wanted, whenever she wanted.

Derek was on duty behind his desk when she emerged into the brightly lit entrance hall.

'Evening Mrs T. You're looking chipper this afternoon. Got a date?'

'I've just had one Derek – you missed it.'

She ran up the stairs, two at a time, energised with a new zest for life. She had plans, she had her own life to lead and she was going to do it her own way. Not to spite Leonard, and not to annoy him. She might end up leading a life he would approve of, or she might not. Suddenly she didn't care. She didn't care what he would think, and she realised she wanted him and his ashes gone. But where? She would need to think carefully about that one.

SIXTEEN

Peggy had been unaware that her self-styled haircut had a name, and had never heard the word mullet in any context. Unaware anyway until a drunken conversation with Fiona from the charity shop after they had both experienced their first pottery lesson.

The tutor was a jolly chap in his mid-forties who called himself PottyJak and operated from an old cottage on the edge of town. He was unconcerned with Peggy's warnings that the spelling error may cause him issues with an email address or website and assured her that he was gaining more followers on his Insta, whatever that was, than his competition, so she shouldn't worry herself about it.

He had enthused about their efforts, and assisted with the more difficult aspects of joining two flat pieces of clay together to form a tube with a bottom circle, also attached using a complicated system of gouging lines into both edges and splashing water onto the clay at regular intervals. They were making a vase.

'It's a bit like making a pie.'

She recognised the voice and that was the first time Peggy had realised Fiona was one of the other nine people in the class. Peggy had arrived late and Fiona had been skulking at the back during the demonstration. She explained herself later in the Lounge Bar of the Black Lion, as they were enjoying their fourth gin and tonic,

'Most sixty somethings end up looking alike and they all wear similar styles of clothing, however individual they think they are. When I walked in, all I saw was a sea of middle-aged women, all looking the same.'

This was the comment that had provoked a close analysis of Peggy's own unique style.

'Mullet? Is that a style?'

'Yes,' Fiona had assured her, 'but not one that anyone in their right mind would request! Who does your hair anyway? I used to go to Mario in Bletchley, but he's put his prices up and, well you know, some cutbacks had to be made. See what I did there?'

Fiona had an annoying habit of laughing raucously at everything she said, and no, Peggy did not see what she had done.

Baffled, she tried asking again,

'So if it's not a style, why has it got a name?'

Fiona set about explaining, comparing Peggy's hair with a few TV presenters from the seventies, some she had heard of although not always for hair-related reasons, and some she did not know. She got the general impression from the descriptions that yes indeed, her hairstyle was definitely in the mullet range and it was probably something she should consider changing.

'Do you not think it suits me then?'

Why, she wondered was she taking styling advice from a woman who showed more calf above her socks than would generally be considered acceptable, and whose own hair was such an abominable mess, she did not know. Fiona was the first person apart from Leonard to have passed any comment about her appearance, but where Leonard's remarks were designed only to be insulting, Fiona did seem to be trying to offer some tips for self-improvement.

'Ladies, we're closing for the afternoon shortly. Can I get you anything before I ring the last bell?'

Peggy looked around to see that they were the only customers, even the other pottery class people had shuffled off without bidding them farewell. The barman was hovering near their table, tea towel in hand.

'One more Peggy? Then we could wander up to Cutz by Jilly and see what she recommends. She's my neighbour, she's always trying to get me to go in and get my own locks dealt with. We could both get done – I got a tax rebate through yesterday.'

Fiona made inverted comma marks in the air, and laughed, as she said the words tax rebate, and while Peggy was wondering what that might mean, and asking herself why on earth she was conversing with this woman who seemed a little unhinged, Fiona was paying for a further round of drinks and peanuts.

'Chin chin Peg. For the old times eh?'

Peggy did not, as far as she could remember, have old times with Fiona, but raised her glass to chink with Fiona's, and watched as the other woman downed a complete gin and tonic in just a few gulps before reaching in for the lemon, and without wincing, ate all the flesh of it away from the peel. She finished off all the peanuts, knotted the wrapper tightly and dropped it into her glass. She then reached out to collect Peggy's glass, encouraging her to drink faster than she was used to.

Was this a good time to be getting a haircut she wondered.

Too late.

Just 15 minutes after the last cold gin had travelled down her throat, Peggy found herself sitting in a large black chair staring at her own reflection, while speaking to the mirror image of Jilly, who seemed keen to get to work, running her hands through Peggy's hair, scrutinising the ends.

'Great condition darlin', so many women find their hair is course and unmanageable as they get older. But this, it's lovely.'

Maybe the combination of compliments mixed with copious daytime drinking influenced Peggy's decision making, certainly Fiona seemed keen to try a new style for her own course grey hair and flicked through a pile of hair magazines while Jilly set to work on Peggy's new look.

Jilly had turned Peggy away from the mirror while she snipped and combed, and added potions and creams, rustling sheets of tin foil, and finally washing, blow drying and ironing the new style.

'There you go.'

Jilly turned Peggy to face the mirror once again. She could not believe the transformation in herself. Her skin looked radiant, her eyes, dark chocolate brown, were shining from her face and as she moved her head this way and that, she felt soft hair brushing against her neck in waves of gentle curls. Gone was the stiff black fringe. In fact all the black was gone. Her hair was now brown with occasional lighter streaks that caught the light as she moved. She ran her fingers through her hair, sweeping it backwards, away from her face.

'You've got a lovely face darlin, I don't know why you've been hiding behind all that hair for so long. What do you think of your friend's hair Fi?'

Wondering if she might wake from this dream at any minute, Peggy turned to Fiona for a reaction.

Fiona, now immersed in her own arrangement of foils with spikes of hair reaching out in every direction, looked up from the June 2014 edition of Cosmopolitan, her mouth dropping open in response.

'Sweet Jesus. It's taken years off you love. You'll be fighting em off even more now!'

This was the closest thing to a compliment Peggy had received from anyone other than her mother or father. The first time for so long that anyone had taken time to look at her properly, and she was unnerved by the raw and genuine care these two virtual strangers were showing her.

She wanted to cry, felt her cheeks redden and a lump appear in her throat – so that was really a thing then, she had always thought it was just a meaningless saying.

She couldn't cry, not in front of Fiona, a woman she had dismissed as just someone dreadful to be avoided and she held herself together while Jilly worked more magic on Fiona with an equally dramatic effect. She held herself together while they walked back up the High Street, while they exchanged pleasantries at the end of Fiona's road, and while she walked through the graveyard, past Derek reading his newspaper and drinking from a large 'Keep Calm it's January' mug, and while she walked three flights up the stairs to her front door.

She held herself together while she took off her coat and hung it on the hook in the hallway, over her discarded boots.

Only when she was sitting in her favourite chair, looking at herself in her hand mirror, did she allow herself to break down. Then every tear she should have shed for the past forty years erupted from her and she cried. Not just crying like when she watched that nice Scotsman reading the Auden poem in Four Weddings and a Funeral, or when she read about Heathcliff and Cathy in Wuthering Heights. No, this was painful, stomach-churning sobbing that went on for a long time as she sat in her own chair, in her own apartment, holding her head in her hands until she finally fell asleep with her new silk scarf from Joe wrapped around her for warmth, for company, and for comfort.

The sharp ringing of her intercom woke her from a disturbing dream where Leonard was wandering around her apartment, sneering at her furniture, at the excessive number of toilets and of course mocking the American fridge. She couldn't make him leave, however hard she tried. At the point when the intercom interrupted the illusion, Leonard was turning towards her, his eyes flashing with hate and his fist raised above his head.

With a jolt, her eyes opened and scanned the room. No Leonard.

She stumbled towards the source of the incessant noise and banged her hand on the entry button, without checking who was there. She checked her appearance in the hall mirror and was astounded at the face looking back at her. Her eyes might be puffy and her cheeks red, but she was looking at someone she hadn't seen for thirty years – someone based in this century, not firmly fixed in the last.

There was a knock at the door and peering back at her from the peephole was a chilly Joe, wrapped in coat, hat and scarf, but shivering and clapping his hands together to generate heat.

If any other face had been visible she might have shouted apologies and sent them packing but steady, solid and friendly Joe would be admitted.

'Wow! You look amazing Peggy.'

She thanked him and stood back to allow him to walk into the hall, feeling the cold air surrounding him.

'Actually, you also look awful. Has something happened? Do you want me to go? Leave you to it?'

No, she explained, she did not want him to leave her to it. She did not want him to go, and no, nothing terrible had happened. Quite the reverse she realised although she wasn't sure if this gentle, uncomplicated man would understand someone having a breakdown because they had been to the hairdressers and their hair looked better than OK.

'Tea? Have you eaten? I haven't and I think I need to.'

Relieved that he wasn't being offered alcohol, Joe agreed to tea and cheese on toast. He sat on a stool in the kitchen and watched as Peggy cut bread, grated cheese, and poured hot water onto real tea leaves in a large brown teapot. He had lots to talk about but it could wait, he wanted to know why she looked as if she had been crying for weeks, and why she suddenly appeared to be a much younger version of the woman he had been speaking to just a few days before.

They ate from trays, perched on their laps as they sat by the fire. Joe on the expansive sofa, and Peggy facing him on her favourite chair.

'Joe, would you drive me to the top of Dunstable Downs one day? It's time to dispose of Leonard's ashes and he hated the Downs in his later years – too near the golf course for his liking and he never saw the point of gliders, so it's perfect isn't it?'

Joe laughed but wasn't sure this represented the best way to lay Leonard to rest. He agreed to drive and they made plans for the following Friday when they felt the place shouldn't be too busy with other visitors.

'You look a bit better than when I arrived Peggy. What's happened? I hardly recognised you – is it your hair? You look, different.'

Peggy was not sure if Joe would understand her reaction to her new hairstyle. Was it just her hair, or was it the compliments, or the kindness of virtual strangers? Or the realisation that after she had judged Fiona so harshly, and still did really, the woman could show such openness, when she clearly had issues of her own, but there was no ulterior motive in wanting Peggy to look and feel better. She was confused and humbled, but was that enough to have set off such a reaction?

'I guess it's been a build-up of lots of things Joe, that's all. Nothing to worry about. Now, what has brought you out in this cold at this time of night? Not just to see my new hairdo surely?'

They both laughed and once Joe had drained his cup, and eaten the remaining crumbs and pieces of cheese from his plate, he coughed nervously and began.

'It's me and Tracey.'

Peggy had recently stopped interrupting people to correct their grammar, after an unfortunate episode with Jean when it transpired she had actually been wrong. Her expression was enough to halt Joe for a second but when no feedback was offered he continued,

'Looks like she wants a divorce. Says I show more interest in other women than I do in her. Says I show more interest in the weekly bin collection that I do in her, she also said that.'

'How do you feel about it Joe?' Peggy had read that it was always good to ask that as an introduction to further discussion. It seemed to have the right effect, getting Joe to question his reaction to this devastating, yet at the same time half-expected news.

'I think it's the right thing. To be honest, I am not interested in her anymore. She's lost whatever it was that kept us together. She just wants to sit and watch telly at the time, and moan. Boy does she moan.'

Peggy had also read that there were always two sides to every tale. She knew that even with her and Leonard, she had allowed him to bully her, hadn't argued against any of his bizarre rules or decisions, and that she had certainly changed from the light-hearted and fun-loving teenager she always felt herself to be. She had quickly withdrawn from him, rarely spoke and certainly never asked how his day had gone. She hadn't cared, so nor did he.

'Is it worth asking her to reconsider?'

Joe's face registered his surprise at this reaction, but his emphatic 'No', let Peggy know that although it was Tracey who had instigated the split, maybe it was laziness on Joe's part that had let things go on for so long.

'Anyway,' he continued, 'two things I need to talk to you about. One is easy, one not so. I'll start with the easy bit. She's moving back to Brum to live with her sister. The boys are staying here and looks like they'll be with me for a while yet. No sign of them moving out. So she wants to sell our house and have her money out of it, and I wondered how you would feel about me buying your house from you?'

Peggy had not expected this. She knew her house was slightly bigger than Joe and Tracey's, but maybe the reason she couldn't live there anymore was the same as Joe's reason for wanting to move out of his house.

'I'll do it properly, get a proper valuation and that. I've checked with John and Melanie and they're not coming back any time soon. The Abbey have said they won't be hiring him again and they don't have roots here. They seem OK where they are now, that's what got me thinking about me moving in permanently. The boys say they'll chip in. What do you think?'

'I think it would be good actually.' She was thinking that once Leonard's ashes were being trod underfoot by visitors to Dunstable Downs, if the house was gone too, maybe his shadow wouldn't be hanging over her and maybe she could move on.

'Let's get a fair valuation done, and move on from there.' She felt her spirits lift at the thought of Joe being master of Leonard's kingdom.

'What else Joe? That was the easy bit, what on earth is the tricky bit?'

If the suggestion about buying her house came as a surprise, Joe's next revelation knocked her Nordic socks off.

She was being cited as a reason for Tracey's miserable marriage ending. Her friendship with Joe, and she suspected with their sons, had been misunderstood by Tracey and her 'eyes on the street' – a neighbour who Peggy had noticed was part of the Christmas revelry gang in the pub when she had met up with Colin. But surely if she was with Colin, why would Tracey think there was anything going on with Joe? Was she being cast as a scarlet woman in the town?

'She says she's heard I've been drinking with you, and apparently I mention your name whenever I talk to her. She flipped when Mark said he'd seen you and Ros in the pub, and you'd been having a laugh with him.'

Had she had a laugh with Mark? Had she done anything to make this woman believe she was trying to steal her husband?

'She's using you Peggy that's all. She doesn't believe any of this, any more than you or I do. She's cross because you're about the same age as her but she's confined herself to the house and a dreary life, and your life seems to have just begun. That's how she sees it anyway.'

'I'll get more tea.'

She collected the cups and plates and retreated to the kitchen, leaving a bewildered Joe flicking through the latest copy of Breathe Magazine.

Waiting for the kettle to boil, she hid herself where Joe could not see her, and covered her mouth so he couldn't hear her laughing. What was she doing to attract so much attention? She thought she had a quiet, hermit lifestyle and here she was, the local siren, talked about in shops and on doorsteps. What would they say when they saw her new haircut?

Joe was engrossed in an article about Imposter Syndrome when she returned with fresh cups and an artfully arranged plate of garibaldi biscuits.

'Dead fly sandwiches! My mum loved these.'

Joe was a man of simple pleasures, the relish with which he received these little fruity treats was heart-warming. Would she have been so gracious with food she had been surprised with? She wasn't sure.

'So, are you telling me this to warn me? Or do I need to do anything? I am sorry if I have caused you any trouble Joe, maybe I have asked too much of you since I've been on my own. I never thought.'

Joe was holding his free hand up to stop her talking.

'No, you've not done anything, stop! This isn't about you, this is her, just grasping out at excuses for why she just wants to go and live with her sister so they can moan together, and she needs it to be someone else's fault. That's all. I'm just telling you so you know what she's trying to do. We're all doing what we can to get her to just go, and not do any of this. I just wanted you to know. That's all. Just in case anyone says anything. Didn't want you taken by surprise; you know.'

She did know.

'I've had to get a solicitor, to sort it all out and he says we should be OK. I'm not going to challenge any of it. She can go whenever she wants – the sooner the better and the less damage she can do when she's gone. The boys will stay in the house for now. Between us we can do both houses up – one to sell and one to live in.

This is the first time in years I've felt in control of my own life you know. I'm feeling good about life. A bit like you I imagine. We'll get

Leonard thrown into the wind, get Tracey settled in Brum and we can both move on. You know, separately I mean.'

He didn't need to add the separately bit and the fact that he did caused a disturbance in the air. He felt it too, and it caused him to rush the last two garibaldis, gulp his tea and he was gone five minutes after voicing the unspeakable. He left Peggy to rub rejuvenating cream around her puffy eyes, and slip into bed with the final few pages of Wolf Hall, fully dressed because who was going to tell her it was wrong?

SEVENTEEN

'I love this view. I'd still always choose somewhere with a garden, but I see why you wanted this flat so badly.'

Thick snow had fallen overnight and unsure about where the graves were, the two women had decided to take their morning coffee on Peggy's balcony rather than inadvertently trampling over remains and memorials in the graveyard.

'It's funny isn't it, the idea of someone building a snowdome for people to sledge up and down fake snow when they could be doing that down the High Street this morning.'

Peggy wondered sometimes at how Ros's brain worked, but usually found it easier just to nod and smile.

She handed Ros her coffee in one of the hand-thrown mugs she had bought from PottyJak. They were glazed in a deep peacock blue, with a loose daisy design painted on the front in green.

'Did you make these then? At your pottery class?'

Peggy laughed,

'No, I made a slab pot, a vase. It did stand up for a few minutes, but it had collapsed by the time I left and I saw PottyJak throw it into the clay bin. It was fun. I don't know why you won't give it a try. You'd like it. Very liberating.'

'I've told you before Peggy, the idea of plunging my hands into wet clay and getting it all under my fingernails gives me the hives. Did PottyJak do your hair too?'

Peggy had wondered when Ros might mention her new cut'n'colour as Jilly had described it. She knew it looked good. Ros had hidden her surprise when she first arrived, and almost twenty minutes had passed before she mentioned it. Peggy maintained a casual attitude, as if a visit to the hairdressers was a regular occurrence for her, not her first experience of a salon possibly ever.

'No, Fiona and I popped into the salon on the way home from pottery.'

'Mmm, so I heard, after a couple of hours getting up some dutch courage in the Black Lion first.'

'Good God! I can't move in this town without being talked about! I didn't know anyone even knew who I was, but now I'm the infamous drunken harlot stealing husbands all over the place. Which of your spies were out yesterday Ros? Was it Jean?'

'Whoah! Take it easy! Jilly used to do Mum's hair. I bumped into her in the Co-op last night. I'd run out of soya milk. She said you'd been in, a bit the worse for wear, with that Fiona from the charity shop, and she'd sorted you out she said. I thought she meant she'd sobered you up.'

She took a sip of coffee and continued,

'It looks nice. Makes you look younger. Less... severe. What's this about stealing husbands?'

Awkward compliments over, Peggy moved on to explaining about Joe's visit, about the prospective house sale, and his divorce, only touching briefly on her own involvement, and making no mention of her slight wobble in the previous early evening.

'She probably got fed up of him giving you doe eyes every time he sees you.'

'He doesn't do that! He's been a good friend and he's been glad of renting my old house while they sorted themselves out, that's all. Final answer.'

Peggy had never been able to raise a single eyebrow as an expression of doubt, but Ros was a master, and she dealt the sucker blow with great effect. She did not believe there were no foundations to the rumours and was not to be persuaded otherwise. The subject was closed on both sides.

Ros filled Peggy in on all the activities she and Jean had been taking part in. There was a Nordic Walking Group, a Beginners' Golf morning and a Ramblers Society.

'That's how come I walked up your stairs this morning. I didn't take the lift. I'm getting quite fit now. Jean's fitness mad.'

Just mad more like, Peggy thought, but did not feel it was necessary to make any comment. Jean was obviously good for Ros. She looked well as she gazed at the distant skyline of Milton Keynes, with a light breeze blowing her straight grey hair around her face. She was wearing bright colours too – not a brown twin set in sight. There was a cerise pink blouse with a grey and turquoise scarf knotted loosely off to one side of her neck, in a jaunty fashion.

The two stood together watching the sun pass over the trees and green fields. Now, the little town where she had grown up stretched out and almost joined up with Milton Keynes. There was a time when new buildings were limited to two storeys but it seemed things had changed and the sky was literally the limit. Cranes littered the skyline where a new budget hotel was being built to accommodate future shoppers and visitors to the theatre.

'This landscape has changed since our grandparents lived here hasn't it? Since the men worked the land on family-owned farms and the women made lace for the upper crust to adorn their posh frocks. Imagine, sitting making lace by candlelight, just to make ends meet. While the knobs in the big houses drank tea and ate cake in their fine clothes. Jean's got me thinking about all that now.'

Peggy rolled her eyes.

'And I thought we were just contemplating the shifting sands of time. Didn't realise this was going to be a speech about the atrocities of capitalism.'

There were more words Peggy wanted to add but she had learnt to keep the more cutting stuff to herself where Jean was concerned. So she didn't refer to her as Cashmere Jean in Ros's earshot, and made no reference to the double standards of someone cadging free food from a recent acquaintance, and moving in rent free, to a property worth half a million pounds at least. No, she listened as Ros continued with her local history lecture, which proved to be quite interesting and they did share a past linked to the area where the women had led vastly different lives to their own.

As she was seeing Ros out of the door a few pleasant hours later, she noticed her friend looking at her hair in the mirror as she was adjusting her faux fur hat, looking away once she realised Peggy was watching her.

'Might you go and see Jilly sometime Ros?'

It was a general and friendly enquiry, designed to be encouraging, and she was surprised by Ros's swift answer, delivered as Peggy was still speaking.

'I'm booked in at two thirty this afternoon. She says she'll sort me out, but I won't need as much black coffee as you two did will I?'

And with that she left.

Peggy walked to her Lounge where she watched Ros walk out of the front door and turn left towards her own flat. She was surprised to see her engaging in an animated conversation with Derek in the driveway. It lasted quite a few minutes and seemed to end agreeably, but there had definitely been a disagreement there. She would send a text and ask what that was all about.

EIGHTEEN

Peggy was having one of those dreams where the dreamer is aware that what is happening is not reality, but they don't have the power to end it.

There was music, Strauss, and she was spinning around a huge dancefloor with a smiling partner who was gazing at her with love in his eyes. They were waltzing, faultlessly among a sea of other dancers, all step perfect. If she could just concentrate on the steps, maybe she would be able to replicate the dance when she woke up, but it was difficult to focus with this handsome companion looking deep into her eyes.

The music changed, into a jarring modern piece with no rhythm, and with discordant voices shouting over the instruments. She was puzzled by the change, the other dancers had all disappeared and she looked up at her partner, wanting an explanation, but the partner was Leonard and he was sneering at her,

'You can't dance, what are you doing here? You've let yourself down, again. You can't dance.'

She pulled away from him and opened her eyes. She was in her own bed and Leonard was not there. She snapped her alarm off; it had somehow tuned itself into a different station, not her familiar Radio 4.

Leonard. Why was she dreaming about him? Was he warning her not to get rid of his ashes?

She threw back the sheets and stood up, speaking to the absent Leonard in strong terms.

'You're dead. You're taking flight this morning off the top of the Downs, landing wherever the wind takes you, and there is nothing you can do about it.'

She got herself ready, dressed in warm clothes with strong shoes, and set Leonard's box of ashes by the door. She didn't want to forget to take him with her.

After a good breakfast of scrambled eggs and coffee, she read her Psychology magazine until it was time for Joe to collect her, then she stood by the window to watch for his arrival.

She found herself smiling as she saw Joe's sign-written van pull up into the car park. His optimistic branding of Field and Sons was not a reality with his boys preferring to either work on the land or behind a bar to a life of painting and decorating, but he obviously felt there was still hope for the family firm. Either that or perhaps it was too expensive, and defeatist, to have them removed.

She watched as he parked the van in a disabled space, and wander over to Derek who shook his hand in a friendly way apparently making no objection to Joe's flagrant rule-breaking. She could not imagine she would have got away with such rebellious behaviour.

She picked up the cardboard box containing all that remained of Leonard and dropped him into a strong carrier bag. She checked all the lights, ovens and hobs were off, and set off down the stairs, swinging the bag with a feeling of absolute joy.

Both men greeted her with a friendly 'Morning', and Derek retreated back into the building, no doubt to continue reading his sports paper and do as little work as possible.

As they drove through the lanes towards Dunstable, Joe anxiously adjusted the heating to make sure she was comfortable, offering a selection of CDs and radio stations for her to choose. She had never been a fan of the whining voice of Karen Carpenter, or the false fun of Abba, and phone in radio stations annoyed her intensely so she chose a friendly and comfortable silence for the journey while Leonard rested on the back seat in his plastic bag.

A cold wind whipped around them as they stepped out of Joe's van on the top of Dunstable Downs, and Peggy busied herself with zipping her coat, wrapping her scarf around her neck and tying a firm knot in the front. Joe disappeared to negotiate the parking ticket machine and almost lost the ticket as a gust blew around him.

He snatched Leonard from the back seat of the van and the pair set off on a long path away from the car park and café, looking for an element of privacy, unsure whether what they were about to do was legal, or even acceptable in civilised society.

They finally found a space and stood behind a tall bush, shielded from the other visitors, ready to dispatch Leonard into the sky.

The box was secured by four brass tacks, but Joe produced a penknife from his jacket pocket and removed them, so the lid could be lifted off and the mess of ashes exposed.

'How do you want to do this?'

Peggy had not thought beyond the images of women throwing ashes into the sea that she had seen on TV and in films. The reality was that the wind was not all blowing in one direction and there seemed to be a danger of the ashes coming back at them. She didn't like the idea of that, but this had to be done.

As she slowly lifted the lid, a few specks floated up into the air and in panic she lifted the box over her head, turned her body around until she felt the wind behind her and tipped the contents out. A gust caught her from behind and both the box and its contents were lifted into the air. The last she saw of the ashes was them blowing in clumps towards the road and the golf course.

'And then he was gone.' She looked round at Joe who was wide-eyed at the spectacle, but at the sight of her expression he started to laugh, and she joined in.

Joe retrieved the box from the side of the road, levered the brass plate off the lid, and after checking that Peggy didn't want to keep it, he pushed it down into a rubbish bin.

'Come on Mrs T – let's get a hot chocolate in the caff. They do a mean flapjack in there too. My treat.'

Without hesitation or embarrassment, he put his arm around Peggy's shoulders. He left it there when he realised she wasn't going to shrug him away, and the two walked into the welcoming light of the cafe, taking window seats and contemplating Leonard's final and very suitable resting place.

It was dark by the time they got back into the van and Joe took a slow drive back to Sovereign Court, finally pulling up outside the open front door.

She was distracted by wondering why the door was open, and how she would question Derek – what was the point of an intercom system if visitors could just walk in when they wanted? Turning to Joe to complain about Derek's lack of responsibility, she was shocked to find he was moving towards her, and recoiled away from him.

'Thank you Joe. I have enjoyed the day.'

She was grappling with the door handle, trying to escape.

'I was just going to say, don't forget your carrier bag, it's on the floor there.'

'So it is, thank you. Really, thank you Joe. I can't think of anyone I would rather have done that with, getting rid of Leonard I mean. You're a true friend.'

Feeling calmer, she managed to pull the door handle towards her and the door opened, allowing her to step out of the car, carrier bag in hand, and she bent in to speak to Joe again.

'Come up for lunch some time. Let me know when you're not busy. My thank you to you.'

Joe smiled, 'That will be nice Peggy, I will.'

As she walked away, she could feel him watching her and concentrated on walking carefully – she did not want to fall over in front of him. She found herself smiling, and thinking about their next lunch. She hoped it wouldn't be too long before she saw him again.

NINETEEN

'Evening Mrs T.'

Derek's greeting was unusually cheery. Peggy knew there had to be a reason. He had gossip to impart or perhaps a little win on the horses to show off about.

'You've had another gentleman caller while you were out. I said you were out with one of the others. He said he'd come back later, about now I should think.'

'Derek!' Peggy despaired at his casual references to her social life, when all it really consisted of lately was a few pointless classes, the disposal of Leonard's ashes, a few visits from Joe, a long-time friend and neighbour, and Colin who had revealed himself to be some sort of brother-in-law.

'They're not gentleman callers for goodness sake. I lead a dull life – I know you'll find that disappointing to hear. There's nothing to tell. Just a few old boys with their own reasons for visiting and not the reasons you're imagining I assure you.'

She was interrupted by a loud cough from Derek and a quieter one from someone behind her.

She spun round to see Colin, standing by the door holding a bunch of battered flowers.

'I fell over again. Do you have a few minutes? Or is it not a good time.'

Peggy tried to express 'see what I mean' to Derek in her face arrangement. Whether she was successful in portraying the correct message or not, she could not tell but he took his seat behind the Reception desk and returned his attention to his newspaper.

'Come up Colin. I've just been out distributing Leonard around the Bedfordshire countryside. I have a busy night on TV tonight but I can spare you half an hour for a cup of tea – any good?'

Colin nodded and followed her to the stairs. He seemed a little unsteady on his feet and she did wonder whether she had been unkind to insist on walking up the three flights, but if this put him off from making these unannounced visits then so be it. She did make the allowance of not engaging him in conversation while he concentrated on his breathing.

Only when they reached her door did she question him about the fall.

'Where did you fall? Look at your trousers! All shredded at the knee. Give me your coat and sit yourself down. I'll put the kettle on.'

As she waited for the water to heat she found herself praying that there would be no need for her to administer first aid. If she'd wanted to be a nurse maid she'd have hung on to Leonard and let him live a bit longer. No, if this Colin was going to prove himself to be a needy sort he could just leave her alone. Nevertheless she prepared a tray of tea and crumpets and took them through to the Living Room where she found Colin inspecting his legs for signs of injury.

'I think the grass and mud under the snow took most of the fall. This is a rip rather than being shredded along the kerb like last time. I was on my way up here and tripped on a headstone. I went flying. That's how the flowers got messed up I'm afraid.'

She wondered why he hadn't just put them in the bin, they were no use to her – just a dozen stalks wrapped in cellophane. Still she graciously accepted them when offered, and made a show of plunging the lower ends of the stalks into deep water.

'I was actually coming here to bring you this. I knew it was in my house somewhere. I searched everywhere for it and finally found it in my suitcase, up the loft. Best place for a travel book I suppose.'

He handed over a pristine copy of a guidebook for Eastern Europe.

'I bought it for my last trip, but it was cancelled at the last minute. I always planned to go back some time. I was there for a few months in 2010, but well you know how it is, life just took over and I never got round to booking it up again.'

Peggy tried to remember what stage she was at with the cancelling and re-booking cycle of her trip with Camerons Travel.

She flicked through the pages with brightly coloured pictures of churches, mountains and tiny streets full of people in traditional dress.

'How do you feel about travelling there?'

No-one had asked her that outright before and she took a moment to consider her answer. There was no point brushing him off with the usual 'I'll be fine'. He had been where she kept telling people she wanted to go, and he may be able to offer some advice. She hoped he wasn't there to persuade her one way or the other.

She looked at Colin properly. Now he was settled into the sofa he was relaxed and comfortable. She felt he could be taken seriously. She couldn't have had an in-depth conversation with the Colin who had arrived with scuffed knees clutching a bunch of flower stalks.

He was waiting patiently for her answer, not butting in, and prompting her in any way, just waiting for her to be ready to answer him.

This warranted some honesty.

'I'll be truthful with you Colin; I don't know how I feel about it. I have booked, cancelled, and re-booked more times than I care to remember. I don't really think they have actually made the booking properly for me yet because there's been no conversations about the arrangements. They just take a deposit, give me a receipt and an itinerary which hasn't changed in all the times I have done this. And I was thinking I'd go to Pleven rather than Sofia. I don't know why. It just sounded more mysterious, less obvious I guess. It sort of epitomises it all for me.'

Colin waved her objections away.

'I understand Peggy, but Sofia is the cultural hub of Bulgaria. In my humble opinion of course!'

He laughed, and then when he realised she may have misunderstood, went on to explain,

'Here, let me have the book, I'll show you what I mean. I think you'll agree with me. You are more likely to find some English speakers there – I know you want to speak the language, but you might come unstuck – it would be good to know that you could fall back on the mother tongue if you needed to and you might need a good local guide, but your hotel would find someone for you, someone reliable.'

He handed the book back to her, indicating several pages for her to look at. She agreed that it did look marvellous and when the book opened on a view of one of the restaurants, she was immediately gripped by the image of cosy tables huddled together, the walls full of shelves housing a bizarre range of antiques and household items – old radios and typewriters, china, textiles, and lamps. Even in the guidebook photographs, there was a thin layer of what appeared to be smoke, laying just above the diners' heads.

Peggy carried on flicking through the pages of the book. She felt unnerved by someone actually taking her plans seriously – even she had not really done that, always assuming either she would cancel it or something would happen to make sure she never left the UK, but what that might be she could not imagine.

'Were you there with your job? Alone or in a group?'

She needed to get some facts straight, about his trip, before she could start making comparisons with her plans.

'I travelled alone; I did visit a client when I was there but just for one meeting. I decided to extend the stay to make it a holiday. You don't need a visa unless you're planning to be there for a long time. I think it's about three months. I imagine they have waited until you definitely confirm your travel dates before they spend their time and energy, and your money, on all the paperwork. It has to be right or you won't get in.'

OK so he travelled alone, but it was a truth universally acknowledged, to quote Jane Austen, that it was easier for men to travel alone than women. How did she really feel about it now someone was taking her seriously?

'Have you done much travelling in the past Peggy? Did you and Leonard get out and about much? I've been wondering where the travel bug has come from.'

'Colin, I'll be honest with you, I've been nowhere. Leonard always said why would you go somewhere to sleep in an uncomfortable bed and eat strange food when you're better off at home, and I always thought we couldn't afford to go anywhere.

No, I have not left this patch of England, ever.

Well, I tell a lie, I went to Dunstable this morning to shake Leonard's remains off the top of a hill and way back there was the trip to Whitley Bay for a family wedding. We were there in a hotel for a whole weekend apparently, but I was only two years old so I remember nothing. Apart from Ros and I popping into London for the museums and galleries occasionally, I've stayed around here all my life, travelling to school and work within a five-mile radius of here. I watched Milton Keynes from its first inception. We had a school trip to the site that would become the shopping centre – it was just fields then – and the teachers told us there would be a huge complex of indoor shopping. Obviously, we took no interest and thought it was all nonsense anyway – the very idea of people going shopping inside one big building sounded ludicrous at the time.

No, that's not travel I know, but I've been thinking about that trip lately and it made me realise that I've sat still and watched a big town arrive and develop and see thousands of new people arrive and make it their home. All that time has passed and I've just been an observer. Yes that's it, I've been an observer, always watching from my window. I'm still doing that now, but I want more. I want to immerse myself in how other people live, involve myself in the culture of other countries. I want to hear real people speak the languages I spent years learning while Leonard was still alive. I've let them go a bit lately but I could pick them back up I'm sure, how hard could it be?'

'Well, you do surprise me.'

Colin expressed this surprise by shaking his head and wearily rubbing his hands across his face. This was going to be more difficult than he had thought.

'What I want Colin, is to be able to face that 11 or 12-year-old girl that I was then, when she stood in that field just a few miles away, and tell her we turned out OK, that I didn't let her down, because right now I feel as if I have.'

Sometimes, Peggy realised, it took a conversation with a virtual stranger to let a person voice what's been whirring around the back of their head for years, and she realised that was the purpose of therapy. She had always poo-pooed the idea of people opening up about their private lives, and paying for the privilege. In fact in the past she had found it all excruciatingly embarrassing and had always known it was not something she would ever be taking part in, and here she was telling Colin stuff she hadn't even known herself until the words were out of her mouth. Now those words were laying in the air between them, ready to humiliate her.

'You're a survivor Peggy, don't you realise that? You lived with a man who mentally abused you for forty years and you survived. I know it because I have done the same. They were the same, my Daisy and your Leonard. Alright they might have been victims of the same mental abuse themselves so perhaps they deserve more pity than scorn, but we were victims too.

That abuse, it made them miserable, but you and I – well we've come out of it and we're not going to let that happen to us are we?'

Colin had stood up and was walking around the room as he spoke, and Peggy was briefly distracted by crumbs falling from his trousers onto the rug. He paced in a circle around her, then back to the sofa, emphasising each point by holding his hands up – stopping the evil of Daisy and Leonard in its tracks. All the time he maintained eye contact with her, his piercing eyes urging her to take a stand against her past.

'All I am saying is, if you want to travel, do it. If you don't want to travel, then don't go putting yourself into danger, or into a situation you won't gain anything from, just to spite a man who is now dead. Dead and gone. There's nothing wrong with wanting to stay here and enjoy the life you've made for yourself, nothing wrong with staying put, if you're doing it because that's what you want. What would be wrong, would be you going travelling if it wouldn't make you happy, whatever your definition of happy is of course.'

He paused long enough to smile reassuringly in her direction – whatever path she chose, would be the right one, if it was for the right reasons. That's what the smile said to her.

'Ask yourself, do you want to get on a plane on your own? Do you want to find your way to a hotel on your own, wander around a strange city alone but at your own pace, not at the whim of anyone else? Eat alone? Look at the sights alone? Sleep alone in a beautiful boutique hotel room? Wonder at the marvels of architecture you have never seen anything like before, all on your own?

If that thought excites you, you've already answered the question about whether you should go or not.

If it terrifies you, ask yourself why. Would you learn from the experience? Would you be overcoming deep rooted fears and therefore enjoy some self-improvement? Fear can be a good thing, but you've got to go with your gut on this.'

He sat back on the sofa, sweeping his hair away from his forehead with both hands, and then folding his arms loosely across his chest, waiting for a response that never came.

'Well that's what I think anyway. You see, for many months I refused to move into my father's house because Daisy hadn't liked what I'd told her about him, but then a friend asked me what I was trying to prove. If I'd won a large Victorian detached house on the main road in a lovely town I'd be over the moon wouldn't I? And there, I had one handed to me on a plate and I stayed, stubbornly remaining in a house that was full of bad memories of Daisy and our life together.

I felt a bit foolish then. I do want to get rid of more of his stuff, but some of it is OK so again, what am I proving and to whom, if I give it all away. He's dead, Daisy's dead and Leonard's dead. We're out of their reach and we mustn't let them do us any more damage.'

Peggy had listened to every word of Colin's speech, digesting each one and questioning herself. What really were her motives for wanting to travel? Was it just to show off that she could speak a few languages? And could she actually speak them, or just read them out loud from books. Did she really want to see these sights, walk around the streets of other countries, sharing other cultures, tasting other foods, and breathing in the aromas of other worlds? Or was she content to view from afar? Virtual tours on her laptop showed her plenty of sights and books were good too.

Her experiences of travel so far had been provided by saints of exploration in her view. The two Michaels, Palin and Portillo, with their foppish good looks and quirky outfits, guiding her gently around the globe, chatting with the locals and eating food she wouldn't really want to try, taking part in activities – some of which looked painful, but which they endured with patient tolerance, for her to witness without leaving her favourite chair.

What would make her happy then? Or even what would make her happier than she already was?

Would lone travel give her something that would be lacking if she shared the trip with someone else, or would that familiar hatred of other people return to spoil the trip for everyone – her included?

'I have some thinking to do don't I? You've been very insightful Colin, thank you. Now you must go, and I must start writing my thoughts down. I find that to be the best way to work out what's going on in my head – not at the front here,'

She tapped her forehead to demonstrate where the everyday thoughts lay,

'but right at the back. The stuff that's lurking, hidden away. You've given those thoughts permission to break through and I need to capture them before they return to the dark recesses. I have no idea what the outcome will be, but I think you have set me on the right path.'

When she realised he wasn't about to move, she wondered if there had been another reason for this visit. She sincerely hoped not, her mind was racing but she knew it would all settle back down if she didn't commit her thoughts to paper pretty soon.

'Was there something else?'

She tried so hard not to be rude, but sometimes bluntness was the only way.

It worked. He stood and handed her his cup and plate. She noticed all the crumbs had missed the plate, and were now beneath his feet on the rug. She must not be distracted by cleaning up after him, she knew where there was a good empty notebook – a Moleskine, another flat-warming present from Ros – and she was anxious to make a start.

'I'll get your coat. You know, I can't thank you enough for this. You've really made me think about what I want to do, and I'm going to get myself some answers, this very evening.'

She managed to get him out of the door without inviting him for dinner. This had become a habit, as if she had to offer her guests a return visit in exchange for their departure. The lunch with Joe on Boxing Day had been a joy and she really did hope he would let her know soon that he was free to visit again. There had been a few pleasant evenings with Ros involving a baked camembert and a set of dominoes, but she lived alone by choice and she must not keep filling the space with other people.

As usual, she wandered to the Lounge window from where she could watch him make his way towards the graveyard, lit by a few council lampposts and flickering solar lights that had become popular around some of the more recent graves. He appeared to remain upright until he passed out of her view around the front of the church.

Relieved, and absolved of responsibility for him, she fetched the notebook from a drawer, together with a selection of coloured pens, poured herself a large glass of tap water and headed for her bedroom. She knew if she was in the lounge she would be compelled to get the mini-vac out and start clearing Colin's crumpet crumbs away – best to remove herself from all distractions and get to work.

She was woken by light streaming in through the bedroom window. Her notebook had fallen to the floor, but she found she was laying on a pen and was annoyed to find green ink had leaked onto her sheets. Her clock was showing 08:13. She rubbed her eyes and wondered how long she had been writing for; how long had she slept for. What day was it?

She reached down and retrieved her notebook. The squared pages were full of notes, some surrounded by cloud shapes, some underlined and some, like the word WHY in large capitals on several pages. There were drawings too, of mountains, churches, and boats. Boats? That was a new one. Had she been writing in her sleep?

Straightening the sheets, she decided to ignore the green stain – no-one else was going to see it were they? If it had been red she might have removed them – no-one wants to go to sleep in a bed that looks like a murder scene do they? But green she decided was harmless enough.

She carried the notebook through to the kitchen, set the coffee maker in motion and returned to her very own en-suite to enjoy a long hot shower, realising as the water touched her head that she had not had to deal with her new haircut yet and panicked, wondering if she was going to be able to achieve the same Hollywood look that Gilly had created. It was too late. Doubtless the unmanageable curls would return to haunt her, but there was nothing she could do about that.

She was right. When she unfolded the towel from her head, her hair was a mass of curls. She scraped her fingers through, admiring the delicious shades of brown and copper and watching as the conditioning cream Gilly had 'thrown in' to the cost of her treatment, settled the normally frizzy mess into something resembling a style.

She chose a red knee length woollen dress and thick harlequin tights for her day at home, and once she had collected bread, butter, and honey on a tray with the coffee pot and a warmed cup, she headed for her chair with the notebook to read what her semi-conscious self had decided about the future.

TWENTY

January was proving to be a cold month, too cold for sitting on a bench in a graveyard where the wind whipped around the walls and through the trees. Their bench was in the epicentre of the mini tornadoes whistling around the gravestones, knocking over dried-up wreaths and mini-Christmas trees adorned with baubles and spray-on snow. Ros had taken to arriving at Peggy's door moments before they were due to meet, preferring the indoor balcony view to a wet bench.

Peggy, delighted that their arrangement was continuing even after the introduction of Jean into Ros's life, was only too willing to keep her slippers on for their daily meet and the two would stand in comfortable silence for long periods of time, watching whatever weather conditions there were, travel across the vast landscape stretching out before them.

'So, what did your notes tell you then?'

Peggy told Ros about the journal (notebook seemed not to quite portray the depth of self-discovery contained within its pages), but had not included Colin's involvement in the process. She thought she knew what Ros would say about that, and was not inclined to start explaining herself.

'My notes,' she began, 'my notes tell me that if I really want to travel, I should do it, but if I would prefer to stay here then I shouldn't berate myself for being dull, vegetating.'

'We knew that didn't we?' For all Ros's saving the planet and let's look after hedgehogs spirit, she had little tolerance for what she might call airy fairy head stuff.

She was chewing a vegan nut brittle muffin, trying hard not to dislodge any fillings or crowns. Peggy had declined the offer. Not because she didn't trust Jean's bakery skills, but because she was less confident in her own ancient fillings and crowns than Ros appeared to be, and had no desire to have her new plans disrupted by visits to the dentist.

'My notes reveal that there are places in the UK where I could achieve some of my goals – visiting Cathedrals and the homes and final resting places of the famous. I'm considering a train trip, on the theme of Arts and Crafts. Just a few days at first to see how I get on eating alone in restaurants, staying in B&Bs or small hotels along the way. See how it feels to be a solo traveller but without the risk of arrest for not having the right paperwork, or misunderstanding a warning sign.'

After dispatching the final crumbs of the muffin, and flicking the remains over the balcony, Ros turned to Peggy, pointing an index finger at her.

'What happened to Bulgaria then?'

'Nothing has happened to Bulgaria Ros, and nothing is likely to happen to it for a while, well hopefully not because let's be honest we'd be caught in the crossfire. All that has happened is that my notes reveal I was planning these trips as an escape. From Leonard to start with, then from the memory of Leonard, then from his sneering expression if he thought he'd won, that I was too useless to do anything on my own.'

Ros had turned from the view, and was facing Peggy, listening carefully and respectfully to this rare and open declaration of acceptance. She had never heard her friend speak of herself in this way. Usually she was all blustering and cynical. If Leonard sneered, then she had a feeling that normally Peggy could have out sneered him. But not this morning. This was new.

'Is that really how you felt? That you had to go all that way to prove something to him? Even now he's dead.'

Peggy looked thoughtful.

'You feel the same don't you? About your mum.'

Ros nodded and retrieved a tissue from her sleeve, dabbing her eyes gently. Her new haircut framed her face perfectly and Peggy noticed, she had good skin, soft, almost translucent. And there appeared to be a trace of make-up – blusher and mascara.

'She's still reaching out to me, even now. I wondered if I'd started a relationship with Jean just to spite her, but honestly it's more than that. It might even have been like that to start with but it's not now. She's kind, thoughtful and puts me first. No-one has ever done that before.'

Peggy's resting face was speaking for her.

'I know you haven't always got on with her. I don't think you've seen the real Jean. She's nervous of you, really nervous. She knows how important you are to me and doesn't want to come between us, ever. That's why she insists we still meet up. I've been very confused, but whenever I feel like I'm getting on with my own life, Mother pops into my head with her "who are you kidding?" or "why would anyone love you?"'

'Oh Ros. Why? Why? Because you're a good friend, because you care about people, and hedgehogs of course, and well just because you're you. Here.'

She turned and put her arms around her friend, pulling her towards her in a gesture she had never made before. She was hugging someone, being hugged, and they stood together until the sobbing subsided.

'I feel such a fool Peggy, breaking down like that. I am so sorry, I..'

'Don't Ros, don't apologise. I did it. That afternoon when I got back from the hairdressers. That mad Fiona, she'd been so genuinely kind, and Gilly – she didn't know me but she wanted me to look nice and she was pleased when I did. I found it all too much. I go about expecting people to be unkind, or to have some secret agenda if they say something nice, then all of a sudden I was faced with some kind of, well just raw niceness. I don't know how else to say it. I felt a bit overwhelmed' I got home here and I broke down.'

This was the most honest the two women had been with each other since their teens, but there seemed to be no reason to stop.

'I felt better afterwards.'

She smiled, and hoped her expression was encouraging.

'Come on, tea or something stronger? It is midday. Has the yardarm done whatever it has to do before we're allowed a drink?'

Ros delved into her bag and pulled out a bottle of cream liquor. It's not the real thing and Jean says it tastes of B.O., but I thought we could share it. Any good?'

'Perfect – B.O. cream and Brandy – that would be my Desert Island luxury item.'

The two women laughed and Peggy fetched tumblers, deciding against the smaller glasses – there was a lot of the stuff to get through while they pored over Peggy's notes.

Each page of the notebook had been split into columns. Points to consider were listed on the left of each page, and there was a complicated scoring system going on, taking up the remainder of the paper.

'What I've done is write down everything I think about, to do with what I want from life from now on. Then, I've scored points according to whether that will be satisfied by travelling to Bulgaria for example, or anywhere else overseas. UK travel was expected to score high because frankly it's easier to do, but Bulgaria keeps coming out on top.'

'On your own?'

'Yes on my own. This all has to be done on my own. I am on my own, and will be for the foreseeable future. I like being on my own – I didn't think that would be the case, but it is. I get irritated by company. No offence.'

Ros's 'none taken' wasn't strictly true but fitted the context of the conversation and she knew that Peggy was difficult company so she was unlikely to find any sane person who would be able to tolerate her for long. That just left the slightly unhinged and she would struggle with them as companions.

'So Derek, rather indiscreetly I must say, was telling me that you have had a series of gentleman callers. I did tell him off, of course. It's not his job to sit in judgement of all who pass before him – that's what I told him. I was rather pleased with myself. Anyway, wouldn't you be tempted to go travelling with one of them?'

Peggy, normally accustomed to hiding astonishment at Ros's more outlandish remarks, was taken aback.

'Gentleman Callers? Joe visits from time to time, and yes he has been for lunch a few times. Colin, Gentleman Caller number two, has been here – it was him that made me question if I really wanted to go travelling, where I should be going, and most importantly – WHY?

But that's it. There hasn't been a trail of flower bearing beaux traipsing up the stairs with romance in their hearts. I intend to speak to Derek, and his employer. What a nerve! He's half asleep most of the time.'

Feeling a combination of fury and delight at this news, Peggy had lost track of her decision-making matrix. She held a hand to her hot cheeks in an attempt to cool them, but it was too late. Adrenaline was coursing through her veins and she felt energised.

'Well,' Ros was relieved that she wasn't in trouble for passing on Derek's comments, 'what must he think of us? There's me shacked up with Jean on the ground floor and you virtually running a high-class hooker service on the top floor!'

Peggy was breathless with laughter, 'At least you are 'shacked up' with Jean – I'm having tea and cake with these Gentleman Callers, tea, cake and polite conversation! I need to get my act together. If I'm being accused I might as well be getting up to something.'

She did laugh but the very thought of any kind of liaison made her feel slightly nauseous. Maybe that's why travel would be good – a swarthy suntanned chap from foreign climes might be just what she needed. Was it? No it wasn't.

She had started to add a point to page 23 of her notebook, but rubbed it out. No need to complicate matters.

'Oh, I haven't laughed like that for years Peggy. Who would have thought we would be the talked about residents here, when there's so much actually going on with the other people living here? Take Sandy from the first floor – she's had more husbands than I've had hot tofu. And I don't know where Elizabeth next to me stashes all her booze, but the Majestic van is out there most weeks making deliveries, Derek never bats an eyelid at her.'

'Back to me Ros?'

Peggy had learnt from some of the TV shows she watched, that lifting the tone at the end of a sentence was sufficient to imply more than the words being spoken.

Ros responded immediately with gushing apologies for moving the conversation away from the main topic. Was there newly learnt sarcasm in her voice? Peggy couldn't be sure but Jean was certainly having an influence on the previously, and comfortably, mousey Ros.

Peggy patiently read her notes out loud, sometimes jotting down new ideas and extra words never intended for Ros's ear. When she scanned ahead and saw Cornwall in a list of suggested trips she could visualise the crashing waves hitting golden sand but realised that culture was missing from the 'benefits' column. She quickly added Minack Theatre and St Ives (Art).

But other suggestions where the benefits column was blank were rubbed out or a thick black line drawn through them. Travelling in a group of like-minded souls was rubbed out completely. She had obviously not been able to think of any benefits at the time and certainly couldn't disagree with herself there. What had she been thinking?

'Did you just say Silent Retreat? You? Silent? You know that means you're not even allowed to offer constructive feedback about the organisation, or the food, or the accommodation, don't you? It means silence.'

This was a valid point. Peggy took a rubber to the word Silent, leaving Retreat intact. There was always yoga, Ros had made no comment about that and she did feel it would do her good to stretch her muscles and joints as she entered her next decade. There was a girl who visited someone on the floor below her, arriving weekly with a mat rolled up under her arm and swinging a long ponytail behind her, but the resident of the flat was rarely seen without walking aids so that might be more of a physio thing. Still it was something to think about, she wrote 'one to one yoga' underneath the retreats section.

Peggy closed the notebook once she had read all the comments intended for Ros to hear and was about to begin her concluding summary when they both heard the sound of cars manoeuvring on the gravel parking space outside.

Against specific instructions, Ros had left the balcony doors wide open, letting cold air fill Peggy's cosy bedroom, and the noise was filtering through to the lounge with the icy breeze. They both leapt up and ran to the balcony, arriving together to see the tops of a long black hearse and a limousine in tandem at the bottom of the steps. Other cars were pulling into the parking area, each waiting patiently as the one before reversed into the spaces normally reserved for residents' visitors.

They could only see the tops of the black funeral cars, but they could see the word GRAN spelt out in purple flowers in the back window of the hearse.

'Not a much-visited Gran' Ros observed, 'I've never seen kids visiting, have you?'

Peggy shook her head, and they watched as two women in black were led by a suited Derek, away from the front door towards the official cars. He then backed respectfully away and walked over to a red car with the front door open, where he bent and greeted the driver.

One by one the occupants of the other cars emerged and after shaking hands with each other, they formed an orderly queue at the back of the procession. First to set off was a serious-looking funeral director, walking slowly towards the graveyard. Then followed the flower-topped coffin, held aloft by men in black jackets and grey trousers, and the trail of black-clad mourners.

'Come on, I've got a spare black coat – it'll be almost to the ground on you but that's fashionable isn't it?'

Peggy rifled through her wardrobe and holding two coats up in front of her, weighed up which was the shorter of the two and threw it towards Ros.

She grabbed her keys and the pair flew down the stairs at lightning speed, only slowing as they reached the front door.

The cortege was disappearing round the corner towards the front of the graveyard, so they took their usual shortcut, heading for their bench where they would get a good view of what was going on.

The service in the church went on for almost an hour, and they had rushed out without flasks or snacks, but they could hear the music – an agreeable mix of modern and classical, and they both nodded agreement at the hymn choices.

'I'd have Abide with Me too. I've told Jean how I want my service to be conducted, and chosen my stone. Look, over there – see the rustic grey one that looks as if it's been hewn from a rock that just happened to be there. And no photos – I've made that very clear. Jean fancies a waterfall picture on her stone but I've said she's on her own there. Plain and simple I want. Yes, like me.'

Peggy was sitting on her hands for warmth, the gloves were in the coat Ros was wearing but if she pointed that out she would have to share them and she wasn't sure how she felt about that – sharing a coat was one thing, but gloves? No, that was a step too far.

'You're pretty serious with Jean then? You haven't known her long, is this all a bit quick?'

Ros nodded to the sobbing mourners emerging from the front door of the church.

'You never know, do you, when your time's up. What have we got? Another 20 plus years of sanity and limited joint movement if we're really lucky, then it might be all dribbling and incontinence after that. I've spent nearly sixty years with my life on hold for one reason or another. I can't blame Mother anymore, if I'd wanted to escape from her I could have, but I think I shielded behind the excuse of her. I can't wait any longer. If Jean turns out to be a wrong'un then what have I lost? Really? And I'm enjoying life, as it is. I want nothing more. That's where you need to be you know.'

They sat, hidden from the mourners, but able to watch the whole burial process. Words were muttered by the Reverend Graham Saunders, soil was thrown onto the lowered coffin, people were hugged. Then they moved away, back to the car park, presumably to be driven somewhere for stale sandwiches that had been stored overnight in an industrial sized fridge, warm wine, and cheap sausage rolls, while they shared amusing stories about the person they had just left in a wooden box, in a hole in the ground.

As soon as the funeral party was out of sight, a council truck was reversed over to where they had been standing just moments before. A team of workers in Hi-Viz jackets jumped from the front of the truck and began heaving soil back into the hole from whence it had come just a few hours before. They piled it up, topped it with all the flowers – GRAN was laid along the length of the mound – and pushed a wooden cross into one end.

The women watched, admiring how quickly the men were working. There was no chatting or joviality, thankfully. Peggy had already drafted an email in her head to the head of the council, berating the disrespectful behaviour of the workmen, but that was deleted when she saw them stand by the grave and lower their heads for a minute of silent reflection. They got back in the truck and drove away slowly. The whole thing was done in an hour and a half.

'Lunch? I had put baked potatoes in the oven on a timer – should be about ready now. There was a spare if you want to ask Jean to join us.'

'Well that sounds ideal Peggy, thank you. I won't bother Jean; she was in the middle of making her special chutney when I left. The flat smelt like a vinegar factory. She won't be done for hours, then she's got a few Archers' Omnibuses to catch up on. She'll hardly know I'm not there. Aren't we going to see who it was first?'

Peggy wasn't sure if she wanted to put a name to what had just happened. It was one thing to know an unidentified neighbour had died, but another to think who that person might have been. Had she passed her on the stairs, snubbed a friendly greeting maybe, or even worse, been downright rude to this person whose life had now ended. She couldn't bear to think of it.

She had no choice, Ros was tugging her towards the grave, then bending to read the name of the wooden cross.

'At least straighten it up while you're down there! They've left it at an angle for heaven's sake.'

'It says she was born in April 1960 – that's a month younger than you, and four months older than me. She was 58 years old Peggy, that's all. 58, and now she's gone.'

Peggy nodded. She understood all the implications of what Ros was saying. How she had neatly managed to tie this woman's death into the explanation of why she was so quick to let Jean move in, why she was trusting Jean, and placing all her hopes in their shared future. Because, actually, why not? As she had said, what did she have to lose? Unless Jean was a confidence trickster and only after her money of course, but even then she was enjoying life and did confidence tricksters really bother themselves with making chutney? The very idea of preserving vegetables was surely an indication that she also had some hopes that she would still be there months later when the first lid was removed, the fruits of her labours laid out on a lunch platter to be enjoyed and shared.

'Anthea Norman. Don't know the name do you? Unless she's that blond woman that plays tennis in the summer with Derek. Do you think that's her? She always looked fit and healthy.'

Ros straightened herself up, brushing soil from the hem of her borrowed coat.

'Well,' Peggy answered, 'if I was to be asked for two words to describe her now, fit and healthy wouldn't be my first choice. Dead and buried more like.'

'Doesn't that just prove my point Peggy? Doesn't that tell you that life is short. Even life for people who think they've got years ahead of them. Even tennis playing women who dye their hair blond to hide the grey. None of us know when we'll be taking our last breath do we? I might choke on your baked spud, and that would be that, but when I get up there I could honestly say, yes I have had a good time, well – lately anyway. I've done my best to enjoy it to the last.

That's all any of us want you to do. That's why I asked Colin..'

Her voice faded away. A penny dropped in Peggy's head.

'Colin? You put him up to that?'

'Not put him up to it, that's not how it was. I asked him to call in and we talked about how we could get you to make some plans. Jean's not keen on him, but he seems to have your best interests in mind. I said she's too suspicious of men, that's all.'

'Did you know he fell over in the graveyard, nearly killed himself? How would you answer him up there then? "Yes I've had a good time but I killed Colin because I wanted him to do some dirty work for me" He could have knocked himself out or anything.

It was a bit devious, that's all. But I suppose it shows you care. Does it? Do you? Care, what happens to me, or do you just want me out of the way so you can get on with having a good time with Jean?'

She knew that wasn't true. She knew Ros cared about her and she knew she had been hiding away from making decisions about her future because she was still coming to terms with having a future she could make decisions about.

'You know that is not true, and you know I care about you. I also knew you wouldn't listen to me because let's be honest here, you don't think I'm your intellectual equal, and Joe knew he wasn't the man for the job for the same reason.'

Peggy opened the front door of Sovereign Court to let Ros through, smiling politely at Derek's stand-in, a small, neat, dark-haired man in a brown suit.

'Wait a minute.'

She stopped while Ros continued up the stairs,

'You've all discussed me? Joe too?'

Ros was on the first landing and still walking upwards. Peggy had to take the stairs two at a time to catch up with her. On the second landing Ros stopped and turned to face her.

'I'll tell you once I have my baked potato served up, with a glass of Chardonnay I brought with me, that's sitting in your fridge door right now. Then I'll tell you all about it, and then you can tell me what you intend to do.'

She turned and carried on walking up the stairs, with Peggy following, three steps behind.

Peggy struggled to take in everything Ros had said. The three of them had apparently met in The Three Cups, served by Mark who had not mentioned any of it to her when she had called in for a mulled cider it seemed, on the very morning after they had all met and been talking about her.

Peggy's plans were not discussed over lunch, they both managed to avoid the subject, focussing instead on the funeral they had witnessed that morning, and how quickly time was passing for them.

Peggy could have sat with Ros for the whole afternoon chewing over their shared memories and wasted years, but Ros was anxious to get back to the Chutney Kitchen, so they cleared up together and parted on friendly terms.

Peggy watched her friend leave the front door and turn left towards the aroma of onions and vinegar. Knowing she would be watching, Ros had purposely not looked up at Peggy's balcony as she normally did whenever she passed, keeping her head down and pretending to pull her scarf around her for warmth. She must remember to take a coat when she visited next time. They might live in the same building, but it was a trek in the cold from one flat to the other, and if she was caught by another resident wanting a chat it could get very cold indeed.

Once Ros had disappeared round the corner, Peggy found herself taking in the full view, across the graveyard with the new grave just visible, over the trees and across the fields beyond. The wind was blowing the clouds, casting fast moving shadows across the landscape, interspersed with weak sun picking out the colours of distant crops and woodland.

This was her home. Home was the one definite that had come out of her note taking, and the conversations with Ros. Her home, hers alone and that, she realised, was especially important to her now. What had become apparent was that she valued her independence above everything else. If she wanted to travel she would, if she wanted to stay home she would do that too. If she wanted to sleep all day and read all night that was her choice to make. No-one could make her do anything she didn't want to do and no-one had the right, or the opportunity, to make judgements about her decisions.

Three people had got together to talk about their concerns for her.

How did that make her feel?

Cross, yes cross that this had happened without her knowledge. That was the thing that made her cross. Not that she wasn't involved, but that she hadn't been consulted beforehand. She would have told them not to do it, she was certain of that, but she would have been wrong to do that, because what came out of it was that she was now in possession of some plans. Plans she would never have made without the intervention of the front man Colin, and the backroom influencers, Ros and Joe. Even Jean had apparently made a contribution of sorts.

But Joe! He had been involved too and he had said nothing of it, although she realised he had recently been asking lots of questions about her plans for the future.

She wondered when he would appear. Was he concerned that their plans had been discovered? Or would he just turn up out of the blue and act as if he knew nothing again. How would that simple and honest man deal with such skulduggery?

She realised she was smiling. So did that mean she was pleased about this revelation of Ros's? Possibly.

She closed the balcony doors and reached for the notebook and pen. Turning to a new page, she wrote SUMMARY at the top, then underlined it.

What do I want?

That was the subheading, and she was reminded of protesters outside Downing Street.

'What do we want? – the answer might be Justice, or a pay rise or something like that. Then,

'When do we want it?' – the answer was always a resounding 'Now'.

'So what do I want?' she asked herself, out loud just because she could.

'I want to see some other towns, some scenery, something to take my breath away.'

What that might be was a bigger problem. She had been watching webcams of a beach in North Devon, watching surfers battling with huge waves, clad from head to foot in black wet suits.

She wrote 'waves' as the first item on the list.

'Bridges' was the next surprising item – she had no idea where that thought had come from, although there had been mention on the radio of the Humber Bridge being closed that morning to high sided vehicles and cyclists. She imagined a cyclist, caught by a strong gust and being thrown into the river below, and shuddered.

She decided that looking at bridges was probably safer and more awe-inspiring than being on a bridge, especially on a bike.

'Sites of historical importance' had notes and ticks in the comments column. She had been reading about travel to Machu Pichu but after hearing about the long trek up the hills at the crack of dawn she wondered if it would be worth it, and would she see much more than she had already seen on TV. Petra, she realised, might fall into the same category as she had read of people fainting in the heat on the way there. There was so much to think about, even now.

By the time her stomach was telling her it was evening, she had a long list of things she wanted to see, and lines drawn through those she had once thought were high priority but practicalities now told her would be more trouble than they were worth.

She tossed pasta in a thick tomato sauce, sprinkling parmesan over the top, and thought she might add 'eating in good restaurants' to the list. She had been worried that the list so far still just involved observation, not taking part, but was that really wrong? Surely observing something could also be defined as being involved in it? And if she was out and about, actually witnessing waves for example, as they crashed onto a beach, then she would be experiencing the smells, the salty air, the drops of spray landing on her, and the weather – whatever that might be.

Eating food cooked by a great chef, that wasn't just observation, that was taste too.

She dipped her finger into the home-made sauce and tasted it. Perfection. Marcus Waring would need to be on top form if he wanted to do better than that.

TWENTY-ONE

Peggy had called the meeting; she had arranged for freshly cut sandwiches and drinks to be brought to the table in the window of The Three Cups.

Her three guests were waiting to hear what she had to say. She had never in her life sat at a table in a bar with more than one person at a time, and in fact was more often to be seen drinking alone, but always in the same window seat.

Her preference was to sit to one side, facing the rest of the bar area, so she could see everything going on in the room, and also keep an eye on who was wandering up and down the High Street. Today however, Ros had taken that seat, she was on the bench in the window, with her back to the High Street, beside Joe. Colin was in the other seat, facing Ros.

At her prompt, they all raised their glasses and chinked together in mid-air.

'To Peggy', the two men both spoke together and she was embarrassed.

She wanted to pinch herself, to see if this was a dream. Instead of sitting enviously looking at groups of people out enjoying themselves, and laughing together, here she was in a group of her own. Her eyes shone with excitement and she knew it.

Joe was the first to speak, 'I am sorry about all that sneaking about. It wasn't done in a bad way, it's just, well we were all worried about you and we just wanted to make sure you have a good life now. That was it, that was all.'

She could see Mark watching from behind the bar, making sure his dad was not making a fool of himself, or worse still that he was on the receiving end of a tongue lashing from her.

The others joined in, reassuring her that their motives were good and honest and that they wanted to make sure she was OK. She was, as Colin pointed out, still grieving.

That made her laugh and at the sound of her laughter they all relaxed.

'Grieving? I have never been so pleased to see the back of someone! You must know that don't you? I'm not in denial here. I hated him.'

Even after all this time, when they all knew what an awful man Leonard was, what a dreary life she had led, how he had alienated her from all her family – not friends because until that very evening she didn't ever think of herself as someone who had friends. Still they did not seem to be aware how much she despised him, to her very core.

'Really, I hated him. If I'm grieving it's for the life I might have led if I had never met him. What might I have become? Would I have had children? Daughters I could go shopping with, or sons to make me laugh. I might have had a career, might have got myself an education. And yes, I might have travelled with a welcome companion. That's what I grieve for, not for him. Hopefully it's not too late for some of that.'

She took a large swig of wine and set it back on the table with a firm hand that might have broken the stem of a more delicate piece of glassware.

'So, what I wanted to say to you all was, thank you. Thank you for caring enough to notice that I was still treading water, still not doing anything. Because if what I decide to do turns out to be nothing, I need to even do that with some certainty and stop dithering about wondering what to do and then not even enjoy not doing it. If you see what I mean.'

They nodded, to confirm they did see.

'And...?'

Ros had finished her first sandwich and was keen to get some answers. Jean was busy at home with an online art class but she didn't want to be out for too long.

'Well I have made some decisions now. I think Bulgaria will have to wait until next year. 2020 feels like the year for foreign travel for me. I'll think about going in February/March time and thanks to Colin here, I am looking at starting in a different city, maybe in the north of the country. It'll be colder I know, but that's OK.'

'And you've spoken to Mr Borthwick in the travel agents?' Ros knew about the confusion Peggy had caused with the poor man, and wasn't sure if he would even still want her business.

'I have. I went in today. Stacey is on maternity leave so I didn't have to face her. Valerie is back in charge and the staff in there seem very friendly now. I've even paid a hefty deposit and he's going to get to work on the visas and all that because I would like to stay for a while – not just have a holiday. I won't back out of it this time, so I'll definitely be going. I'm sure nothing can go wrong.'

'And this year?' Joe was confident that he was not in the firing line for any blame or repercussions and was enjoying a night out with sandwiches thrown in. He knew his question was a good one.

'This year Joe, it's the UK. I have a list of places I want to go to, and I will tick them off. They're not everybody's cup of tea, but they are places I've read about and I have whittled them down to the ones I think will be better than seeing them on TV. Lovely Michael Portillo does get to the root of places, but he doesn't quite do it like I would. I won't be confining myself to Bradshaw's views of travel.'

Revealing that she had got herself a provisional driving licence, she felt like the Queen announcing the New Year's Honours. Her audience was gripped. OK she hadn't driven since she was 17 and as Ros pointed out, she would probably need a bit of a refresher, before taking a test but that wasn't the point. Joe offered his services, suggesting they practise manoeuvres around the big town car park one evening, but Colin was adamant that a professional should be involved too.

Washing her hands in the Ladies, and catching sight of herself in the big mirror above the sinks, she hardly recognised the face looking back at her. She had definitely changed, and not just her hair. She looked less fearsome, but also less dull. Less like a miserable and cross old lady and more like a butterfly emerging for the first time.

She, Peggy Thomas, was in a pub with friends, yes friends. She was making plans and they were interested to hear what she had to say. She didn't imagine for one minute that either Colin or Joe had any other agenda than friendship, but what if they did? Would she mind? She still wasn't sure about that one.

There were more drinks on the table when she returned to the window seat. Ros seemed fidgety to get home, but the two men were settled in for the evening, chatting about football and rugby, sometimes cricket and a lot about the refurbishment of Colin's dad's house. It seemed he was intending to move in permanently and as they say on all the TV makeover shows, 'put his own stamp on it', whatever that meant. She hoped Colin wouldn't be taking advantage of Joe's good nature and be expecting cheap rates.

'This will be my last for the night,' she announced, raising yet another glass into the air for a group-chink.

'Ros needs to get back, and I will walk up with her, but you two stay if you want to.'

They did. The two women made a noisy exit from the pub, cheerily waving goodbye to other drinkers and all the bar staff, while the two men stayed in the window, moving on to shorts.

'Come on ladies, I'll see you home. Dad's settled in for the night.'

Mark laughed as he squeezed between them and linked arms with them both.

'I'll come back for Dad, but he wanted me to make sure you got home safe and weren't ravaged in the graveyard.'

There followed the usual, 'we should be so lucky' and 'chance would be a fine thing', comments that were normally bandied about in these situations but they both appreciated a chaperone and genuinely believed they provided interesting conversation on the way home.

'Nice boy, isn't he?'

Ros's voice wasn't as quiet as she imagined, as they stood on the front steps and waved Mark off, watching him until he disappeared into the graveyard.

The two women embraced as was their recently acquired custom, and went their separate ways. Ros to find Jean and admire her drawing; Peggy to her luxuriously empty flat on the third floor.

TWENTY-TWO

April had begun with sunshine and little sign of rain, Peggy was packing mainly warm weather clothing for her first trip in the camper van she had bought just two weeks before, and named Caroline after her mother. The van was a late birthday present to herself.

Driving lessons had gone surprisingly well. She had explained to Ros over coffee one morning that she had already had four lessons from the intensive two-week course and was progressing.

Her instructor, Jim, who she had at first thought to be a rather feeble and limp individual, had displayed nerves of steel on the back roads around the town and she had warmed to him, even if his opinion of her appeared not to change.

'His face,' she exclaimed in delight, 'is white with fear at the start of every lesson, and things don't improve for him until he drops me off back here. He has five more lessons to put up with me for, before he sends me off onto the streets alone.'

Ros had seen Jim's little silver car pottering around the town as he taught the local teenagers how to drive. He must have thought an old lady would be an easy few hours' money when he had taken the booking over the phone. His opinion soon changed after he met Peggy. Ros knew he still lived with his mother at the far end of town, near the woods, and felt sorry for him, wondering if he might hang up his L plates once Peggy was off his hands.

The feeble Jim had proved himself to be a first-class instructor, even if he was unlikely to maintain any form of relationship with his latest client after the course. Thankfully for him, after a test that took her around Bletchley with one of the stiffer examiners, Peggy was finally in possession of a full driving licence, which permitted her to drive a vehicle on the road. This in addition to endless hours of practice with Joe, gave her the freedom to take herself off in her new camper van, whenever she wanted to.

Shortly after the celebration evening, Ros arrived at Peggy's door with a bundle of paperwork full of notes and message exchanges with Peggy's missing brother. She had found him within ten minutes of beginning her search on social media, living in the Cotswolds, and working as a tree surgeon. She had contacted him on the pretext of having some trees she wanted cutting down and had engineered a conversation with him about where he was from and who his family were.

He did not seem to be concerned that he had lost a potential customer when Ros announced who she really was, and said he was keen to meet up with Peggy.

She had burst into Peggy's flat before the door was fully open, pushing Peggy to one side and thrusting a wilted bunch of stocks into her hands.

'Derek says you'll need to start taking these flowers yourself. He says he feels like he's working in Kew Gardens. Who are they from anyway?'

Peggy took the flowers and put them straight into the bin.

'I've given up even looking. Your Mike from the Book Club sends them occasionally, and so does Laurence from the choir – I think his are a form of apology for his rudeness when I tried to join him. Even naked Peter sent some. I don't even like flowers indoors anyway – they're dead within a day or so and start to smell.'

Accepting the offer of a glass of plain water, with ice, Ros began to spread her notes over the kitchen worktop, excited for Peggy to see every photo and piece of evidence.

'This is your brother, Paul, he lives in Chipping Norton with his wife and their three children – well not children anymore. Two girls – that's Eleanor there, she is 22 years old and lives with her boyfriend in Birmingham and here's Caroline, named after your mum I imagine, who is 17 and doing her A levels – quite clever it seems. Then this is Joel. He is 19 and just started at university studying – wait for it – Russian! Slightly different from Bulgarian, but similar – it runs in the family Peggy!'

Peggy scanned the photographs, looking for her young brother, and there he was. Looking just like her father, but suntanned and laughing, more relaxed than she ever remembered seeing her father look.

In many of the images Ros had printed out, Paul was surrounded by his family, or among a group of laughing men about his age, standing with golf bags, and wearing a familiar uniform of golf attire.

Paul's son looked exactly like their older brother Ray, tall and dark with wide smiling eyes and thick brows. The girls, she was hesitant to admit it to herself, but Ros spoke first,

'Those girls are the spit of you Peggy – both of them. Look, long dark hair, different glasses obviously, but same shape of face. They're lovely looking kids aren't they?'

The compliment hung between them, waiting for comment, but none came.

Once the photos had all been checked over, and scrutinised for detail and background information, Ros stacked them all together and stood back, pleased with herself.

She had provided Peggy with names and addresses, plus plenty of information about the family's friends and where they had been on holiday for the past few years.

'People provide every detail about their lives on social media don't they? Do they not worry about so many people knowing everything about them?'

Ros shrugged, 'That's how it is nowadays Peggy. That's what people do. You can get as involved as you want, but you're right, some people do give a lot away about themselves.'

She paused, waiting for a reaction, but Peggy was still gazing at the bundle of photos and addresses.

'You should be thankful, I wouldn't have found him otherwise, would I?'

Ros had sent Paul a message, via his profile page, asking if she could have his phone number to pass on to Peggy, and giving him Peggy's number – she was fairly sure he was a family man and not likely to be a serial killer.

His text messages were short, but kind. He asked about how her life had been, not mentioning Leonard, in fact writing as if Leonard had never existed and perhaps that was the best way to approach this new relationship.

After a few tentative text messages, Peggy had summoned the courage to call Paul one Sunday evening, during The Antiques Roadshow. She had been distracted by the apparent greed of one of the visitors who was clearly disappointed with the sensibly low valuation on an item she had recently paid a higher price for. These people annoyed Peggy, and she snapped the TV off, deciding this would be a good opportunity to speak to her brother before another week began.

He had been delighted to hear her voice, and as they spoke the years melted away. He brushed away her apologies for not being around for so long. He understood and assured her their mother had understood, although she had worried about Peggy, knowing she would not be happy with Leonard. The family had hoped that Peggy would return to them once she realised who Leonard really was. How sad, they agreed, that their parents had not lived to see Peggy's return from isolation.

TWENTY-THREE

Peggy had been hoping to start her UK tour in St Ives in her new camper van, taking in some of the artwork in and around the area – there had been much talk on a recent show with Michael Portillo, of the colours of St Ives and she was keen to see this for herself. No longer did she feel willing to just take Michael's word for it.

Her sketchpad and pencils were packed along with a new set of watercolours she had bought from Nicky Reilly who was keen to know her plans. Peggy had maintained an air of mystery and would not be drawn into disclosing what or where she would be drawing and painting.

After speaking to Paul, she had decided that he and his family would be her first port of call. Cornwall could wait. She had vague memories of lovely scenery in the Cotswolds, from the works trip with Leonard, although she had spent most of the journey reading about the area, rather than watching it roll by for herself. This time she would take it all in, and would make sure to capture it in her sketch pad.

It had taken many more pub meetings for her to finalise her plans – both Colin and Joe were deeply knowledgeable about travel, in their own ways. Colin offering tips about where to stop along the way and all the must-see places to visit. Joe's advice was mainly centred around the maintenance of the van, and what checks would need to be carried out to ensure she would not be needing to call upon the breakdown services he had insisted on arranging for her.

She intended to meander her way back home, in the van, staying on camp sites if she didn't want to tackle the whole journey in one go, and stopping whenever she wanted to take in the sights, or to make a cup of tea in a layby (this small task was definitely on the bucket list). The whole trip should take one month from the moment she left until she arrived back at Sovereign Court with Caroline the Camper Van.

For a woman in her late fifties who had rarely left the town where she had been born and lived all her life, this felt like an enormous undertaking, but she was confident that if she didn't look like a woman who had never been anywhere, then she could fool herself and everyone else into believing it was possible.

A week before departure, Joe arrived at Peggy's unannounced and with no apparent reason for the visit.

He was wearing a new brown shirt and thin jumper. She had never seen the shirt before, but then she imagined he must have clothes she hadn't seen. He had shaved too and smelt strongly of a citrus after shave, so unlike the pine forest of Leonard's fragrance cabinet in their old bathroom.

'Before you go Peggy, I want you to come to my cottage and I'll cook for you.'

She knew this invitation was long overdue but the thought of stepping over the threshold of the house she had shared with Leonard for so long made her freeze in terror.

'You won't recognise the place, I promise. No ghosts.'

It wasn't really ghosts that terrified her, more the memories of him, and his last hours in particular. She could have saved his life, or at least tried; she knew that now. She had thought about that morning so often, how she had told herself he was already dead so it wouldn't matter that she had ignored his fall.

She could see herself moving around the kitchen, making lunch, lighting a fire in the living room, hoping that if she carried on as normal he would just go away. But he wasn't going away and that first time she had set off up the stairs, she could hear him mumbling. When she checked a third time everything was quiet, then she knew he was finally going to die. She would be rid of him. Only then did she call an ambulance and tell the operator that her husband had taken a fall.

Why had Joe brought the subject up now, just when she was setting off on her adventure?

'I'm sorry, I shouldn't have said that now should I? Only,'

He shifted in his seat, uncomfortable,

'I want you to see what I've done to the place. I think you'll like it, honestly. Tomorrow night, Mark says he'll join us when he's finished on the farm, and Liam will be there to start with. He's going out with a new lady friend. She sounds nice actually, not his usual type.'

'This isn't the best timing, Joe, I've got a lot to think about.'

They sat in awkward silence, Peggy fiddling in her bag, checking again that she had packed her purse in there, and shiny new driving licence, Joe staring at his hands.

Joe continued with his pitch.

'I know you're busy packing and that, but you have to eat, and why not eat with me, and the boys? Nothing formal, just a wholesome meal to set you on your way. You won't even recognise the place. The boys helped, but I've managed to – what do they say on those programmes you watch? I've put my own stamp on it.'

He waited for a response but none came.

'You'll like it. I hope you will anyway.

Well, I just wanted to come and ask you that, but if you don't want to come then that's fine. I can pop over on the morning you set off to say goodbye, and to wish you well – meeting your brother and all. I'm excited for you, and I'll be watching for you and Caroline to come chugging up the hill when you get back.'

He weathered the storm of the silence and carried on, regardless.

'Think about my invitation. I'm a good cook.'

Finally she looked up at him and smiled.

'Of course Joe, I'd love to. I can't keep letting Leonard stop me doing things can I, and as you say I do have to eat. Tomorrow you said. What time? 7?'

Joe's relief was obvious – he had survived the exchange, and he had a dinner to look forward to.

'I'll send Liam to pick you up. Great.'

TWENTY-FOUR

Liam was waiting for her by the front doors of Sovereign Court at 6.45 exactly, as promised.

'You look very smart Liam – do you have a date?'

'I was going to say the same to you Mrs T! Not the date bit obviously, but you look very lovely, if I'm allowed to say that.'

What a lovely boy he had turned out to be. She knew he had been a worry to his parents in his teens, a bit of a tearaway, but he had turned into the sort of young man any mother would be proud of. She wasn't sure if Tracey saw it that way. They hadn't seen much of her since her departure for Birmingham, but she knew Joe was proud of both his boys, even if they weren't prepared to join him in his family business.

They walked down to the cottage, chatting about the weather, what crops were being grown in the fields, and what Ros had been up to. Nothing too embarrassing, just chat. She felt the evening breeze in her hair and she focussed on just enjoying the walk, trying to forget the destination. There were delicious cooking aromas floating towards them and she felt glad they were coming from where she would be eating that night.

'Here we are Mrs T.'

Liam held the door open and for the first time since leaving the home she had shared with dead Leonard, she stepped into the front room.

'Wow! Joe, you're right, I would not recognise this as the room where I spent so many unhappy years.'

She had never thought about what Joe did for a living, beyond driving his dusty van around the town and turning up at her house splattered with paint. He had transformed the room into a cosy space, taken out the nasty fireplace Leonard had installed when they first moved in, and in its place was a brick fireplace, with a log burner, already lit. There were two small terracotta sofas facing each other on either side of the fire, with a table between them, laid with bowls of olives and peanuts.

'I got the olives for you.'

Joe emerged from the kitchen, wearing a black apron embroidered with a large J in the centre. He was wiping his hands on a tea towel and beckoned her to go through to the kitchen,

'See what I've done in here.'

Her old dark wood cabinets were gone, along with the ancient freestanding electric cooker and rusty fridge. The glossy white cupboards were spotlessly clean and polished to a mirror shine, there was a huge white sink with a single curved tap, and a double oven set into the cupboards.

'I got a fridge like yours – it does ice.'

Joe was beaming, like a new father showing off his first child.

'See, no sign of Leonard.'

He was right. The transformation was complete. Not only was there no trace remaining of Leonard, nothing of her remained either, and she was glad. Glad that the Peggy who had been so miserable, hiding away with her books in that grim dark cottage had evaporated. Gone forever.

'You've done a fantastic job in here Joe. I am almost speechless. Almost.'

They laughed together and Joe poured her a glass of white wine, setting it down on the granite worktop beside his glass of beer.

'Cheers!'

Peggy took a sip, 'Delicious. What are we eating? We could smell it as we came through the gate at the end of the fields, it's making me feel hungry!'

She watched as he worked his way around the kitchen, stirring and straining, tipping pasta and a meaty sauce into four bowls, finally sprinkling shaved parmesan over the top of each.

'Choose a bowl Peggy and follow me, Liam! Ready.'

She picked up the bowl nearest to her, and set off behind Joe, wondering where they could be going. He seemed to be heading towards the stable door that led to the garden. Holding two plates, he reversed against the door and pushed back, letting Peggy go through before him.

She was confused, it was a pleasant evening but surely not warm enough to eat outside.

'We are eating in my new Conservatory.'

Instead of the grubby paved area and unkempt garden she was expecting, she found herself looking at a large room, with windows on all sides, looking onto a small, neat garden with lights all around the perimeter.

'I always wanted to do this next door but Tracey wasn't having any of it. Here,'

He had dressed the table with a centrepiece of candles and flowers, and was pulling a chair out for Peggy to sit down.

'You are so talented Joe. When do you find time to do all this? It's an incredible transformation. You've added thousands to the value of this place I should think.'

'Well next door is done up just as nicely, but without this. It sold for good money, and there's a nice couple living there now, with their littlun. Cute little lass she is. So instead of two miserable households, there's two happy ones now.

We're alright here aren't we mate?'

This was addressed to Liam who had walked in carrying a bottle of wine, and his own bottle of beer.

'Careful Dad, me and Mark won't want to leave if you make us too comfy!'

The three laughed together and ate their pasta, Peggy refused seconds but both Joe and Liam helped themselves to another plateful.

'There's enough for Mark, don't worry, he won't starve.'

After a suitable break, Joe disappeared and returned with a bowl full of profiteroles, topped with a thick chocolate sauce, which he ladled into four bowls, setting one aside for Mark and handing out the other three.

He brought through coffees and a box of Ferrero Rocher which none of them could face and Liam took the opportunity to make his escape, off to meet the new lady friend Joe had been so complimentary about.

As he left, Mark appeared, and sat with them eating his microwaved meal, but refusing the profiteroles.

'It's been a lovely evening, thank you Joe. You were right, I hardly knew I was in my old home. You've really changed the whole atmosphere of the house.'

'I'll take that Peggy, thank you. Not sure Colin would agree, he's a bit nit-picking with the work I'm doing for him. Still, I'll do my best.'

Peggy was surprised to hear criticism of Colin who had created for himself an almost saintly reputation in their little community. Only Jean had expressed a dislike of him and she hardly knew him after all, but Joe's comments ignited a tiny thought in her head. She had misgivings about the near perfect Colin who she felt seemed too good to be true, but she thought that was just her being cynical. Maybe not.

TWENTY-FIVE

On the morning of departure, Peggy thought she would slide away unnoticed. There had been no witnesses as she loaded her suitcase into the back door of the van, or when she had hauled the cool box containing milk, butter, and white wine into the side door, or as she decanted a box full of tea, coffee, and sugar into the tiny cupboard above the back seat.

Backwards and forwards she trotted, in the early sunshine, with everything she would need for her planned four-week absence. Only when she appeared at the front door for the final time, did she see Ros and Jean standing with Joe beside her van, waiting to say their goodbyes.

Jean handed over a basket full of cakes and jars of chutney and Ros settled a box containing six bottles of wine into a space under one of the seats,

'Not when you're driving obviously!'

'Of course not Ros – just at night when I've parked up, then I can pick up my new guitar and have a sip while I learn to play.'

'Well I hope you're on a deserted camp site then! These aren't vegan brownies Peggy, I found a special non-vegan recipe for you – less sticky,'

They all laughed and helped Peggy into the van with the last of her supplies.

Ros and Jean both wished her luck, gave her their customary hugs, and stepped back.

Joe remained, unsure what to do, so she reached forward and gave him a hug, whispering 'Thank you Joe, I couldn't have got this far without you, I want you to know that.'

Without thinking, and maybe he had thought she was Tracey and he'd stepped back to a time when they were happy together. Whatever it was, he had kissed Peggy on the cheek. He had never done that before and in the instant he realised what he had done, he had time to wonder how she would react.

She kissed him back, just on the cheek, but it was a kiss with such affection that it took them both by surprise.

'I have brought you these Peggy, it's a selfish gift. Postcards with stamps on – I'm hoping you'll keep in touch so I know where you are, and if you're OK.

I know, I know you will send texts and stuff, but I can't stick a text to the side of my fridge can I?'

Of all the gifts she had ever received, she felt more touched by this little wad of postcards than she remembered ever feeling before. She reached into the van and tucked them into the glove box, where all the contact details for breakdown, insurance and emergency numbers Ros and Joe had put together for her, were stashed in a little folder.

'Thank you Joe, I'll make sure you have enough postcards to fill the side of your fridge, then I can start filling up the front with the next trip.'

They had another brief hug and she stepped into the van, started her up and set off, waving at the trio out of the open windows.

She did spot Colin making his way through the churchyard. He had obviously got the timings wrong. That wasn't her problem, she no longer felt responsible for anyone but herself.

She turned the dial on the old radio and listened to Saint Saens Dance Macabre as she drove along the High Street on her way to the Cotswolds, to her brother, and his family. Her family.

TWENTY-SIX

How strange her town looked, driving back into it after just a few weeks. She had hardly looked at the houses when she left, concentrating so hard on driving Caroline and keeping her on course, looking out for hazards along the way – vehicles approaching from side streets and pedestrians with their unexpected launches into her path. These were the obstacles the patient Jim had alerted her to, but on the journey home she was more relaxed, aware that while she did need to keep half an eye out for hazards, she could occasionally look off to one side or another, her to take in the surroundings.

Lights were blazing in the windows of Colin's house – upstairs and down. Perhaps his cleaning lady was there, polishing and sweeping, not caring about the cost of electricity.

Fiona was outside her charity shop, hefting bags of donations in through the front door, and the outdoor seating area at The Three

Cups was full of people enjoying chilled drinks in the warmth of a late spring evening.

She smiled at the drinkers, pleased with her town, and pleased to be home after a successful trip, and with a glove box containing no postcards. She had sent them to Joe of course, but had also sent some to Ros and Jean, letting them all know where she had been, who with, and what she had eaten.

There was a homemade bollard in her parking space outside Sovereign Court, reading 'Reserved for Caroline' and before she could switch the engine off to climb out and move it, Ros and Jean came running over waving and shouting.

Jean grabbed the bollard and the two women stood back, watching Peggy pull into the space, parking Caroline perfectly within the lines. She swung the door open and was greeted by two beaming faces.

'Colin said he saw you drive past about ten minutes ago. Jean only finished painting the bollard last night – some of it is still a bit wet!'

The two women laughed together, giggling like children. She had only been gone for a few weeks, had she lost Ros in that time?

'I was so excited when Paul phoned yesterday to say you had set off. Joe's on his way – he's just finishing a decorating job at Colin's. He's been decorating upstairs, been there since before you left.'

No, nothing had changed. She still couldn't move in the town without the town criers sending messages all around, letting everyone know what she was doing; Ros was still excited to see her; and Joe was still playing Jeeves to Colin's Wooster.

'It's good to be home Ros, and thank you for the bollard Jean. I haven't had to do much parking in tight spaces while I've been away – I have been wondering all the way home if I'd be able to find a space here on a Saturday.'

She reluctantly joined in with Ros's suggestion of a Group Hug, something she had thought only went on in the TV reality shows Paul's family were so fond of, and once that had ended she was happy to accept Ros's offer of help with her bags.

'Wow, you've been doing quite a bit of shopping Peggy! This is lovely.'

Ros had hauled a huge terracotta plant pot from the side door of the van.

'Be careful Ros! That's a gift for you, and Jean of course, for your garden. I thought maybe you'd get a good lot of herbs in there Jean.'

The acceptance did not go unnoticed. Jean took the pot from Ros, and disappeared round the corner of the building with it.

'Thank you Peggy, that was a perfect present for her. People are still buying her wine as presents, they just don't understand. She'll be really touched that you have acknowledged how hard she is trying.'

Peggy accepted the undeserved compliments. So Jean wasn't drinking any more. Was Ros? So there had been some changes in her absence.

'We got your postcards. Chipping Norton sounds interesting. How were Paul and his family? Did you all get on OK?'

'You two still gassing?' Jean had re-appeared, dusty from carrying the plant pot and, Peggy noticed, a more healthy-looking version of the Jean she had left behind a month ago.

'Come on, let's get Peggy's stuff into the flat and let her settle back in. Dinner tonight Peggy? I've had a shoulder of lamb slow-roasting all day – it's a big one so there will be plenty to go round.'

She grabbed a suitcase and holdall, leaving Ros with a few bulging carrier bags and set off for the front door, punching in Peggy's code and pushing her way into the reception area.

'She's not plant based any more. We had a talk. The doctor was worried about her. Said she needed to stop the vegan diet. And...'

She held her hand up to stop Peggy's protests,

'she knows your code because I just told her it, as we walked out just now. She's got a memory like a sieve. It'll have gone from her head by the time she gets to the top of your stairs.'

'Dinner at 8?'

Peggy nodded and both women beamed as they set off for the stairs. She closed the door once they had disappeared from view, and looked around her neat and cosy apartment.

'Home', she said out loud. 'My home.'

Everything was as she had left it, tidy and clean, and not a trace of Leonard anywhere. She had wondered, as she slept in the hard spare bed at her brother's house, whether Leonard would have moved in while she was gone, seeped Pinewood and hair cream into the soft furnishings, and pounded her new furniture with his bony backside. But there was nothing of him. His ashes were gone, and he was gone.

She poured herself a large whisky with one cube of ice. There wouldn't be much drinking that evening if Jean was off the booze – it wouldn't be right to even take wine with her, would it? She wasn't sure of the etiquette of being around new abstainers. If she buried a bottle at the bottom of her bag she could always retrieve it if Ros was drinking, and otherwise it would stay in the bag and come back with her.

She absent-mindedly unpacked a few bags and was jerked back from her mental meanderings by the buzzing of the intercom. Who on earth?

'Welcome back Peggy, it's me.'

Me was Joe, and she pressed the button to allow him to walk into the building. Would he be taking the lift, or the stairs? Either way she had a couple of minutes to remove her empty whisky glass to the kitchen before she heard him knocking at the door.

There were traces of grey paint on his hands and arms, but his smiling face was paint free.

'Welcome back. Good trip?'

She followed him into her own living room and sat opposite where he had positioned himself on one end of the long sofa.

'I've come to walk you down to Ros's. She phoned and invited me for dinner, Colin too.'

Did he look disappointed that Colin had also been invited?

'Come on then, tell all. How was the trip? Did you need the breakdown service? How was Caroline?'

She answered the van related questions but wanted to save the details of her trip until she could tell Ros too. Joe didn't seem to mind, he had answers to the stuff he was interested in, and was still smiling while she talked.

'I knew she was a good buy.'

Peggy found him funny, such a relief after three weeks in the company of her tense brother and his wife who was more concerned with her social media presences to strangers than the comfort of her house guest.

The spring wreath on Ros's door was wilting slightly and a few of the artificial daffodil heads fell off when Joe rattled at the knocker. Peggy watched as he kicked them into the pile of logs.

'I saw you!'

A laughing Colin appeared at the gate,

'All the crocuses fell off when I did that last week – there won't be much left soon.'

'Much what?'

Jean had flung the door open, wiping her hands on a flowery apron, and looking around to see what they might be talking about.

'Much sunshine, I was saying it's nearly dark.'

Colin was an easy teller of an untruth, the lie slipped off his tongue without hesitation and something in the back of Peggy's subconscious was whispering to her.'

She pushed the thoughts away, pleased to see Ros happy, fussing around her guests with canapes and pouring alcoholic drinks to everyone except herself and Jean. They all listened politely while she recounted the details of her break in Chipping Norton, skimming over the tensions between herself and Paul's wife, but saving the best nugget until the last.

'It was interesting,' she began, 'that Paul's middle child, Joel, is at university studying Russian. We had a few video calls with him and we managed a simple conversation – me in Bulgarian and him in Russian. He will be living in St Petersburg next year and he is going to take a trip to Bulgaria in the term break. He has suggested I time my visit for when he is there, and he will be my guide.'

The reality of a much talked about trip that they had all believed would never happen, involving someone else who was making serious plans, silenced the group into deep thought while they all concentrated on the melt in the mouth slow roasted lamb.

'When will that be Peggy?' Joe was first to finish his meal, leaving most of his spicy tabbouleh on the side of his plate.

'January next year. I don't plan to stay for long, just a holiday, no visa required, then I'll be home for my big birthday and ready to settle down to a quiet life in retirement. Don't worry, I've spoken to Borthwicks and it's all OK.'

She laughed and once the others realised it was ok, they all joined her.

'Retirement from what?'

'Quiet? Compared to what?'

'You can laugh, but Caroline and I are going to tour the UK from now on. Bulgaria is not a holiday destination for me – it's going to be a challenge, and to have someone showing me round who can speak some of the language – I can't pass that offer up can I?'

'It makes sense Peggy and if it actually happens, I for one will wish you well. Cheers, to Peggy in Bulgaria.'

Colin laughed, held his glass up and they all followed, cheers-ing the plans that now seemed they would actually take place.

'I think,' Colin continued, 'it's lovely for you that someone is prepared to take you seriously and entertain your plans for this big journey. It's very kind of him isn't it, to go along with it all. Bless you both.'

'Well Colin, that's not patronising at all is it?' Jean was laughing, but Peggy wasn't going to let her spoil the evening.

'And what has happened here, while I've been away?'

Much conversation was made of not much and the group carried on talking until Ros's new cuckoo clock pronounced that midnight had been reached.

'He only comes out at midnight and midday. It's a design fault.' Jean looked at Ros and the two laughed together. Again Peggy had the warm feeling that her friend had finally found what she was looking for. She raised her glass,

'Ros and Jean, great food and great company. Thank you all for welcoming me home from my travels. Cheers.'

They all raised their glasses and drained the last drops, before agreeing that it was time to head home.

'I'll walk you up the hill Peggy. I insist.'

Had Colin always been overbearing? Peggy was not one to be told what to do, and his insistence that he should be the one to walk her home stirred a warning but she couldn't work out if it was the wine, or her own stubborn nature, or something else that made her lie.

She flicked a glance at Joe and hoped he would go along with her,

'No, it's fine Colin thank you. Joe has already said he would walk back up with me. I'm lending him some books and he said he would collect them on the way home.'

Then, to ease any awkwardness, 'I'm sure I only need one chaperone.'

Ros was frowning and Colin picked up his jacket from the sofa, thrusting his arms into the sleeves with some force before once buttoning it up slightly askew, making a comical sight with his thick brows knotted together in annoyance.

'Well I hope you'll be safe with our ladies-man Peggy. Watch him!'

There was something sinister about his laughter, but Ros and Jean were joining in with the general humorous chat. Maybe she was imagining sinister laughter where there was none. Only Joe seemed to notice the malice in Colin's face and rather than shrinking from it, Peggy was pleased to see that his shoulders went back and he responded firmly but politely. After all, they had shared a pleasant evening together, this was no time for a playground tiff.

'I'll be on my absolute best behaviour Colin, ladies. I will make sure our traveller gets home in one piece.'

As they wandered through the graveyard on the way back to Sovereign Court, Peggy was explaining that her brother Paul had been showing her the constellations through his magnificent telescope. She was looking up at the stars to see how many she could identify,

'He lives on a farm you see. They don't farm, they just have a few chickens and his wife uses the barns for her business, selling baby equipment from her website, 'Babeez'. Why people have to use a z and misspell everything these days I don't know. Anyway she seems to make quite a bit of money. She buys stuff in second hand, cleans it up a bit and sells it on her website. People come from all over. She has what my mum would have called 'a face like a slapped arse'.'

Joe laughed out loud, 'I wasn't expecting that! What sort of face is that then?'

'You know, pinched. She said it about Leonard when I first took him home.'

'Oh I see it now, like this?'

He pursed his lips and screwed his face up; his eyes were almost closed.

'That's it! Well that's her, Jennah her name is. Spelt with an 'h', but I think she added that on herself when she was at school. She did explain why but I wasn't listening. I wasn't keen on her, but I'm not going to let that stop me having a relationship with my brother now I've found him.'

'I'm glad to hear it Peggy. You've wasted too much time not being with your family. Sounds like you got on well enough with him, and their kids.'

'Yes, the kids are great. All interesting, and interested in every-thing. Anyway, there is no light pollution where they live, and when there was a clear sky we could see thousands of stars, not just the few we see from here. See that glow,'

she pointed across at the orange sky over Milton Keynes,

'that glow knocks out all the stars, that's what Paul was saying anyway. I loved it and he really knew his stuff. It was fascinating.'

They stood in the shade of the church, looking upwards and pointing out stars they knew the names of. Peggy had not remembered everything her brother had told her and Joe demonstrated a good understanding of the midnight skies. It was in comfortable silence that they eventually set off towards Sovereign Court until they reached the front doors, when Joe bent and kissed Peggy gently on the cheek, and gave her a quick hug. He watched her punch in the familiar code, and once she was safely behind locked doors, he headed off for home.

Still breathless from running up the stairs, she abandoned her jacket and shoes in the hallway and made her way to the kitchen window where she eventually saw the tiny shape of Joe in the light of the new lampposts wandering towards the cottage where she had once lived with Leonard. He disappeared into the darkness of his front garden, and she clambered into her own comfortable bed, fully clothed – because who was going to question her?

TWENTY-SEVEN

'In and out Mrs?'

'Yes please.'

Peggy had watched the two drivers in front of her respond in this way, and understood that it meant Caroline would receive a thorough wash on the outside, windows would be cleaned, and the inside of the van would be treated to a thorough vacuum. The sign indicated that this would cost her £18 as Caroline was not a normal sized car. She had a folded £20 note folded in her hand and intended to offer a £2 tip to the enthusiastic boy scouts who were raising money for repairs to their hall.

She could see that a car had drawn up behind her, but was concentrating on watching the boys cleaning wheels and sponging foam over Caroline's roof.

'Long time no see Peggy.'

At the sound of her name she spun round and was faced with a beaming Colin.

'It's only been a week Colin. I've had jobs to do at home. Not intentionally avoiding anyone I assure you.'

Although he was smiling, Colin's words had felt like an accusation and she knew her response was probably over defensive, but he carried on, oblivious to any awkwardness.

'I've tried to call on you a couple of times, but Derek said you weren't receiving any visitors. He was unusually protective of you.'

She smiled. Paul had advised her that Derek would be a good person to have 'on side'. He had suggested an occasional gift of a crate of lager, and she was delighted that the first of these gifts had been well received. He had been agreeable to turning visitors away from the front door for her, and had been very willing to help her to the local tip with some of Leonard's stuff that had been lurking in the cellar. It had been £12 well spent.

'We get along OK now. We understand each other a bit better these days I think.'

Colin didn't need to know about the lager.

'I'm glad I've seen you. I wanted to invite you to a night out.'

He reached into his pocket and took out an envelope, handing it to her with a flourish.

'A proper choir, proper orchestra and proper music. Karl Jenkins' *Armed Man*, it's truly marvellous. I think you will enjoy it. Dinner first?' Or after?'

She might be living a more liberated life since Leonard's departure, but eating after an evening theatre trip? What was he thinking of?

'I'll check my diary Colin. It does sound interesting.'

'Well you keep your ticket, so you have all the information, and you can let me know if you want to eat too. Honestly, you will love it, I know you will. Someone at church was at the premier, at the Albert Hall – blew his mind apparently.'

After what seemed like hours, the Scout Leader handed her keys back and she handed over a rather sweaty £20 note in exchange for her keys.

Colin had moved back towards his own car and was manoeuvring towards the sponge wielding scouts so she was able to make her escape without the necessity for ridiculous excuses, but at the level crossing the Bedford to Bletchley train's arrival allowed her the time to peek into the envelope to see when Colin's cultural trip was due to take place.

'It's this Saturday! Not much notice is it?'

Peggy had called in to Ros's flat hoping for some advice and words of encouragement, but had found only Jean at home, stripping wallpaper from the kitchen wall.

'You haven't got anything else on have you?'

Jean was not the most patient confidante. She stepped down from the kitchen chair and dumped strips of wet wallpaper into a large pink bag.

'You just have to decide if you want to see the show, whether you trust him enough to be out in his company alone, and whether you'd rather be out with him or at home on your own. Simple enough. Tea? Ros won't be long.'

Peggy nodded and considered Jean's words. She had been listening to the CD of the performance for months; had nothing else planned and had never considered whether he was to be trusted or not.

'He's very considerate you know.'

Jean's look was difficult to comprehend. Was she jealous?

'I'll be honest Peg, there's something about him I don't like. Can't put my finger on it, but something doesn't ring true. Just my opinion. You make up your own mind.'

The front door swung open and there was the sound of carrier bags being dropped onto the hall floor.

'Oh how lovely – my two favourite people, together in one room.'

Ros's obvious joy at finding her talking to Jean in a civilised way, made Peggy feel guilty. All the woman wanted was for the two of them to get along, but they seemed only to wind each other up without even trying.

'I won't stop Ros, thank you. Jean did offer me tea, but I've just had an invitation to the theatre for Saturday night. Jean has helped me make the decision to accept so I'll get along home and let Colin know it's a yes.'

She managed to escape further questions from Ros and after clambering over piles of carrier bags, she was soon out in the open air and walking with a spring in her step towards her own front door.

She decided to text her response, rather than involve herself with small talk over the phone, and was delighted to get an immediate reply confirming that he would pick her up at 4pm so they could have an early supper before taking their seats in the theatre. She collected two postcards from her pigeonhole, both from her nephew Joel with views of Exeter, where he was at university, and full of Russian words. She would need to concentrate on translating them properly and working out how to write a good reply – she could tell him about her theatre trip!

Colin had been right about the music; it was very much to her taste, and so well performed by the local chorale. He had not been right in his choice of supper, as she had pointed out,

'Spaghetti Bolognese is a dish best eaten alone or with a person one is extremely comfortable with.' His white shirt still showed signs of tomato staining, despite his frantic efforts to clean himself up in the gents toilets with a burgundy paper napkin. The napkin had shed it's colour on top of the stain. He had not quite recovered from the episode.

If his evening had been ruined, hers hadn't. She enjoyed the taxi ride into town, the busy pub where they had eaten and was enthralled by the music, humming along to some of the easier tunes on the journey home.

'Pull up here, this is fine.' Colin's barked instructions to the driver seemed premature. They were still on the edge of town, nearer to his home than to hers. They stepped out of the car, and at his insistence, she followed him in through the gates to his house, and stepped through the front door.

'Has your cleaning lady not been for a while?' Peggy was shocked to see the dull, dusty banisters, and grubby carpet.

'Yes, silly girl. A stupid misunderstanding. I've been too busy to do anything and this is how she has left me. I always thought she was a bit unhinged, and I was obviously right. Still, her loss.'

Something jangled at the back of Peggy's mind, some memory was clawing at her, desperate to be heard. Colin had walked into the hallway and had thrown his linen jacket onto a chair where other coats and hats had been discarded.

She kept her hand on the doorknob, unsure what to do when Colin's smile returned,

'Come up and see Joe's handiwork in my bedroom Peggy. He's worked wonders, he might not have much up top but he's a whizz with a paintbrush.'

'No Colin, I think I need to get back now. I have a busy day tomorrow, mustn't be too late home. I'll walk, it's fine.'

She had her back to him, wrestling with the doorknob, trying to open the heavy oak door, when she felt Colin grab her arm, squeezing tightly.

'No Peggy, you're not going yet.'

He was hurting her arm and the more she tried to struggle free, the tighter he gripped her. His face was close to hers and there was a fury in his eyes she had not seen before.

'You're no different to the rest of them are you? You, Daisy, that stupid cleaning girl, you're all sweetness and light while things are going your way aren't you? Then you turn and think you can just walk away. Well Daisy found out that's not how it works, oh yes she did, and you're going to play things my way, so_'

His words were cut short by a sharp banging on the door and Peggy could see the shadow of a woman through the glass.

'Jean?'

'What the bloody hell does she want?'

Colin had loosened his grip and Peggy managed to throw the door open, to see a shocked Jean standing on the porch step.

'I found this, on the pavement. Peggy, it's your phone, with the picture of you and Ros on the back.'

Peggy threw her arms around Jean in thanks and relief, pushed herself away from Colin and his house, and marched her towards the lights and safety of the High Street.

As soon as she was out of sight of Colin, standing in his doorway, she crouched down, put her head in her hands and sobbed. Jean bent and crouched down with her, resting her hand on Peggy's back, and waited for the shaking to subside.

Peggy accepted the offer of a tissue without questioning its provenance, and dabbed at her eyes.

'I never liked him.'

Peggy knew. She knew Jean hadn't liked Colin, hadn't trusted him with his flamboyant generosity and superficial kindnesses. She also knew that she hadn't liked or trusted Jean, yet Jean was clearly more able to make good judgements about other people than she was.

'Stiff drink? For you obviously, not me – Ros would never forgive me, but she would also never forgive me if I let you go home in this state. Come on. We'll call into The White Lion – the last thing we want right now is to bump into any of the Field men.'

Jean was right, and when a warm brandy was finally working its way through Peggy's system, she relaxed and felt able to consider what had just happened.

'I'm no psychiatrist Jean, but I think the evening went wrong when he spilt his dinner down his front. He was showing off at how to scoop spaghetti up 'the Italian way', and a big lump dropped down his shirt. He was livid and the evening went downhill fast after that. He hated the fact that I was more familiar with the music than he was, and embarrassed when he started clapping in the wrong place.'

Jean was nodding, allowing Peggy to mull over the events of the evening without contributing.

'I think it was important to him that he thought he was teaching me something I didn't know. It didn't suit him that I enjoyed it, and that I knew the order of it all, you know – what was coming next. I've always longed to be taken to a musical performance by someone who knew their way round the whole business, but it turned out I knew more than him.'

Jean shook her head sympathetically, not really understanding the implications of Colin's actions during the performance, but sharing the disappointment.

'So what happened in the house? What was going on?'

'And what, Jean, would have happened if you hadn't arrived when you did?'

Peggy nodded at the barman, signalling that more drinks were required and he brought them over, accepting Peggy's cash and returning a few moments later with a small silver dish containing her change.

She tried to explain the events from Colin's abrupt instruction for the taxi to stop, until Jean knocked on the door, trying to recall his words, and what they might mean.

'What do you think he meant about Daisy? Do you think he did away with her?'

'Careful where you go with that one Peggy. There's doing away with someone, and there's not rushing to help someone and leaving them to die.'

Peggy took a large swig of her brandy, and placed the empty glass back on the table.

'Is there a difference? I'm not criticising you for it Peg. Your Leonard was a monster, everyone knew it, and even people who didn't know you very well have been thrilled to see how you've found yourself since he went. You don't know it but you're an inspiration round here.

Colin had no idea what he was taking on did he?'

Parting at the double doors into Sovereign Court, after a walk home arm in arm, Peggy hugged a surprised Jean, and thanked her,

'For knocking on Colin's door when you did, for your wise words, for loving Ros, and well, for everything.'

'OK, OK, go on in and get yourself into bed. And tell Derek not to let Colin in, under any circumstances. I'll talk to him in the morning too, and I'll explain everything to Ros. I'll leave you to decide whether Joe and his boys need to know.'

Peggy turned and opened the door, but Jean had one more piece of advice to impart.

'Tomorrow morning Peggy, I want you to do an internet search on the word 'narcissist'. I think you were married to one, and I think Daisy was married to one too.'

Peggy remembered an early conversation with Colin,

'I've done that before Jean – Colin told me to do it. He said Daisy was one. It was him.'

Jean showed no surprise.

'Well I am convinced it wasn't Daisy that was the narcissist in that relationship. None of this is your fault, remember that.'

TWENTY-EIGHT

She woke, fully dressed again, to the sound of the intercom buzzing repeatedly.

'I need to stop this. People don't go to bed in their clothes.'

'Joe, not this morning. I'm not up yet.'

'Let me in Peggy please. It's important.'

Resigned, she clicked the button to let Joe in and waited for him to appear on the landing.

'Tea?'

'No tea thank you. Can we talk please?'

She led him through to the Living Room, and sat on her chair, waiting for what she knew he was about to say.

'I need to talk to you about Colin Peggy.'

She sat back and waited, anxious not to show any emotion that might provoke him into doing something he would regret.

'OK, this isn't easy.'

He shifted in his seat.

'I went to see my Financial Advisor yesterday afternoon.'

This was an unexpected turn, but not for the reason Joe seemed to think.

'I know, blokes like me don't normally have a Financial Advisor, but I had to get one. I had a big win on the lottery last year, didn't tell anyone, I was a bit embarrassed about it to be honest, but anyway they gave me this local chap, Brian, and we've become sort of friends over the last few months.'

Joe, a millionaire?

This was absolutely not what she thought he had called on her for, and she could not imagine where it was headed, but she relaxed slightly, sure that she was not going to be called upon to deal with any testosterone issues.

'Anyway, he was telling me about one of his clients – I know, he shouldn't have been telling me, but there were no names or anything. This chap, his wife had died. She'd owned the house and left it and all her money to charity, so he'd been turned out of his own house. Then – this is where it gets interesting – he'd moved into his father's house, but he's got a gambling problem this chap, and he's got to sell it, to pay off his debts. He owes Brian a fortune. He used to work with him.'

There was a pause while Joe waited for a reaction to his big news.

'I'm sorry Joe, why are you telling me this?'

Joe threw his arms up in the air,

'Because, Mrs Trusting, the bloke is Colin.'

'Are you sure?'

'Yes, and do you know when I realised for certain that it was him? When he told me that the bloke had said he'd found a merry widow who'd come into a bit of money and he was sure he could get his hands on enough to pay everything off without having to sell his dad's house.'

A penny dropped.

'And that was me?'

'I believe so, and I also believe that I am the mug that was doing the house up for him. He hasn't paid me and I don't imagine he ever will.'

There was no need to tell Joe her news. What good would it do anyone?

'Let's go back a bit here Joe. You won the lottery?'

His frown quickly turned to laughter.

'I did. Took me a while for it to sink in. That's how come I bought myself that nice coat at Christmas. You know, treated myself. Brian says I should pay off my mortgage, but if I do that I reckon Tracey will find out and want half of it, even though I bought the ticket after she'd gone to her sister's and she told me it was over. I only told the boys the other week. Brian's been helping me work out how to get them on the property ladder without giving them a big tax bill. He's a good bloke.'

'If a little indiscreet?'

'He never mentioned names, still hasn't. He was a bit upset when he realised I had cottoned on to who it was. See he deals with him in Newport Pagnell, didn't realise the dad's house was here.'

'Or the merry widow either eh?'

The intercom interrupted them, and a few minutes later Ros and Jean arrived, carrying a tin of freshly made brownies and a bottle of gin.

'You've told Joe then?'

Ros refused to be silenced by Jean, and sat herself next to a confused Joe, thrusting the open tin towards him.

'They're this morning's batch, still a bit warm. So, what do you make of our dark stranger now then Joe? Jean always knew, didn't you Jean? He had the rest of us fooled though. Unbelievable.'

'I think,' Peggy started, 'I think Joe has something to tell you two, and I think I have something to tell Joe, but can I get some tea first please? I've experienced those brownies before, and nice as they are, they do require the assistance of hot liquid to remove them from your teeth. I'll leave you three to exchange information, and no-one leave until I get back please.'

Peggy spent some time staring out of her kitchen window, down towards Ribbon Factory Lane, and the little row of cottages where Millionaire Joe now lived in the house she had shared with Narcissist Leonard. She had searched again for the word on the internet before she had fallen asleep the night before, and Jean was right, certainly about Leonard. She would never know who the guilty party was in Colin and Daisy's relationship and accepted Jean's thinly veiled warning against pursuing her suspicions about Daisy's death. If Colin was guilty, then so was she. She could have saved Leonard, at least for a while, but she had no regrets and anyway nothing was certain.

She looked down at the cottages and remembered the shadow of herself occupying number 45 Ribbon Factory Lane; her life on hold while Leonard lived, and she was glad he was dead. Obviously, she wished she had not married him, and lost contact with her family, but she had Paul back now and she looked forward to a future with him and his family.

As for Colin, what a terrible judge of character she was. Swayed by his appearance, his clothes, and his polite behaviour that all disguised the monster he clearly was. Jean had seen it, but she had been blinded by her judgement of Jean.

The kettle was boiling and she poured steaming water onto four teabags in her biggest teapot, counting quietly to 120 before she gave it a quick stir and put the lid on.

'So you all know everything?'

They did. Joe had been persuaded not to pay a visit on Colin, and to leave well alone. He was not convinced but was apparently frightened of Jean so he agreed, although he refused to vouch in the same way for his boys.

'No-one must approach Colin about any of this please. I mean no-one Joe, especially not your boys. No more lives can be ruined by Colin, or Daisy or Leonard. They are all out of our lives and they must stay that way. I won't have your boys getting into trouble over this foolish old woman who was swayed by an expensively dressed man who displays polite manners.'

'But who falls over a lot!' Ros's impersonation of Colin falling was cruel in its accuracy, but they all laughed. She had managed to reduce the image of Colin to a clown in their eyes.

It was another two weeks before Peggy felt able to venture beyond the perimeter of the Sovereign Court gardens. Joe had persuaded her to go with him to visit Brian, his financial advisor, and had promised lunch on the way home at his favourite pub beside the Canal.

He was right, Brian was good at his job, and had some good advice, for which she agreed to pay a modest fee. She had been sworn to secrecy about Joe's lottery win, but had of course told Ros, and they had both agreed there was a more confident air about this quiet and kind man.

He managed to eat his Ploughman's lunch without spilling any pickle or crumbs onto himself, and although he stuck to orange juice, he was insistent that she should choose a good wine to accompany her crab cakes. They sat in comfortable silence under a parasol, at a table overlooking the canal and watched holidaymakers slide slowly through the water in their colourful barges.

'There's no getting away from the glare of onlookers on one of those things is there?'

Joe laughed.

'They only do about a mile an hour. They say it's relaxing but I'd be getting anxious about the next lock gate as soon as I'd left the last one.'

'Thank you for this Joe. I needed to get out of the flat, and this is perfect. Warm sun, chilled wine,'

'And the relaxing sound of the pub's extractor fan belting out the stink of chip fat.'

Peggy hadn't noticed the extractor fan or the chip fat. She was glad to be out, happy to be in the company of someone who wasn't trying to impress her, or educate her, or improve her in any way. And he didn't seem to want anything in return.

She swirled the wine around in her glass, watching as it caught the light.

'How's the plans for Bulgaria going? Any news from Paul's lad?'

Peggy had received more postcards from Joel, the latest few were from St Petersburg where he was settled into student accommodation just outside the city. He was still talking about when she would visit, and had sent details of some good hotels through to Val at the travel agents.

Peggy was excited about the trip. There were times when she wondered if she should still be going, the business with Colin had knocked her confidence and made her think she wasn't capable of making the journey alone. That's what Leonard had done, made her feel inadequate, but other people – including young Joel – thought she could do it, so she had stopped herself from sending her usual 'cancel the trip' messages, and was slowly gathering all the clothes she needed for the cold climate.

'I wanted to go in March next year, but I've decided January might be better, then I can be back in time for my birthday. I'll be 60. It's a big one.'

'People are saying 2020 is going to be a good year. You'll finally get your trip done, then you can set about travelling around the UK in Caroline. You'll have a great time. Maybe you'll be able to go back to Bulgaria again, before Joel comes back, you know – see the place in the summer.'

'Joel has plans for museums, and a few of his friends will come with us too. We'll be quite a party.'

She enjoyed talking about her plans, now they were real. Looking back, she realised that when she had been arranging the trip before, she was doing it to spite Leonard, not because she wanted to go anywhere. But even if he was alive he wouldn't have cared. He would have tried to talk her out of it, told her she wouldn't manage without him and she would have agreed and cancelled everything. Just like she had done after he had died.

These were plans that had been made because she wanted to go. She wanted to spend time with her new nephew, to make up for time she had missed with his dad when he was younger. She wanted to see another country, soak up some culture, eat different food and see different sights.

And yes, she realised, she wanted to do that on her own. Joel would show her around and help her with some of the arrangements, but she would be in her own hotel room, eating breakfast alone and sitting on the plane on her own. A solo traveller. That's what excited her. She was no longer terrified at the thought of it. She could not wait.

Peggy continued to visit Joe in his cottage and allowed him to cook for her. He never behaved in the same way as Colin had, and any ghosts there had been after Leonard's death, she knew, had been of her own making. It was she who spoke to him, told him how much she hated him and the life she had shared with him. He no longer answered her, or made a light flicker, or moved any objects around the house. Leonard the ghost did not exist, and probably never had. She was no longer nervous about going back into the cottage now Joe had transformed it into a modern, clean, welcoming home.

They spent many evenings together, either in her flat or sitting in his squashy sofa in front of a fire he knew how to light, and keep going, playing Scrabble or chess, or just talking. Sometimes they listened to music and sometimes they sat quietly watching the flames until they died to an orange glow, then either he would leave and wander home alone, or it would be time for him to walk her through the fields back to Sovereign Court and see her safely in through the front door.

She had been fearful for so long about going back. That's what it was. Going back, and seeing how she would be when she got there. That's what had frightened her, but she realised that was nonsense. She could now face up to the stalled life she had led in those four walls, hardly ever speaking to anyone in the town, although they had all clearly known who she was. It was her own past she was frightened of, not ghosts, and certainly not Joe.

At last she had given up on all the clubs and classes of the previous year, realising she actually preferred her own company and if she wanted to sing she would do so, in her own time and to her own tune.

Colin had not been seen since that evening after the theatre trip, but they had all seen vans pulling up outside his father's house, taking furniture away, and Jean had watched from the pavement as a truck had towed the Jeep away. She had laughed because they had tried to take the neighbour's Mini away too. There had been a huge argument in the street and the police had to intervene. Jean said she had to hide in the doorway of a pub so she could have a good view and not be drawn into any of the goings on.

A For Sale board was reported and a few days later it had been replaced by a Sold board. When that disappeared they knew that either the house had new occupants, or a sale had fallen through, but by that time they agreed they didn't really care.

It was Brian the super discreet Financial Adviser who had passed on the news of one of his clients being arrested although he was not able to furnish them with any names or further details. They would, he said, need to wait until it was in the papers or on the news and they waited, until they forgot about him.

'Are you and Joe, you know, an item?'

Peggy had agreed to a catch up with Ros on their old bench in the churchyard in the week before Christmas. Ros was obviously building up to discussing the arrangements for Christmas lunch and Peggy was trying to avoid the issue.

She handed Ros a cup of coffee and slowly screwed the cap back on to the flask.

'I am sorry to disappoint you Ros, but we are not as you so commonly describe it, an item. We are companions, we are friends and we enjoy each other's company. There's no excitement there for you to tell Jean. I am very fond of him, but there is no more to tell.'

Ros's eyebrows registered her disbelief.

'Can we talk about something else?'

'We could talk about Christmas. Would you like to come to us for lunch again?'

The very thought filled Peggy with dread. She still bore the scars of watching the two of them scoffing their dried-up lunches, with condensation pouring from the windows, and Jean falling asleep at the table.

'I'm fine on my own thank you. I have a ready meal in the freezer already. I'll come down for the service in the morning so I can call in for a drink with you then, but if you don't mind I will leave you to it, and head home after that. But I am agreeable to an exchange of gifts this year if that would make you happy.'

It did. And Christmas passed without a cross word. New Year was celebrated quietly, apart from a brief and enlightening sortie into the world of Karaoke at The Three Cups in the early part of the evening, and with just a tiny shudder, 2019 disappeared to be replaced by the hope of 2020.

Peggy had a visit from her brother Paul in early January with his two daughters. His wife had taken a turn in the morning and had pulled out of the trip at the last minute. She introduced them all to Jean and Ros, and then to Joe, Mark and Liam and they all had lunch together in The Three Cups. Paul had brought a suitcase of clothes for Peggy to take with her for Joel, and he opened it up so she could see there were no drugs or other illegal items stashed inside.

'They ask you at the airport if you packed the case yourself and I remember from years ago how rubbish you are at lying. I don't want you arrested!'

It was like they had never been apart.

He and his girls were impressed with Peggy's flat and the girls spent most of their time standing on the balcony saying it was like being on holiday. She had no idea what sort of holiday might involve a balcony, but she was happy that they were enjoying being there. They promised to visit when she got back, saying they could sleep on the floor.

She had her family with her, she had good friends and she was about to go on the trip of a lifetime, something she had dreamed about for years.

When Paul and the girls left after their visit, they all hugged and promised to keep in touch, asking her to give Joel a kiss for them, and report back on how he was doing. She agreed to take lots of photographs and send them on. It had not occurred to her that she was providing some comfort to Paul and had no idea how worried he had been about his son taking off for a year to another country. How thoughtless she had been. To her, his being in Russia when she wanted to visit Bulgaria had suited her well. She had never given any thought to how it must be for a parent to be without their child for that length of time, with no idea of how or where he was living. This thought gave a new purpose to her trip, she had a reason to be going there. She was doing something for someone else and it gave her a good feeling.

She stood with Ros, Jean and Joe and waved her family off, watching as the car disappeared from view, and felt an unfamiliar emotion wash over her. Happy, but tearful. She had never experienced anything like that before, and she wasn't sure what to make of it.

TWENTY-NINE

On January 31st, a new version of Peggy Thomas trundled two suitcases through customs at Heathrow Airport, with just a vague, but fond memory of Joe watching her disappear into the Departure Lounge just two weeks before.

She had seen everything she wanted to see, she had spent time with Joel and his friends, in bars and restaurants, eating new foods and realising the extent of the gap in her knowledge of the language. If she lived to be 100, and read her books every day, she now knew she would still only know one tenth of the language. There was more to it than just yes, no, have you got a table for one by the window, and how much is the bill please.

She had seen snow, and ice, rain and felt the sting of Bulgarian winds on her face and neck. She had not been prepared for just how cold it would be, and how warming a shot of the local spirit could be in those conditions.

She had not got lost, not mislaid papers or passport, money, phone, or camera and had conversed on friendly terms with the staff at her hotel.

This Peggy Thomas could take on the world, once she was home anyway.

As she turned the corner and saw the sea of people behind the barriers, just one familiar face was looking her way, and waving.

She took off the face mask the airline had insisted she wore for the flight home, and walked towards him before she realised that he was not the only one there to meet her. Ros and Jean obviously, Mark, Liam, and Paul with his two daughters, all beaming at her and all reaching out to take her suitcase from her.

She could hardly make out what anyone was saying, so many excited voices asking had she had a good time, what was the weather like.

They chattered and gabbled all the way back to the car park, and finally split off to their own cars, leaving her with Joe.

'It's good to have you back Peggy. I've missed you, more than I thought I would.'

'It's good to be back.'

'They want us to stop on the way home, for something to eat. Do you mind? Paul's been over a few times. We've become quite a gang really, but our ringleader has been missing.'

He loaded her case and coat into the back of his van, and walked round to open her door for her, but before she could step in, he bent and kissed her on the cheek.

'Ah Joe, it's good to see you again.'

'I wanted to do that as soon as I saw you come through those departure gates, but you know, I wasn't sure if it was quite right.'

'And do you think you want to do it again Joe?'

'I think I do if that's alright with you.'

And Peggy nodded, 'It's definitely alright with me. I've missed you too, much more than I ever thought I could miss someone.'

Acknowledgements

Peggy was born in Devon, during an Arvon tutorial, and was inspired by a *Diane Arbus* photograph, 'Lady in a Rooming House Parlor, Albion, NY'. She arrived fully formed. The photograph reminded me of a lovely aunt who passed away this year aged 96. The character of my Peggy, and her life, bear no resemblance to my aunt who was kind, sociable, elegant, educated, and enjoyed a happy life with her husband and son.

My thanks go to Russ Litten and Tiffany Murray for your inspiring tutoring and wise words, to Arvon for an amazing week of writing, food, wine and chat, and to my fellow writers for making a cold rainy week in January 2020 so memorable. How lucky we were to snatch that magical time just before we were hit by the rest of 2020.

Special thanks go to fellow Arvonites Charlie and Georgia for the zooms and timely reminders to 'just get it done'. I also need to mention my draft-readers Ann, Diana and Lyndsey.

Finally, enormous thanks to my amazing family for your unwavering support and encouragement.

About the Author

Carole L Pollard was born in Carlisle, England and lived her first few years with her parents and grandparents in their family garage, Moorville, surrounded by the smells of motor oil, tyres and Capstan Full Strength cigarettes. The family moved south in the sixties, to Dunstable, but Carole has lived for most of her life in Milton Keynes, with her husband Roy, and three children.

Carole has worked and studied at The Open University, gaining a BA in English Literature and Creative Writing in 2017, and an MA in Creative Writing in 2019. Now the studying is all done she has returned to her first love, writing. She has had several articles published, and for many years produced and wrote *Local Craft Matters*, a magazine dedicated to the incredible crafters in and around the Milton Keynes area. This is her first novel.

Printed in Great Britain
by Amazon

42060782R00199